Down to Earth

a novel

David Elston

ISBN-13: 979-8-9894776-4-7

Cypress Press
670 Albemarle Dr, Suite 1200
Shreveport, LA 71106

Cover art licensed from Adobe Stock
Cover design by David Elston

This is a work of fiction. Names, characters, places, and incidents are either used fictitiously or are the product of the author's imagination.

CYPRESS PRESS
an independent publisher

Dedicated to

Shreveport,
home away from Home

One

Something's wrong with me, or so I'm told. I don't doubt it's true, though I'm not sure that's all there is to the story.

I got baptized at seven but was informed later that day that it didn't take. I tried it again the next year to the same effect. In fact, I went under the water a total of six times between the ages of seven and fourteen - just about every time Brother Ronny planned a revival. I didn't get it - it seemed to work for everybody else. They'd get dunked and come out clean as a scalded pig. Me? I repented with all my might. I walked the aisle as sincerely as I knew how. But just as soon as I came up out of the water, would you know it, I couldn't help but find the nearest mud to wallow in. And there was always someone around to catch me in it. I must be pretty good at fooling myself but apparently not anyone else.

When I attended my final revival at Mt. Sinai Community Church, as I said, I was fourteen. As you might imagine, I wasn't too happy to be there. I sat in the back pew with my head down. A three-day affair, the revival was a crescendo of sorts, with Brother Ronny starting off easy and gentle on day one, hammering us with the Law on day two, and then binding up our wounds with the offer of forgiveness on day three. Wary of being caught up in the drama again, I planned to watch it all from afar.

"Folks," Brother Ronny began, shuffling his feet and shaking his head, "I suspect I better humble myself before we get going. Ol' Ronny hasn't always been the fine gentleman you see before you today. Lord knows it. There was a time when I was a man of the world, you see. I was overfond of alcohol and smoking them cancer sticks like a locomotive. Chasing after loose women, gambling and dancing my life away. And - my greatest regret - I took the Lord's holy name in vain every chance I got."

He raised his large arms, showing us palms the size of bear paws. "Now, hear me out, don't walk out just yet. That's not the end of the story, you see. Because as I was coming home on one such night of drinking and debauchery, I drove myself into a ditch, my truck flipping right on over. I lay there in my upside-down pickup with a broken nose, looking out my shattered window and - the Lord knows it to be true - I heard him speak to me. He says to me - honest truth, folks - just as clear as you hear me now, the Lord says to me, 'Ronny, what you fooling around with all this mess for? It's time to grow up and be a man. Quit running from me, boy. I got big plans for you.' Honest truth, folks, his words exactly. And I tell you, from that day on, it's been the straight and narrow road for Ronny Hampton. I been following the Lord's call ever since. Preaching that name I used to blaspheme. Not a drop of poison water has touched this tongue, nor a puff of smoke entered these lungs. And as for chasing girls, I found myself a godly woman and settled down with her. Look at her, folks. Bonnie, stand up and let them see you. Look at her - bone of my bone and flesh of my flesh. Bonnie Hampton, folks, my sister-wife in the Lord. She's not one for the spotlight, but you know what? I feel the Spirit leading me to bring her up here in a little while to give her own testimony. She don't mind. Do you, sugar? All right, you can sit back down."

I was not really paying attention, in part because I'd heard it all before, but also because there was a girl named Georgia Hampton across the aisle, I was making eyes with. That's right, *Hampton*, as in the blessed daughter of Reverend Ronny himself. Boy, don't I know how to set myself up for some trouble. I have sometimes asked myself, knowing all that would unfold from that moment, would I do anything different? And no, I wouldn't, but I might have at least counted the cost.

I'd been fond of Georgia for a while, but she was strictly off limits, protective as her daddy was. Before that day, it had never been more than a word here, a look there. Yet, by some work of grace, she was not sitting next to her momma as usual that day, and before the end of the first hour, I got her passing notes with me. I wasn't so glum over being stuck at the revival anymore.

After further recounting his life as a traveling evangelist and leading us himself in a handful of hymns, we broke for the evening and went home, many families in great anticipation of things to come. In the car that night, my parents, who had long hoped for the salvation of my soul, asked what I thought. "One thing I don't get," I said. "How come we plan revivals?"

"What are you talking about, son?" Daddy said.

"Don't seem like the kind a thing a man could plan, seeing that it's a work of the Holy Ghost. How's Brother Ronny know what the Lord plans to do? When and where a revival's gonna break out?"

This was not what they were expecting to be on my mind that night. "Boy, that man's anointed," Daddy said. "He's called by God. He knows things we don't."

"But I thought the Holy Ghost was like the wind, blowing

wherever it wants. A revival planned by a man seems like nothing but than a man trying to bottle up lightning. Trying to make wind himself."

Dad looked sharply at me in the mirror. "Don't you got enough iniquity in that heart of yours to be worrying about Brother Ronny?"

"Yessir," I said. Momma reached over and stroked Daddy's hand on the console.

The next morning, Brother Ronny started to preach from the Sermon on the Mount. Georgia was across the aisle again, sitting next to a friend. She opened her eyes during the prayer, turned a little and saw me looking at her, and then closed her eyes again, trying to hide a smile. On the back of a tithing envelope I wrote, *You like to fish?* and tossed it to her while Brother Ronny was looking down, reading the Beatitudes. During a gospel song a little later, I felt her slip the note back into my palm while everyone else was standing and singing with their hands raised. It said, *Don't know how. Never been before.* I wrote back, *We should go some time. I'll teach you.* A little later I got a note from her during a prayer that said, *Careful or Daddy will get you.* Not really the words I was hoping for, but just having her pass notes with me felt like such an achievement, she could have written *Get lost,* and I'd still have counted it an honor.

She was right though. Sure enough, about mid-morning Brother Ronny picked up his Bible and continued where he left off, "Ye have heard that it was said by them of old time, Thou shalt not commit adultery: But I say unto you, That whosoever looketh on a woman to lust after her hath committed adultery with her already in his heart."

Then, no longer easy or gentle, he slammed the Bible on the pulpit and shouted, "You hear that, Elijah Youngblood! The

Lord's got his eye on you, boy!"

That's me. Elijah Youngblood.

I just about fell out of the pew. Poor Georgia went red as riverbed clay. My parents turned around, Momma's eyes wide with embarrassment, Daddy's with outrage. They motioned for me to come sit with them. The rest of the revival, I felt so ashamed and torn up with guilt I thought for sure I'd finally repented. Saturday night I lay in bed, terrified I might die in my sleep before getting to wash away my sins the next day. I also couldn't help but marvel - Brother Ronny got me again. I kept my thoughts off Georgia as best I could.

On Sunday, it was time for him to comfort sore sinners like me with the offer of forgiveness. "Only one condition, my friends," Brother Ronny said. "You got to surrender it all. Not fifty percent. Not ninety-nine percent. You got to surrender it *all* at the foot a that old rugged Cross." When he disappeared a little later to don his baptismal hip waders and white gown, the choir began to sing, *This is my story, this is my song, praising my Savior all the day long!* The baptistry was front and center of the chapel, up behind the pulpit with a little opening where people could watch the sinner's old self drown in the waters. Brother Ronny kept it filled at all times, saying he didn't want to be caught off guard when the Holy Ghost broke forth. The deacons walked among the pews like bird dogs sniffing out fallen game.

When Brother Ronny finally emerged and gave the altar call, I walked the aisle one last time and got in line behind a few others. The choir continued to sing, *Perfect submission, perfect delight, visions of rapture now burst on my sight.* When it was my turn, I stepped up the stairs and through the narrow door into the baptistry. I saw Brother Ronny through the opening, his massive frame filling the small space like some kind of water giant. I felt like David stepping next to Goliath. When I started to descend into the water next to him, he put his hand out, stopping me. "Now, hold on, Elijah. We've been here too many times. You got to be sincere, boy. You got to mean it. Don't step in these here waters if you ain't surrender it all."

"Yes, sir, I mean it this time. Promise. Like you said, I'm feeling the Spirit's compunction. Please, I'm afraid of hell, Brother Ronny. I gotta wash away these sins before they get me."

"Well then, if that's the case," he said, leading me down into the frigid, waist-high water, "I baptize you in the name of the Father, the Son, and the Holy Ghost." He leaned me back. He seemed to leave me underwater a while longer than the others. When I came back up, he slapped me on my wet back and said, "Now go and don't sin no more, you hear?"

As I changed clothes and resumed my place next to my parents, I felt good. Clean. Scalded of all my impurities. I felt like I belonged in that place finally. Hair wet and skin moist, I sat in the pew in wonder. Whether it was the work of the Lord or Brother Ronny, somehow these revivals always got me, no matter how hard-hearted and stiff-necked I tried to be.

The service ended after a few more hymns and a concluding prayer. Then it was time to gather next door in the fellowship hall for a potluck celebration. While we were crossing the parking lot, I told my parents, "I'm gonna go dry off in the sun before coming inside, if that's all right."

There was an open field next to the church that was used for picnics and games. I found a pine tree on the edge of the field and put my back against it, facing the south where I could feel the sun. I needed to think before the waters of baptism were dry. Beyond the field in front of me were the woods and, even further, the lake where I spent every spare moment I had, where I was most fully myself, the only place I'd ever felt at home. I tried to imagine what life was supposed to be like for someone born again. "What next?" I said aloud as the wind passed. A little disturbed, I was not sure how to answer the question. I realized this was where things had always gone wrong after previous baptisms.

Hearing the church doors open, I turned my head and saw Georgia come out, walking around the building toward the fellowship hall. A sudden gust of wind blew her long brown hair wildly and cast her light blue dress in a train behind her. Waiting to make sure she was by herself, I called her name. I think she recognized my voice because she was already smiling when she turned. I waved her over.

"Wanna sit for a minute?" I said when she got close.

She paused and looked over her shoulder. "All right," she said, sitting next to me in her long white stockings, smoothing her dress over her legs. "I saw you got baptized again. That's great, Elijah."

"Thanks. Hoping it takes this time," I said with half a smile.

"Maybe it took the first time."

"Yeah, well, tell that to your daddy." I straightened up. "Sorry for embarrassing you yesterday. I hope I didn't get you in trouble."

"It's all right, I didn't mind. You got the worst of it, I think. I tried to warn you," she said. "Anyway, what are you doing over here?"

"Oh, I was just wondering..." Watching her brush a strand of hair out of her face, I forgot what I was going to say. Georgia didn't wear a bit of makeup or jewelry, on account of being inventions of the Devil, but she didn't need either one.

"What were you wondering?"

I had to look away to collect my thoughts. "Well, Brother

Ronny - your daddy - tells us what *not* to do once we're saved - 'Don't sin no more,' he always tells me. But what *do* we do?"

She tilted her head a little. "I haven't ever thought about it like that," she said. "You mean, like, besides church?"

"Right. The way he talks, my life's nothing but sin and lust and worldliness. And the world's nothing but firewood for judgment. If he's right about that - and who am I to question the Lord's anointed? - then I have to leave all that behind. If all that's true, how am I supposed to live now? It don't seem like I can take a breath without falling into worldliness. This is where things always go wrong."

"Well, I don't know. I guess I've never let myself wonder those kinds of things. You sure know how to speak your mind."

"Sorry, just admitting my doubts I guess."

"No, I like it. It's . . . refreshing," she said. "Doubts aren't allowed in my house."

We stared out at the field in front of us and the forest beyond it. I could be wrong, but it seemed like she moved a little closer to me. I could hear her breathing now. She smelled like lavender. Looking back toward the fellowship hall and then at the field again, I said, "I mean, let's say, just for instance, I wanted to kiss a pretty girl. You think I could do it without lusting in my heart? Is it even possible to do that kind of thing without falling under judgment?" I swear it was an honest question, but I saw her turn red and realized how it sounded.

"I don't know," she said, "What do you think?"

I paused, thinking how to clarify my motives. "Depends on how pretty she is. Girl like you? Shoot, I'd be afraid to try. Doomed from the start."

My compliment only made things worse. She laughed a little and leaned toward me and said quietly, "I've never done a thing like that."

"Well, don't worry. I wouldn't dare kiss the preacher's daughter," I said. And then, as if spoken by another person, I heard myself say, "As much as I'd like to." *There you go again, boy, wallering in that mud.*

"Well," she said, looking over her shoulder. "I don't mind. Anyway, Daddy don't have to know."

Completely unprepared for that response, I felt like a rabbit spooked in the woods, my heart rate through the roof. In disbelief at the progression of the conversation, I said hoarsely, "You sure?" She nodded.

I checked once more that we were alone. No souls in sight, I did it - I leaned forward and kissed her. Now, don't get the wrong idea. It wasn't one for the movies. There weren't enough heat and moisture to have fogged up a window. No hands on the face or rolling around. Just a simple kiss. But hidden within that ordinary, outward act was nothing less than a bolt of lightning. I was surprised - it didn't feel wrong at all. And if I'm not mistaken, she felt the same. After lingering for a moment, Georgia pulled away and said, her green eyes bright, "Were you able to do it without, you know . . . How was it?"

"Like a baptism of fire."

She laughed and said, "I've never met a boy like you, Elijah Youngblood." She looked back at the fellowship hall. "I better head inside before Daddy comes looking for me." She stood, tucked her hair behind her ears, and said, "Bye, Elijah." I watched her until she made it around the corner of the sanctuary.

I had to wait a while to stop smiling before going into the potluck. When I finally did go in, the first thing I saw, seated across the hall, was Brother Ronny with a mouthful of barbecue brisket, staring at me with the same look as when he preached on the Lake of Fire. I looked away, made my plate and took my place next to my parents. While I was working on a cob of corn, minding my own business, he came up behind me and gripped my shoulder with his iron hand. He bent down and said in my ear, "Looks like that baptism didn't take this year neither." He patted my shoulder, smiled at my parents, and walked away.

You might think I was offended or discouraged by the comment, but the truth is, I didn't mind. In fact, I'm glad he said it. Because with his judgment in my ears and his daughter's blessing on my lips, the dangerous idea came to me that maybe Brother Ronny was wrong about some things. I decided for good that his voice and the Lord's weren't the same after all. Gambling my eternal soul on it, I left the fold behind and embraced exile. Having orphaned myself, I'd have to find my own way, but at least I was free. With nothing more than a shrug, the great burden I'd labored under for so long slid off my back and fell away.

As to whether the baptism took, I'm not one to differ with a man called of God, but I'm not sure I agree with the Preacher. Heck, I still can't say for sure, but I'd like to think if there's more than one way to skin the flesh off a coon, the same could be true of a soul.

Two

Brother Ronny loved to preach about free will, but apparently his daughter wasn't allowed to have one. Especially not in relation to the opposite sex. Georgia was strictly forbidden to speak with boys, even in groups and at church events. I got her in trouble a few times not long after my last baptism for talking with her directly, and Brother Ronny came down hard on her and embarrassed her in front of everyone. I couldn't take the sight of her tears, so I straightened up as best I could. I also became the most faithful participant, attendance-wise, in the whole youth group. Anything for a chance to rub shoulders with that girl.

Besides the binding will of Brother Ronny, since I went to the local high school, and Georgia was homeschooled by Mrs. Bonnie, we had almost no chance to talk. Even so, like a vine of poison oak, once our relationship started, it didn't need much to keep growing. An occasional glance, a passing touch, a note placed in the palm and, rare but best of all, a secret in the ear. We both knew how word could get around, so we were very careful in those early days. For the most part I abided by the rules for the first year and let the vine grow on what naturally occurring sources it could find. But when spring came around again, I couldn't help but pine for more. I decided to try something new.

One Friday night, not long after she had turned fifteen, I sat next to her during youth group. Normally that was impossible, since Brother Ronny was either teaching or at least overseeing the group. This week, however, he was out of town for an evangelistic tour, and one of the veteran deacons, old Mr. Hank, was speaking instead. The entire youth group sat on the carpet in front of him. He stared until we were all quiet and then began, "What'chall know about being fishers of men?" He looked around at us, already disappointed. "Anybody tell me what that means?" Nobody answered. "Come on, who's got a guess? I'll write it on the board behind me while you think on it." He walked toward the chalkboard.

I leaned over. "Georgia," I whispered.

"Yeah?" she said without looking away from Mr. Hank.

"I'm going fishing tomorrow. You wanna come?"

She paused. "I'm sorry," she whispered, "Momma'd never let me."

"I get it," I said, knowing it was a long shot.

"Elijah! Looks like you got something to say," said Mr. Hank loudly, having turned around. "What's it mean to be a fisher of men?"

I cleared my throat. "I suppose it's kin to saving souls, sir."

"There you go! Well said. Now, how about it, Elijah, you want to be a fisher of men?"

"Not really, sir." The whole youth group turned and stared at me in astonishment.

"What do you mean you don't know? Course you do."

Reading again what he had written in chalk, I said, "How's a man of flesh gonna save a everlasting soul?"

"Afraid I don't understand," he said.

"All I mean is, I think I'd rather be the rod or tackle or a little swim jig, maybe, and let the Lord do the angling. I'm nothing but a worm, Mr. Hank. I think I'd be better off on the hook than holding the pole." The whole class broke into laughter, but I kept staring at Mr. Hank.

"Quiet down boys and girls," Mr. Hank said, irritated. "Say what now?"

"Seems to me like nobody's fit to fish for souls but the Lord himself."

"A man can do anything by the power of God." He pointed at Georgia. "Just look at Brother Ronny."

"But do I gotta fish for souls? What if I just want to fish for bass?" Everyone laughed again, but I was serious.

"If you want to follow the Lord, you ain't got a choice." I could have kept arguing but shrugged instead, which seemed to aggravate him even more. I suppose I spoiled his point and was relieved when he moved on to the rest of his lesson. When he started reading aloud about the calling of the disciples, Georgia leaned over and said softly, "I'll come fish with you."

"Change your mind?" I couldn't believe it.

"Yeah. I'll find a way. Just tell me when and where."

"Meet me in the woods east of the church, just past the field. Five-thirty tomorrow morning."

"I'll be there," she said.

I don't know that I slept a bit that night, but I had no lack of energy when it was time to get up the next morning. At five I dressed and went to the kitchen. I put some peanut butter crackers and a bag of grapes in the tackle box, grabbed the thermos of hot chocolate I'd made the night before, and left the house. My parents were used to me leaving early on Saturdays and heading to the woods. They wouldn't have said it, but I think they may have even preferred to have a quiet morning without me. Closing the back door gently behind me, I thought of Georgia sneaking out of the parsonage and began to sweat.

I cut through the forest behind my neighborhood and walked the mile or so, as the crow flies, through the dark woods from my house to the meeting place. The flashlight reflected off the eyes of various nocturnal creatures - a lone coyote, a family of possums, a pair of raccoons. They all either froze or darted away. All kinds of critters were hurrying to bed before the light drove out the darkness, a time which may be frightening to some but always gave me a little thrill.

The parsonage where the Hamptons lived was on the lot on the west side of the church. On the east side was the field where Georgia and I had sat after my baptism, surrounded on two sides by woods. I waited behind some brush, just out of sight of any cars that passed on the road. A fog lay on the field in front of me from the night chill meeting the warmth of the gray morning light. Out by the highway I could barely read the Mt. Sinai Community Church sign. In block letters below the name it said, GOD WANTS FULL CUSTODY, NOT JUST WEEKEND VISITS.

Nervous and cold, I trembled a little. I checked my watch - 5:25. I kept waiting, watching the field in front and the trees behind, wondering if maybe Georgia had decided against it. Or if I'd heard her wrong. I questioned why she changed her mind in the dialogue with Mr. Hank. At 5:30 I said to myself, "Maybe it's too soon for this kind of thing." Doubts swarmed. At 5:40 I heard a twig snap in the gray woods to my right, turned, and saw a blurred movement. Half a minute later, fifty feet away, walking towards me with the silent grace of a doe, was Georgia.

"Dadgum," I said under labored breath, setting my things down. "You came," I said, when she got close.

"Morning," she said. She was wearing a green hoodie and jeans, rolled up at the bottom and showing her ankles. Her long brown hair ran down her back in a French braid.

"I didn't know you were allowed to braid your hair," I said.

"I'm not," she said, touching the back of her head. "Sorry, I can take it out if —"

"Not at all, keep it. Don't bother me at all."

"That's why I was late. I'll take it out before I get home. You all right?"

"I'm good. What? I look spooked or something?"

"Yeah. You afraid I was Daddy?"

"I'm not scared of your daddy. It's you that makes me nervous." I lifted my bag and gear from the ground. "Come on, I got a spot picked out for us."

We walked through the woods slowly, Georgia following close behind me. Being late spring, there was a lot of undergrowth to navigate. Everything was gray, the yellow sunlight not quite making its way through the trees yet.

"How'd you get out the house?" I asked her, holding back a branch for her to pass.

"I told Momma last night I planned to go on a prayer walk when I got up this morning. She does the same thing when she needs some time to herself. She was all for it and just said be back by eight for breakfast." Georgia paused for a moment. "Daddy'd never let me leave if he was home. He'd see right through the lie and start interrogating me."

"Lie? Oftentimes out here is the only place I can pray. Most time in church my soul's clamped shut like a box turtle, can't pray for nothing." A squirrel skittered up a nearby tree after its friend, chattering toward us.

"How come?"

"Aw, well ... I'm sure the Lord's there, but people are so big and loud I can't hardly hear and see him."

"By people you mean Daddy?"

I shrugged.

"You know where you're going?" she said. "In the woods, I mean. All looks the same to me."

"Course. We're halfway there. It's not but a quarter mile ahead."

The brush began to lessen, and we could finally see the light of the sunrise coming through the trees ahead. I helped her over a fallen pine tree and then suddenly the woods opened, the lake, still and smooth in front of us.

She gasped quietly. "Well, this is a first," she said, surveying the place. "Didn't even know this was here."

"Not many people do. This is my own little sacred grove."

"No," she said, "I mean the lake."

"Seriously?" I said, baffled. "That's hard to believe. You've missed out." It was beginning to dawn on me how truly sheltered she had been for the last fifteen years. "Walk out here with me, there's a spot on this little peninsula where I like to cast."

The water now surrounded us on three sides. "This is a good time of day to be here. The water's like a mirror of heaven, don't you think?" She nodded. "So. I guess you've never fished either, huh?"

She shook her head, her braid moving back and forth.

"Here, I got a beginner's pole that's just right for you. This was my first pole. I already got it rigged and all. Can I show you how it works?" She nodded. "All right, see here? There's this little button here you push and hold down, and you cast it like this, taking your thumb off as you cast." The tackle landed about forty feet away, disturbing the still water. "Now with a jig like we got on there, give it a few seconds to let it land on the bottom ... then reel it in quick like this." I brought it in and showed her once more. "Now, once you get that down, twitch the end of the pole around when you're hauling it in, like this. Do that and you'll be sure to catch one. You ready?" I handed her the pole and stepped back.

"I'll try." She took a deep breath. Turning her whole body, she pulled her arm back.

"Hang on," I said, standing on my feet. "It's not like throwing a ball. You're mainly just flicking your wrist." She looked at the pole for a moment and tried to cast, but the bait landed a few feet in front of her, just barely in the water. She wrinkled her nose a little. "Well, you have to bend at the elbow, too."

"Flick the wrist, bend the elbow," she said to herself. Then, surprising even herself, she cast the line about twenty feet into the water. "Like that?" she said.

"That's it. Now that the line has settled, reel it in ... hey, not bad." I stood back and watched as she cast a few more times. "Like watching a hour old fawn just stand up and walk."

I got my thermos out and poured some hot chocolate. Sipping from the metal cup that doubled as the top, the warmth filled my insides. "Hot cocoa?" I said, holding it out to her.

"No, thanks. I'm going to keep working on my cast."

I took my pole out and began to fish alongside her. "Love a good fog over the lake," I said.

After a dozen casts, she put the pole aside and sat with her back on the cypress tree behind us. She poured a cup of hot chocolate and sipped it slowly. "Still hot," she said.

"In a thermos like that, it'd stay warm 'til kingdom come."

She smiled and shook her head. "Can't imagine we'll need hot chocolate when the kingdom comes."

"Says who?" I said with a cast.

She quietly observed the place while I continued to fish. A gentle breeze blew in from the lake. "Look!" she said, tapping my leg. A miniature whirlwind had risen from the lake, swirling the fog, riding the wind across the water. "I've never been out in the wild like this, not in my whole life. Only in dreams." The water next to us was speckled with the tiny splashes of swarming minnows. A stout, blue, crested bird came and perched on the top of a cypress tree that hung overhead.

"See that?" I said, pointing. "That's a kingfisher. Watch it for a second and you'll find out why they call him that." He pointed his beak downward at the water, shifting his feet on the branch every so often. He flew to another tree and shuffled around again. "Keep watching," I said. Finally, he leapt into a freefall, nose diving into the water, and disappeared entirely for a moment. Georgia gave a little gasp just before he reemerged with a little silver fish in his mouth and flew away.

"She's so graceful," she said.

"I know, effortless. That was a male, though. In the world of birds the boys are the pretty ones and the girls aren't much to look at. Opposite you and me. That bird puts our fishing to shame, don't he?"

We both stood and cast for a while. She got her line caught in a tree, and I showed her how to yank it free. Usually, it was a pretty good fishing hole, so I was a little disappointed when an hour went by without a bite. I plucked a green cypress ball from the branch above me and crushed it, getting sap on my fingers. I threw it into the water as a wish or prayer or something and watched the oil spread on top of the lake. Maybe it was a coincidence, or maybe fish like the smell of cypress oil, but not a minute later I saw her pole get yanked into a curve. She gave a little yelp.

"You got one," I said.

"Here, you take it," she said, trying to hand the pole to me.

"Naw, you got it. Just keep reelin' it in."

"I think he's pulling the line out."

"I know, but he'll get wore out before long." And then, just as quickly, the line went slack. "Shoot," I said, wondering if I ought to have done it for her.

Eventually I managed to hook one. I reeled it to the bank and lifted it out of the lake. "Not exactly a lunker. This is what you call a white perch. Now, after you pull it out the water, you just grab it from underneath the belly like this. You have to hold it tight or else she'll flop right on back into the water. Then you just take the hook out her lip, taking note of the barb."

"Her? It's a girl?"

"See her belly here? How it's kind of rounded? She's full of eggs," I said. "Now that I've got the hook out, I'll just slip her back in the water, easy and gentle."

"You're not keeping her?"

"Not today. Plus, she's got thousands of eggs in her that she's about to lay in a nest somewhere around here. I'll be catching her offspring for the rest of my life, more than likely."

She smiled at me, not seeming to mind that she hadn't caught one. I let the fish slide into the water and washed the slime off. Turning back to her, I was surprised to find her smile gone, her eyes round with fear as though I were a black bear. "What's the matter?" I said.

"Elijah, let me ask you something."

"Sure," I cast my line into the lake. "Anything."

She turned away from me and said, her voice trembling, "I've never felt so torn up in my whole life."

"Oh no, what'd I say? Torn up how?"

"Between you and Daddy." She began to cry now. "Between all this and my life at home."

"I see. Feeling guilty?"

"Yeah, but it's more than that. Being out here, being with you - nothing's ever made me feel this way. Alive and free. But I can't have all this without lying and deceiving."

"Yeah," I said, removing some lakeweed from my bait. "I get it. I'm sorry, it's not fair of me. I shouldn't put you in this situation."

"Doesn't it bother you? To be hiding from Daddy like this?"

"Naw, not really," I said.

"How can it not?"

"Listen, if I was up to no good with you, that'd be one thing. That'd weigh on my mind. But I don't mind shading the truth to go fishing with you."

"Isn't that that still lying? Isn't that a sin?"

"I guess so. And just like passing notes with you at that revival, I'll probably pay for one way or another, but it's worth it to get to know you. The way I see it, I can either strain out a gnat and swallow a camel, or the other way around. Look, as a hunter, I go after big game, even if it means a belly full of gnats."

She wiped her eyes with her sleeve and laughed a little. "So, I'm big game, huh?"

"Don't get any bigger than you," I said. "But listen, let me take you back home. Can't have you torn up. Come on."

"No, not yet. Say more about the gnat and the camel."

I sat down next to her. The fog had lifted from the lake,

which was now rippling in the wind. "Here's how I see it. Your daddy don't trust boys. And he don't allow you to be alone with them - why? Because he thinks they'll corrupt you, body and soul. Can't say I blame him. But I don't have any plans of the sort, except to treat you with dignity and kindness. Guess I don't mind breaking his rules as long as I'm doing what's at the heart of them."

"Daddy would never see it that way."

"Reckon not. Neither would my parents. You realize you're talking with an outlaw, don't you?"

"I think that's the reason I came with you." She thought for a moment, her tears drying in the breeze. "My whole life is nothing but law. Can't help but take interest in an outlaw."

"My parents' laws, maybe yours too, are all about the gnats, I said, "But I'm a camel guy." She laughed. "It's kind of like that braid of yours. You don't mean anything sinful by it, even if it is against the rules. You're just displaying your God-given beauty." She ran her fingertips across her hair. I decided to stop while I was ahead.

After some thought she said, "You talk about the Lord in ways I haven't heard before. Where'd you learn to see things this way?"

"You spend enough time alone in the woods, just you and the critters and the Good Lord, you're bound to end up a strange bird."

"Hm," she said.

"Well, why don't I take you back home?"

"No, it's not but seven."

"I don't want you feeling tore up on account a me."

"Like you said, as long as you treat me right, I'll be fine. Long as we're not up to no good. I trust you."

"I don't know that I trust myself, but for you? I can behave. This morning's nothing but a boy teaching a girl to fish. I won't even kiss you this time." I felt awkward after saying that and a little regretful. "Well, hey, you hungry? I got some crackers and grapes. You want some?"

"No, just sit and talk to me for a bit. Put the pole down. I want to hear more about the wild things."

I told her everything I could think of. I pointed out the holes in a dead cypress tree where the ducks roosted. I explained the difference between drakes and hens, between mudpuppies and mudcats. I told her how to find fatwood and use it to start a fire. She asked how Lake Robicheaux came to be, and I explained how the Red River created it a long time ago and fed it ever since. Normally I considered myself fairly ignorant, but she was so eager and appreciative, I felt like maybe I did know a thing or two. "What's the name of the gray wispy stuff hanging everywhere?" she said.

"Spanish moss? Georgia, are you telling me you lived in Louisiana all your life and never knew that?"

"I know," she said quietly. "Sad, isn't it? Got half the book a Psalms memorized but can't name the moss hanging in my front yard or the bird singing out my window."

"Sorry, I don't mean to offend you. It's not your fault. I'm just surprised. As much as your daddy loves the book of Scripture, he don't seem to care much for the book of nature."

She didn't say anything but watched a grey heron swoop over the water. I checked my watch. "Hey, it's almost seven-thirty. Let's go ahead and get you back."

"All right," she said. We stood, and I began moving back toward the woods.

"Aren't you going to grab your things?" she said.

"Nah, I'm coming right back to fish some more. Plus, I didn't get much sleep last night. Might doze a little. Nothing better than a nap in the woods. Like resting on the bosom of Abraham."

She shook her head. "This is all so new to me. I never even knew people lived like this."

"Most people don't," I said. "Told you I'm an odd bird."

We headed back through the brush, the air warm now. She walked beside me this time. Shaking her hair out of its braid, she combed it with her fingers, releasing a scent of lavender, and put it up in a ponytail.

"Never known somebody like you either," I said, kicking a stick off the path.

"How so?"

"Don't know that I can explain it. Too embarrassed to try."

"Try," she said.

"Well, you see . . . I . . . I'm nothing but dirt. And you —"

"We're all made of dirt, Elijah."

"I have my doubts."

"That's why I like you." She grew flushed and animated. "Not a speck of dirt's allowed in my house, even though not one of us is clean. We just pretend. But I don't have to pretend to be clean when I'm with you. Matter of fact, I didn't even know I was pretending until I met you. I can be myself with you, dirt and all."

"I'd like to say the same, but all I've done this morning is try to impress you."

"You done good," she said.

I stopped walking once we got to a thick patch of brush and lowered my voice. I knelt down and pointed. "Look, there's the church, no more than a hundred yards away. You can see the steeple if you get low and look through the trees. See it?"

She knelt next to me. "I see it." She ran her fingers through

27

the leaves and pine straw beneath her, then turned to me, her hair touching the ground. "It's never going to be long enough, is it?"

"You'll get tired of me before long like everyone else."

"I'm not so sure. When can we do it again?"

Still kneeling next to her, I said, "When's your daddy out of town next?"

"Not until August, I think. He's going to visit the Holy Land."

"Aw, I been there before," I said.

"Really?" She tilted her head for a second, confused.

"Sure," I said. "Just this morning."

She smiled and shook her head.

We stood up. "Well," I said, unsure how to see her off. "August, huh?"

"August," she said, walking backwards toward the church. "Bye, Elijah."

THREE

In high school, I didn't give a fig what anybody thought of me. I wasn't rebellious or angry. I guess I just accepted the general consensus that I didn't belong and, like I did with the church, eventually gave up trying altogether. In fact, I liked being in exile. It could be lonesome, for sure, but at least I was free. Besides Georgia, the only people whose opinions mattered to me were Virgil and Shaw.

They lived at a trailer park just outside of city limits and had been bosom friends since learning to walk. I had known of them for years but was always warned about spending time or associating with them. "They're not proper folk, Elijah," Momma said, "Your daddy's worked hard to provide a respectable life for you. What do you want to get caught up with trash for?"

"Aw, Momma, what's wrong with living in a trailer?"

"It's not so much that. They don't got jobs, son, they just sit around and cook meth and drink and fornicate while living off the teat of the government. Off *my* tax dollars."

"How do you know so much about them?"

"Everybody knows about them, Elijah. And there's not a soul at church or in town that respects them. Don't go nowhere near those two boys or you'll become just like them."

Despite the opinions of my parents, what Virgil and Shaw lacked in respectability, they made up for in other ways. For one, they were outdoorsmen, knowing their way around the water and woods better than anyone I knew - boy, man or dog. For a guy like me, there weren't many virtues I prized more highly.

Now, some of what Momma said was true. Shaw's dad was a deadbeat alcoholic. And by the age of ten, Virgil had lost his daddy to suicide and his momma to meth and had to be raised by his grandparents. But here's the thing. They could have thought themselves victims and become just like their parents, but instead they took it all on the chin as their share of suffering in this world. Like orphans, they learned to take care of themselves early in life and made do with what they had. True, they were not on a path of earthly success and didn't count themselves as any better than a deer tick, but I can't remember one time they ever complained about the lot they'd been assigned, as if they deserved better.

Shaw's first name was actually Walter, just like his daddy's, but he couldn't stand how formal it sounded, so he went by Shaw, his momma's maiden name. And Virgil, well, he didn't find out until he was fourteen that his legal name wasn't Virgil. He wouldn't tell anyone his real name, not even Shaw. After he heard about the Roman poet, he began to say the name was given for his song-writing skills, but he had the name long before he ever picked up the guitar and even longer before he could read and write.

I first met Virgil and Shaw just a couple of weeks after fishing with Georgia, bumping into them in the woods. At first, we were a little suspicious of each other, knowing we weren't from the same walks of life, so we just shot the breeze for a minute and moved on. Another time they saw me walking to a spot on the lake not far from their trailer park. I could tell they were assessing me while we talked, checking to see if I really knew anything about fishing. I doubt they were impressed, but I think I passed the test.

Finally, a month later, just before school let out, I ran into them one Sunday afternoon, running a trotline on the lake. We chewed the fat for a while, our boats bobbing in the water side by side. "Hey, what'chu usin' for an anchor there?" Shaw asked. Tugging on the rope, I pulled a long, hollow lead pipe from the lakebed and out of the water.

"It's called a 'Cajun anchor,'" I said, "Shallow, muddy lake like this, you just throw it in like a harpoon and it goes right down in the mud and grabs hold like a 'coon and won't let go." I suppose that must have won me some favor, because shortly after Shaw invited me to join them the next weekend. And that set the pattern for the years to come, where we spent almost every Saturday morning and Sunday afternoon fishing on the lake or goofing off in the woods.

Summer, of course, was more of a daily affair. Near the end of that first summer together, just before school started up again, there was one particular August morning that turned out to have some far-reaching consequences.

Having fished for a couple of hours at dawn, I headed to meet Shaw and Virgil in the woods at a shack-like cabin they called "the House" that had once belonged to a sharecropper. They stumbled upon it when they were only boys, repaired its two rooms with odd scraps of wood and sheet metal over the years, and practically lived in it now. As I neared the House around mid-morning, before I could see them through the brush, I heard them arguing, loud enough that they couldn't hear me approaching.

"Virgil," Shaw said, smearing axle grease on an old rusty cage trap with his finger. "What'd you bring for bait?"

"Jar a peanut butter," Virgil said, opening his pack.

"Peanut butter? Bubba, this ain't no 'coon. Bobcats are carnivores. I need fish guts. Deer heads. Meat!"

Virgil said, "Well? You ain't bring no bait." They both sat back on the leafy forest floor, staring at the rusty trap.

"What are y'all doing with a cage trap?" I said, coming out of the brush.

"Shoot, Elijah, you scared the scat outta me," Virgil said.

Shaw said, "We got a bobcat terr'rizing the place, stealin' our game. What'chu got in your hand there? Nutria?"

I lifted the animal by its long, rat-like tail. "Yeah, he was messing around in my fishing hole this morning so I popped him with the twenty-two. I was gonna skin him and tan the pelt, but you can have him if you need him."

"Perfect," Shaw said. "Give 'em here." He reached out his hand. "Dang, Virgil. Why can't you be like Elijah?" He turned to me. "This fool brought peanut butter."

"Shut up, Shaw," Virgil said. "I don't see you towin' no nutria." Shaw laughed and tossed the carcass to the back of the cage.

Testing the trap a few times, Shaw said, "It'll do. The grease helped." We walked a few hundred yards away and placed the trap on a little game trail that ran through the brush.

"Let's take a breather back at the House," Virgil said. We headed back to the shack and sat on a stump and two cinder blocks around an ashy fire pit. Shaw went inside the shack for a minute and reappeared with a pack of cigarettes. He put three in his mouth, flicked a lighter and lit them. He held one out to me and one to Virgil.

Virgil took a long first drag and then looked intently at Shaw for a moment, who nodded back at him. After exhaling a stream of smoke, Virgil put a loose strand of his long, dark, greasy hair behind his ears and said, "So, Elijah." He paused and looked at Shaw again.

"Go ahead, Virg'," Shaw said.

"Shaw and me been talkin'. It's always been the two of us, y'know. For a long time, we've been lookin' for a third. A third who's like us. Who fits—"

"Misfits," Shaw said.

Virgil continued, "Who misfits. Someone who's kin."

"Only thing is, you ain't like us," Shaw said, looking me up and down. "Well, you is, but you ain't. You think 'bout things way more'n we do, like some kinda philos'pher. Sometimes I see you lookin' at us, or lookin' out at the woods, and it's like you ain't there no more. Like you seein' a vision or somethin'. It gives me the creeps a little, but in a good way."

Virgil shook his head. "What we're tryin' to say is we want you to be our third. We think you're the guy, the one we been waitin' for. We need you. And, I reckon, you need us."

"So, what'cha think?" Shaw said, leaning forward to ash his cigarette over the fire pit.

I glanced back and forth at the two of them while it sunk in. For the first time in my life, I felt naked and unashamed. Known in full without exile. By people I respected, to boot. "Fellas, there's nothing I'd like better."

Shaw flipped open his pocketknife. "All right, hold out your hand. You know what a blood oath is?"

"Shut up, Shaw, and put the dadgum knife away," Virgil said.

He turned to me. "He's just playin'. Welcome to the club, Elijah."

"All that's ours is your'n now," Shaw said. "These woods, the boat, the guns and goods. And, a course, the House. Use it how you want, no need to ask permission. You can sleep here, store your fishin' pole, hideaway from your daddy if he's wantin' to slap you 'round. Play hookie. Or," he said, raising his eyebrows at me, "Iff'n you need a quiet place to be with that myst'ry girlfriend a your'n."

"It's not like that. She's a good girl. Anyway, fellas, I don't know what to say, except - well, I'm in, and it means a lot. I've never belonged anywhere before."

The three of us looked at each other with anticipation, feeling as if something new and big was beginning. Shaw finished his cigarette and tossed the butt into the fire pit and then broke the silence. "Well, we got Virgil, the Redneck Poet. And Elijah, the Redneck Prophet. What about me? What's my title?"

"Just the Redneck," I said.

They laughed. "Fine with me," Shaw said. "Less of a name to live up to. Good luck livin' up to your'n, Elijah Youngblood."

I went home for dinner after spending the day in the woods with Virgil and Shaw. When I opened the door, I heard Momma call from the kitchen. "Elijah, that you?"

"Yes ma'am," I said.

"Come here," she said. I came into the kitchen and sat at the breakfast table. She had her hands in the sink, washing a pot with a sponge. "Aren't you gonna greet your Momma?" She held her cheek out to me. I kissed her and heard her sniff. I sat back down.

"Where you been? Daddy needed your help this morning."

"I was with Virgil and Shaw. We were running a trap for a bobcat. There's a cat's that's been –"

"What you smelling like smoke for?"

"'Cause we smoked cigarettes."

She turned off the faucet and wrung out the sponge, placing it on the back of the sink. "I don't like that, child. You know I don't. What's worse is you aren't even ashamed."

"Aw, Momma, it's just for fun. It's not like that."

"That's how it always starts. This time next year you'll be at a pack a day. Before your eighteenth birthday you'll be cooking meth with the rest of them. Go talk to your Daddy." She pushed open the screen door that led out to the carport and garage. "Frank! Frank! Elijah's coming to talk to you. He's been out with them boys again, smoking."

I got up and went outside, where Daddy was shining his Harley-Davidson next to his truck, which he had just washed and waxed. Momma closed the back door. Without looking up he said, "Boy, why you upset your momma like that?"

"It's just a bit of fun, Daddy. Sitting around the firepit and what not."

He squeezed a spray bottle and began to buff the chrome engine. "Sounds to me like you're caught up in worldliness, son." He shook his head. "Sometimes I fear you won't be on the right side of judgment."

"You mean the Lord don't allow us to hunt and fish?"

"He called his disciples to drop them fishing nets and follow him. To leave it all behind. What are you gonna do when he returns and you're sitting by the shore with that net in your hands?"

"I don't know about that, Daddy. He sure didn't mind blessing St. Pete with a mess a fish."

Daddy withdrew the dipstick from the engine and wiped it on a rag. He checked the oil and nodded to himself, satisfied. "You got to have that mind of yours set on the things of God, Elijah."

"Don't the rivers and trees clap their hands in praise?"

He snorted. "What kind of liberal nonsense you talking? Who told you that?"

"That's in the Bible, Pops."

"If you care so much about the Word of God, forget about them fish next weekend and come to the revival. Brother Ronny's gonna ask about you." He took a step back and looked at the machine, his eyes twinkling.

"You think there'll be Harleys in heaven, Daddy?"

Finally getting his attention, he looked at me sharply. "Boy, what's that supposed to mean?"

"I just saying, you got your motorcycle. How come I can't have my woods and water?"

"For one, 'cause you smoking them cancer sticks out there."

"I'm not so sure that's a sin. Maybe it is. One thing I know for sure, though - there's gonna be woods in heaven. And a river running through them. If they're important enough to be in heaven, surely there's no harm enjoying them here."

"You gotta make it there first, Elijah. That's all I'm saying." He sighed, the twinkle gone from his eyes. "Dadgum, son, you wear me out."

"Sorry, Daddy, I don't mean disrespect."

"Let's just wash up and eat," he said, tossing the rag into the garage and walking past me. "Momma's waiting on us."

FOUR

The relationship with Georgia was no worse for having to remain hidden. As a secret, it was safe, and probably the only thing in Georgia's life she had to call her own. And the promise to keep it pure, mightily as I wrestled with it, kept our consciences clean enough for it to continue. I think it also gave the relationship a depth unusual for a teenage romance, forcing us to find ways to relate that weren't physical. If we had been allowed the freedom of a public relationship and to indulge our desires, who knows whether it would have even lasted. As it was, the whole thing, hidden and forbidden, bound us together like a vow. I suppose I have her daddy to thank for it all, in a way.

In early August, two weeks before school started again, Brother Ronny said farewell to the congregation at the end of a Sunday service. "As y'all know, there's nothing more essential to the Lord's return than the state a Israel. They need our prayers, folks. They need our support. And I want y'all to know - sending me there to help hasten his return is just as noble as if you were going yourself. I'll be back in two Sundays to give a full report. If y'all need something, feel free to reach out to the deacons, all right? And I already know without asking that y'all gonna look after my wife and baby girl while I'm gone." The deacons came up and laid hands on him, commissioning him. It was never quite clear what he would be doing there, but whatever it was, the congregation was filled with awe and eager to see him go forth. I was too, for a different reason.

That night after supper, when daddy had gone to watch TV, I helped Momma clean the kitchen. "Momma," I said, "Mrs. Bonnie and Georgia are probably gonna be lonesome while Brother Ronny's gone."

"Maybe so," she said.

I stacked the plates and put them next to the sink. "He said he expected us to look after them."

"That's right," she said, turning on the faucet.

"What you think we should do?"

"That's sweet of you, Elijah, thinking about them like that." She flipped on the garbage disposal for a moment, then said, "I suppose I could bring them a meal tomorrow."

"That sounds nice, but . . ."

"But what?"

"Still sounds lonesome."

"All right, well," she said, handing me a pot to dry. "I could ask Daddy about having them over. That what you're thinking?"

"Don't matter to me," I shrugged.

"I'll call Bonnie in the morning."

At six o' clock the next evening, there was a knock at the door. I let Momma answer.

"Hey y'all," Momma said. "Come on in. Elijah? Elijah! Come say hello, child. Bonnie and Georgia are here."

"Hi, Mrs. Bonnie," I said, walking into the foyer.

"Evening," she said warmly. "Elijah, you know Georgia, don't you?"

"Yes'm, we've met. Hi, Georgia," I said with an awkward wave.

Mrs. Bonnie said, "Your momma told me it was your idea to have us over. I just thought that was the sweetest thing. I'll be sure to tell Ronny about that."

"Aw, I heard what he said on Sunday. Want to make sure we're doing our duty to the Reverend."

Bonnie smiled, and Momma led her out of the foyer. "Elijah," she called from the kitchen. "Don't go running off outside. Be social and keep Georgia company in the living room while we finish up supper."

"Yes ma'am," I called back, trying not to sound too eager.

Georgia and I sat on two wingback chairs with a small circle table in between us. Unused to fraternizing in public, it was hard to know where to begin. "So, Elijah," she said with a smirk. "I hear you like the outdoors."

"That's right."

"You grow up doing that kind of thing with your daddy?"

"Nah, he's more of a car guy. You know, hot rods, motorcycles. Classic cars. Got a whole garage full. Ten dollars says you get a tour before the night's over."

She smiled. "How'd you get into it all then? The outdoors, I mean."

Momma came into the room and touched Georgia on the shoulder. "Sweet tea, honey?"

"Yes ma'am, thank you." Momma walked off without asking if I wanted anything. A moment later she returned and set the drink on a coaster next to Georgia.

When she left, I said, "Well, behind our neighborhood is a

big patch of undeveloped land, maybe a thousand acres that backs up to the south side of the lake. No fences or anything, just woods, creeks, a few hills. Same woods that're behind the church. My house is just a mile or so northeast."

"Who's it all belong to?"

"Good question, don't rightly know. Probably some investor over in California that's plumb forgot about it. Most of the cabins and rich folks live on the north side of the lake. Anyway, to your first question, when I was about five or six I wandered into the woods one morning when Momma wasn't looking. That evening close to dark, a neighbor found me playing in a creek, stuffing a stick down a crawdad hole. Momma spent the whole day thinking I'd been kidnapped. I got a good whooping for it, but it didn't do any good, I just kept going every chance I could, and Momma finally made peace with the habit. Been roaming the woods alone for ten years now. 'It's the call a the wild,' Daddy used to tell Momma, 'He'll grow out of it.'"

Georgia sipped her iced tea. "Don't seem like you've grown out of it yet."

"Not yet."

"I hope you don't."

"I'm not planning on it." I pulled a loose thread from the fabric on the chair. "Well, enough about me. Tell me about you. I mean, besides being a preacher's daughter."

She looked down and thought for a bit, pursing her lips. "I don't know that there is much else."

"Come on, now."

"There's not much to me, apart from church."

"That's a lie if I ever heard one."

"Sorry," she said with a wan smile.

"That's not right, Georgia. Aren't you made in the image a

God? Nothing on earth's more full of mystery than a human being."

She shrugged uneasily.

"Let me ask you this," I said. "You ever do something that makes you feel alive?"

"Alive how?"

"Alive like . . ." I thought for a moment. "Alive like a kingfisher might feel when he dives in the water and comes out with a fish. Like he's doing exactly what his Maker put him on earth to do."

"Oh," she glanced around the room and then back at me. "I know, sure. I feel like that when I paint. If it's something for school, it doesn't mean as much. But sometimes when I'm alone I'll paint different kinds of things."

"What kind of things?"

"Whatever's on my mind. Could be an empty road with leaves blowing across it. A girl sitting alone on a pew. A boy fishing under Spanish moss," she said, pausing. "The more of my heart I put into it, the more I feel what you're talking about. Alive."

"I bet it's a graceful thing to watch."

She smiled. "Maybe I'll paint you one sometime. I've never had the courage to show them to anybody."

"I'd rather have one of them than a Rembrandt."

She smiled, pleased. "Maybe you will one day."

"See now, you're not just a preacher's daughter. You're an artist."

"I play violin, too," she said with surprise, as if realizing it for the first time.

"And that makes you feel the same way?"

"It depends."

"On?"

41

"My lessons are classical. The old European church composers, you know? Bach, Vivaldi. And they're fine, I appreciate them. The music's pretty and all . . ."

"But . . ."

She lowered her voice close to a whisper. "Classical don't feel like me."

"What does?"

Still whispering, but excited, she said, "Well, one time when Momma and I were shopping, there was a festival in town, you know that Cajun one every spring? And there was a man on the street playing an instrument, sounding like nothing I'd ever heard. It made me want to laugh and cry and dance all at the same time. I couldn't quite see on account of the crowd around him, so I asked Momma what he was playing. She said 'That's a violin, honey. Same thing you play.'

"'Doesn't sound like it,' I told her.

"'He's just playing it like a redneck,' she said. 'They call it a fiddle when you use it that way.'"

Georgia leaned forward, her green eyes filled with light, and said quietly, "Ever since, when Momma and Daddy are out the house, I try to play like that man. Momma wouldn't approve, and Daddy'd condemn it as worldliness. Haven't quite figured it out yet, but even just *trying* to play like that makes me feel the same as when I first heard that man at the festival."

Watching her talk like that, I knew exactly what she meant about the fiddler. "It's a shame you don't get to share that with anybody, Georgia. It's not right. Like a bird that's not allowed to sing, except when no one's listening."

I heard the backdoor open across the house and Daddy shout, "Burgers are ready. Let's eat, y'all."

She reached over and squeezed my hand before standing.

"Guess I am more than a preacher's daughter, aren't I? Thank you."

I headed into the kitchen behind her, feeling a little taller.

At supper, Mrs. Bonnie made the fatal mistake of asking Daddy about his car remodeling hobby. Not realizing her interest was feigned, he spent most of dinner giving the story of how he acquired each car, and the pains he took to restore them. As soon as we were done eating, Daddy offered to give Bonnie a tour of the cars in the garage. I winked at Georgia. While he was among the cars with Momma and Bonnie, Georgia and I stood by the back steps. Low clouds moved slowly above us in the night sky.

"How's your summer been?" I asked.

"Lonesome. Dull," she said, leaning against the railing on the steps. "How about yours?"

"Most days I escape to the woods 'fore my parents wake up. Most of the time I'm with my buddies Virgil and Shaw. I do get lonesome for a different kind of company, though." I glanced over my shoulder at the garage, then back at her. "Thinking about swimming tomorrow morning, with it so hot and all."

"Oh yeah? What time?"

"I usually head out around five thirty or so when the water's still cool. Beat the heat. Sometimes there's a little fog at that time."

Georgia turned her ear toward the garage, where Daddy was carrying on about a leather seat he'd restored. Under her breath, she said, "Same time as my prayer walk."

I nodded and felt my blood pressure begin to rise.

Georgia walked past me to the garage, giving Momma a chance to finally interrupt Daddy. "Frank, I expect Bonnie and Georgia need to get on home."

"They're very nice, Frank," Mrs. Bonnie said. "Impressive

collection." She glanced at Georgia. "I suppose it is late. Let me grab my purse and we'll go." We followed them into the house.

"Thank y'all so much for coming," Momma said.

"Course!" Mrs. Bonnie said. "We'll have to have y'all over next time. Maybe when Ronny gets back from the Holy Land."

"Sounds delightful," Momma said.

"See you, Elijah," Georgia said.

"Yeah, see you," I said.

Momma closed the door behind them and said after a moment, "Well that was nice, wasn't it? And Elijah, thank you for behaving yourself. I think you really made Georgia feel welcome."

"I'm sure it's mighty lonesome when her Daddy's gone."

"You better respect that girl, son," Daddy said, eyeing me. "Don't go messing with a preacher's daughter."

"Aw, in my dreams, Daddy. She's nowhere near my league."

Over the next two weeks, while Brother Ronny was on his crusade, Georgia and I met up as many times as we could get away with. We swam at a nearby abandoned deck a couple of times and fished at the old spot. I also gave her a tour of the two rooms of the House once when I was sure Virgil and Shaw weren't there. She found it fascinating. For the most part, we just walked and talked in the cool of the day.

The last day before her daddy returned, we met at the usual place in the woods near the church. This time there was no fog, only a layer of morning dew and a few mosquitos. I sat with my back to a tree, a little pack beside me. I saw her a long way off, stepping carefully through the forest debris.

"Morning," I said.

"Morning," she said, watching where she placed her feet.

"Can we walk a little slower today?" she said. "Kinda mosey our way? It's our last time for a while. I want to savor it."

"Sure," I said. She stepped beside me and reached for my hand. "Hang on," I said, wiping my hand on my pants. "Sorry, still not quite at ease with you." I reached for her hand again and we began to walk, side by side.

"Where you taking me today?"

"What would you think about meeting Virgil and Shaw? I think they're at the House this morning."

"Would love to," she said.

"I hope you'll like them. Prepare yourself, they're not polished church folk like you're used to."

"That's all right. Neither are you in a way," she said.

"True, but . . . you'll see."

The morning light was shining through the east, behind us, casting an amber light onto the trunks of the trees and the ground beneath us.

"You hear that?" I asked, stopping briefly.

She tilted her head. "What?"

"All the birds waking up. It's a good time to be in the woods. You won't never hear them sing this loud and clear later in the day."

"How come?"

"There's not enough light to look for food right now. That's my guess. They're too busy the rest of the day. Plus, the air is quiet and still. I think they know they've got the stage. Some folks call it 'the Dawn Chorus.'"

"Sounds like the name of a hymn," she said. "The Dawn Chorus. Huh. Sounds familiar somehow." We stood still and listened. "There's so many. Is that an owl?"

"Yeah, that's right. It's his bedtime though. Hear the one

going *cheerio, cheerio?* That's a robin. They're like the rooster of the woods, waking up all the rest."

"What else?" she said.

"That one saying *tea kettle, tea kettle* - that's a wren. They're funny little birds. They can talk all kinds of gibberish."

She squeezed my hand, which was now comfortable and dry. "What's that one? It's like *chicka-dee, chicka-dee.*"

"That's a chickadee."

"Oh," she smiled. "I love it. I never knew the woods had its own music." She closed her eyes and kept listening. "Where'd you learn all this, Elijah, if not from your daddy?"

We started walking again. "I had some help from books here and there, but mostly just looking and listening. All the time I spent out here, hopefully I learned something." I pushed some brush aside so she could walk through.

"You ever get lonely out here?"

"Not really. I do at home though. And I get awful lonesome at church."

"Me too," she said.

"You? That's surprising. Everybody loves you."

"They love me as the preacher's daughter. Brother Ronny's little girl. I got a part to play, you know?"

"I see."

She put her hand to her mouth. "I've never said that out loud before."

"Secret's safe with me, but what's lonely about playing a part?"

"Well, think of somebody in a movie. People may love the person on the screen, but there's no relationship there. They don't know the actress, just the character. People don't know me, just the character I play."

"Can't you just quit playing the part?"

"You *would*, Elijah. That's not so easy for most of us."

"Aw, I'm sure I'd be playing the part if I could. Guess I'm not a very good actor."

We were quiet for a minute. "Sorry for the mud," I said, helping her jump a creek.

"That's OK," she said, "Your friends know we're coming?"

"No," I said, holding down a vine of stickers while she passed. "No telling what we're heading into. We're almost there. I can already hear them."

"Woop!" I called out just before we got through the brush.

"Sooie!" A voice said in response.

"What was that?" she said.

"Just a way to let them know it's me. So they don't shoot me or something."

We made it into the clearing and saw them sitting around the fire in front of the House. Virgil, picking at his guitar, said, "Well, well, w—" stopping short when he saw Georgia step out from behind a tree.

"Fellas, meet Georgia."

Virgil set his guitar aside and threw his cigarette into the coals. He ran his fingers through his long, dark hair and came to shake her hand. "Name's Virgil," he said.

"Hi there," Shaw said, staring at Georgia without getting up. He nodded to her. "Shaw." He had no shoes or shirt on, only a pair of cutoff jeans. He was tending a cast iron skillet on the fire in front of him, a jar of lard and sack of flour by his side. Shaw enjoyed cooking, in part because it gave him a reason to make a fire, his first love. "Care for a hotcake? No syrup or nothin'."

"Thank you, I'm all right," she said.

"Here, have a seat," Virgil said, motioning towards an

upside-down paint bucket as if he were a gentleman pulling out a dining chair. I took a seat next to her on a stump.

"I'll take a hotcake, Shaw," I said.

"I didn't offer you none," Shaw said with a side eye glance. His buzzed head glistened with sweat. "Miss Georgia," he said. "I gotta tell you somethin'."

"Sure," she said, seeming a little nervous. I was, too. For the first time I was bringing together two parts of my life that I'd always kept separate, and I wasn't sure they would pair well together. Sensing that Shaw was in a funny mood, I was already questioning my decision.

"Virgil and I been hearin' bout you. 'Bout how purdy and sweet you was, how the sound a your voice could make a dove cry. 'Bout how just the thought a you works up this boy like a buck in the rut. We been sure 'Lijah was makin' you up all this time. But now I see, he didn't share but half the truth. He been holdin' out on us. Never 'magined he could woo him a girl like you."

I groaned and was about to respond, but Georgia surprised me. "You know, Shaw," she said. "Elijah told me about you, too. He said, 'I can tell they think I'm making you up. Just wait, the moment Shaw lays eyes on you he's gonna flirt with you.'" She was smiling but a little red as she spoke. "Flirt if you want, but it won't do any good."

"Son," Virgil said, "that girl busted you."

Shaw shrugged. "I ain't sorry. Flirtin' or not, jus' tellin' it as it is. Don't let my s'perior qualities worry you, 'Lijah, I got a doe a my own." He took a hotcake off the skillet with a spatula and flipped it into my lap.

"Anyway," I said, eager to change the subject, "What're y'all up to this morning?"

"Aw, little this, little that," Virgil said, shifting around on the cinder block beneath him.

"Virg's composin' a new song," Shaw said.

"It ain't nothin'," he said quietly.

"Georgia's a musician, too," I said.

Virgil said, "I ain't a musician, just a fella with a guitar."

"You write songs?" Georgia said. "Play one."

"Nah," he said, glancing at his guitar.

"Folks, suddenly the Redneck Poet's lost his nerve on account a this lady here," Shaw said. "Show's over. No refunds, sorry. Y'all go on home."

Virgil shook his head and picked up his guitar. He plucked a few strings and adjusted the tuning, starting to strum. "This is a new one. Real simple song. Jus' a sketch, really. No color or nothin' on it yet. Still needs a bridge 'fore the last verse."

"Jus' play already!" Shaw said.

"It's called *Another Moment or Two*," Virgil said. He began to sing, a ragged, earnest voice coming forth.

I ain't askin' for much to begin
Not a friend, a fair wind, nor a fam'ly to tend
Not Solomon's mine nor a sign, divine,
Not to wine and dine in a shrine on cloud nine
All I'm askin' from you
Is another moment or two

I ain't askin' to conquer the earth
For mirth, self-worth, nor a virgin birth
Not ease, a cool breeze, to be Hercules
For the seven seas nor thanks and please
All I'm askin' from you
Is another moment or two

I ain't askin' a lot from you
For sky blue, much ado, nor among who's who
Not to play, swept away, a surprise birthday
A Monet, a buffet, nor a cafe' latte
All I'm askin' from you
Is another moment or two

I ain't askin' for too many things
Not a ring, offspring, nor to spread my wings
For frankincense, nor a white picket fence,
Sixth sense, two pence, nor intelligence
All I'm askin' from you
Is another moment or two
Just a chance to be with you
For another moment or two

He stopped singing and hummed for a while, continuing to strum. Shaw said finally, "Sound like the cry of a heartbroke bear, don't it? He ain't bad, 'specially considerin' his humble or'gins."

I said, "I'm always surprised to hear the kind of things that come out of your head, Virg'. You got a gift. You write that one about a girl?"

He continued to pick the tune on the strings without answering.

"No," Georgia said, watching him for a while. "I don't think it was about a girl."

Virgil didn't say anything, so I said, "How do you know that?"

She shrugged. "It's not just about the words, Elijah. There's meaning in the sound, too. The song didn't feel romantic to me."

"She's right," Virgil said without lifting his head.

"'Bout his fam'ly, I bet," Shaw said with a nod.

Finally, Virgil set his guitar aside, gave a sad smile and said, "Well, that's 'nough a that."

Georgia said, "Thank you, Virgil. I've never heard music so honest and lonesome before. I think I needed it."

"Course," he said.

"Georgia plays the fiddle," I said.

"No kiddin'?" Virgil said.

"'Play' is too strong a word," she said. "Trying to learn."

"I got a neighbor who used to fiddle," Virgil said. "Back when the trailer park was a hot track. She ain't right no more though." He cracked a few twigs in his hands and tossed them onto the smoldering fire, watching them burn. His face looked long and ashen.

"Virgil, you OK?" I said.

"Aw," he said. "Don't worry 'bout me."

"He's in one a his spells," Shaw said. "Here, maybe some food'll help," he said to Virgil, tossing a cake to him. "Hey, 'fore I forget, y'all ain't goin' west are ya? Towards the park?"

"No. Why?"

"Virg' and me got some traps set over by the creek. Foot hold kind. Jus' be careful if you head that way."

"For the bobcat?"

"Yeah, we still ain't caught that thing. Sucker's been robbin' our other traps for — how long now, Virg'?"

"Too long."

Shaw continued, "Too long. It ain't jus' the bobcat though, them traps could catch 'bout anything. Deer, hog, coyote. They're big and strong. I'd bet you a shebear couldn't get outta these heifers. Got 'em bolted to a tree root."

"No, we're not heading that way," I said. "Shebear, huh?" I said, looking over at Virgil with a smile.

"For once, Shaw ain't exaggeratin'. They're big."

Shaw said, "I don' care so much 'bout you, 'Lijah, but I'd never forgive myself if I ruint them ankles a Georgia in a trap. Sure you ain't hungry, Georgia?"

"Oh, why not?" she said.

Shaw laid a hotcake on a little blue tin plate and brought it to her. "Might wanna blow on it first," he said, returning to the fire. He slid some lard off a spoon onto the cast iron skillet and moved it around a little with his finger. Pouring some more batter, he lit a cigarette. "What I wanna know, Miss Georgia," he said, taking a long drag, "Is what you see in this redneck here, Elijah Youngblood."

She looked at me for a moment. "Well, I've never known somebody so down to earth."

Shaw nodded. "Yeah, but look at me - ain't I down to earth? More'n him, I reckon."

She thought for a second and said, "It's more than that. Least for me, he helps me see this life for what it is. In my house, this world's nothing but a dirty waiting room for heaven. My daddy's like Noah building that ark, waiting on the rain to come, preparing for judgment. And there's not one reason to put down roots. 'This world ain't nothing but a sinking ship,' he likes to say, 'don't get caught up polishing no brass.'" Still talking to Shaw, she turned to me. "But Elijah . . . he's not waiting on anything. For him, the rains have come and gone, and he's stepped off the boat onto the new earth and started naming and taming animals and planting a vineyard. He don't mind the dirt. Judgment's passed, and eternal life's already begun, even if it's not what it will be."

Shaw laughed. "Can't say I understand ever'thing you just said, but I think that's what we mean when we call 'em the Redneck Prophet. He don't like the name, but it fits. It's like he straddles the horizon, one foot in heaven, one on earth. Poor fella don't quite fit in neither one." Shaw grinned at me. "Anyhow, I'm just relieved to know we feel the same way 'bout our guy here." He blew a stream of smoke at me. "Don't gimme that look, 'Lijah, you know I'm jus' lookin' out for you. Makin' sure you got the right girl. Seems like a keeper to me."

"I hear you," I said. "You could have a little more tact, though."

"Tact!? Come on, you know better'n that. You 'spect tact from a guy who's barefoot in the woods in cut off jeans and a cig'rette hangin' out his mouth?"

"Point taken," I said. "At least Georgia knows how to put up with you."

"He's just looking out for you," she said, putting a hand on my arm. "Even if it's not with manners."

"I know," I said, "I reckon I'd rather loyalty than manners."

Virgil said, "A roof rat's got more manners than Shaw, but I don't know anybody as loyal. Shaw's somethin' fierce when it comes to his people."

Shaw stirred the food in the skillet. "Keep goin', I like this. What else you got?"

"That's all you get today," I said. He shrugged.

We talked and ate for a while. Georgia asked them questions about their summer, about school, about their families. Shaw did most of the talking, with Virgil adding or editing some things here and there.

Virgil said, "It's all purdy diff'rent than your life, ain't it?"

"Sure is," Georgia said.

"Compared to you, we prolly live like animals," Virgil said. "We got less culture than a armadillah."

"Not at all, I think y'all are fascinating. And you're wrong about the culture. You got heaps of that - even if it's not the usual kind. It's refreshing. Culture's not allowed in my house."

"No 'ffense, but I don't know how you breathe in a house like that," Shaw said. "I'da run off first chance I got."

"There's something else about y'all, too," she said, "I can't put my finger on."

"Stank?" Shaw said.

She smiled and shook her head.

"Friendship?" Virgil said.

"No," she said thoughtfully, "Help me out, Elijah."

"It's the freedom," I said.

"That's it," Georgia said. "I feel it most being with Elijah, but I also feel it listening to you two."

"Freedom, huh?" Shaw said, revealing a mouth full of food. "I ain't ever thought of that."

"There's a trade-off," I said. "If you want freedom you gotta pay a price."

"Oh yeah?" Virgil said. "What's the price?"

"Exile," I said. Georgia, staring into the fire, nodded slowly.

"Huh," Shaw said, "I guess I was born free then. Choice was a'ready made for me." He scratched his glistening head and wiped his hand on his shorts. "What time'd you say you got to get back?" he said.

I checked my watch. "We better go," I said, "It'll be eight before long. Thanks, Shaw." We stood up.

"Nice meetin' you, Miss Georgia."

"Can't believe it," Shaw said without getting up, "The myst'ry girlfriend wasn't made up after all."

"Remember," I said, "Nobody else in the world but you two knows about us."

"I'd just as soon get my foot caught in that trap than spoil a thing as right as you two," Shaw said.

"Don't mind us, 'Lijah," Virgil said. "Sounds like it's her daddy you gotta worry 'bout."

"I'll be back after I drop her off. Then you can show me the shebear traps."

We started back through the brush. I heard Shaw say something followed by laughter.

"Well, what'd you think?" I asked her when we were beyond their ears.

"I'd a lovely time."

"You held your own against Shaw. Proud of you. Figured he'd stir the pot."

"I think he's sweet," she said.

"Sweet, huh? That's a first," I said. "I was nervous about bringing you. Put it off for a long time. Didn't know what I'd do if you and them didn't get along."

"They're your people, for sure," she said. "Maybe they're mine, too."

"Appreciate what you said about me. Almost like you know me better than I know myself."

"Course I do. Works both ways."

Passing under a row of pines, I said, "It's harder this time, letting you go after spending so many days together. When's your daddy leaving again?"

"Not 'til the first week of the New Year."

I counted the months. "Almost half a year. I'll be sixteen by then."

"Yeah," she said quietly. "I've been storing up these last two weeks so I can ponder them in my bed at night when I'm lying awake and lonely. And paint them when I'm by myself and wanting to be near."

"I guess it's the only way for now," I said.

"As long as I'm the preacher's daughter, it's the only way," she said.

"Speaking of," I said, pointing through the trees. "Church is right there. Time's up."

"Not quite," she said.

Kissing under the shadow of that steeple brought me back to our beginnings. Not just the lightning and the fire of the first time, but the blessedness of it. Both times I expected it to feel wrong somehow, but instead felt only wonder and surprise, like being handed a gift from another world.

"Gotta go," she said, stepping back. "Bye, Elijah."

"That all right? Don't want you feeling tore up on account of me."

"Too late for that. I'm tore up in all kinds of ways." She turned toward home. "Mostly good, though," she said over her shoulder.

FIVE

By the time Momma and Daddy realized how close I'd gotten to Virgil and Shaw - about a year after I'd become grafted into the fellowship - it was far too late. The friendship had set for good and established roots. With all that our trio had come to mean to me, I never thought twice about giving them up. I also never lied to my parents about them, which I think kept me from further trouble and more severe punishments.

Even so, for the last two years of high school, at least once a week at supper or in the car one of my parents would bring up the subject. I knew they were only trying to look after my good, so I listened, only rarely disagreeing with them aloud. A lot of their arguments backfired, though. I don't mean that in the typical way of teenage rebellion, as if I wanted to do the opposite of what they said, simply for spite or to prove that I could. No, they would talk about Virgil and Shaw's folks as outcasts, village misfits, "the town pariahs." "That place is nothing but a leper colony, son," Daddy said. "That what you want? Leprosy?" I say such things 'backfired' because when they described them that way, it reminded me of the way people at church and school talked about me. Without knowing it, my parents were building up the trailer park in my mind as a refuge for misfits like me, a whole flock of black sheep where I could be at ease as myself. In our years together, Virgil and Shaw had never taken me to Lakeside Estates where they lived. Always finding an excuse not to, I think they were too embarrassed to bring me. Yet without ever even laying eyes on it, I felt drawn to the place and kin, somehow, to the people.

The night I graduated high school, my parents took a different strategy towards my undesirable friendships, suggested by none other than Brother Ronny himself. "Elijah, I want you to invite those boys to church," Momma said in the car after the graduation ceremony. "It'd be good for them. If anybody can turn them around and get them on a different track, it's Brother Ronny. Even Judas wouldn't have been too far gone for him."

"You don't understand, Momma. Might as well bring an alligator to church. There's nothing further away from their natural habitat." I rolled down the window and felt the evening breeze on my face.

"Exactly, they need converting. Those old trashy ways got to die if they're gonna walk uprightly. No matter, the Lord can make them respectable."

"But Momma, what's respect got to do with it? The Lord himself wasn't respected when he walked the earth. The church in his day had it all upside down. That's why they kilt him."

She turned and looked at Daddy for help, who was busy navigating the traffic in the parking lot. "Frank," she said, tagging him, "I can't tell if he's speaking blasphemy or just being smart with me."

"All I'm saying is this," I said. "Those two boys are rooted to this earth like oaks. Let's say Brother Ronny was able to work them into surrendering somehow - speaking from experience, I don't doubt he could. But the way he goes about it, he's gonna make them trade in every good thing they got, all they ever known, just to get his stamp of approval on their ticket to heaven."

"Course he is!" Daddy said, "They got to deny themselves and take up that cross if they want to follow the Lord. That's just the way it is, there's a cost to it, son."

"I know there's a cost, Daddy, but sometimes I think Brother Ronny asks folks to pay a price the Lord's not asking for. Actually, I think he asks them to give up things the Lord wants them to keep."

"Like what?" he said, defensive.

I put my hand out the window and felt the wind pass through my fingers. "Their humanity."

"Their *what?*" he said with a little laugh, glancing at Momma, incredulous.

"Humanity. Brother Ronny'd tell them their whole lives on this earth, from beginning to end, aren't worth more than a pile a bear scat. The way he sees it, if Virgil's not playing *Amazing Grace* on his guitar, that thing's just kindling for the fires of hell. All the time Shaw spends setting traps and climbing trees and frog gigging? Just storing up judgment for himself."

"Sounds about right to me," Daddy said.

"Not to me. The Lord gave Virgil the gift of music. Made Shaw with the love of nature. Don't seem like the Lord would want them to despise what he's made and called good. Just the opposite, seems like he'd want to bless it. But they'll get no blessing from Brother Ronny. They'd feel like he's trying to take away their God-given dignity. They'll leave feeling like every good thing they've ever known is nothing but trash."

Daddy raised his voice, "How you know that's how they'd feel? Huh? How you know?"

"Cause that's the way he makes me feel."

"Oh!" Momma said, covering her mouth. She acted like she was about to faint.

"Daddy, imagine how you'd feel if Brother Ronny said you aren't allowed to restore and collect cars no more."

He slammed his hand on the center console. "That's not the same and you know it!"

"Elijah!" Momma shrieked. "Enough! I can't listen no more!" She reached for the door handle for a moment, like she was about to get out of the moving car, then put her hands up in the air. "Don't answer a fool according to his folly, Frank."

"No," Daddy put up his hand and pulled the car to the side of the road, parking it. "I got one last question for the know-it-all high school graduate." He turned around in his seat. "You talk like you got something better to offer them." He pointed at my face. "What you got? Hm? You got a better word than Brother Ronny?"

"I don't have a word for nobody, 'cause I'm not a preacher."

"Then what are you, Elijah? Tell me, cause I've never been able to figure you out."

"I'm nothing but a human being, Daddy, but seems like somehow that's against the rules, even though the Lord himself don't mind being one."

Daddy stared at me in bewilderment. Momma was shaking her head and trembling. He finally said, "You need to invite them boys to church, you hear?"

"Yes sir," I said, "They won't come, but I'll do it."

"Promise me."

"Promise."

The next day, I met Shaw and Virgil at the House, where they were weaving together a little fish trap to put where the creek met the lake. Not wanting to delay my dreaded duty, shortly after arriving, I said, "Y'all want to come to church with me tomorrow?"

They turned abruptly. Shaw looked alarmed and angry, like I'd fired a shot at him. Virgil looked wounded, like I'd shot his Granny.

"The hell you ask us a thing like that for?" Shaw said.

"Sorry, my daddy made me promise I would."

"Elijah," Shaw said, "Think about it. If you feel like a fish outta water there, what's it gon' be like for us? You at least got a air bladder like catfish and can keep breathin' for a while. Me and Virg' here, we'd be gaspin' an' floppin' 'round like a perch on a hot deck."

"Plus," Virgil said, pausing and looking over at Shaw, who nodded back to him, "We been to church before."

"You've been? I didn't know that."

"Well, church came to us, I guess," Virgil said.

"That was a hoot, wasn't it?" Shaw said. "Pretty sure it was the same guy, too. Georgia's daddy. I don't 'member his name. Big ol' fella with a boomin' voice? Dark, slicked hair? Smiles at you like a cat at a danglin' mouse?"

I smiled at the rightness of the description. "That's him. When was that?"

Shaw looked uneasily at Virgil for a moment, who shrugged. He said, "I'll tell you the story. 'Bout five years ago, no, maybe closer to ten. . ."

"Closer to ten. Wasn't but a year or so after Grandaddy's

accident."

"Well, while back, one Sundy afternoon, buncha folks descend on the trailer park like buzzards on fish guts. A whole team of 'em, handin' out flyers and carryin' on 'bout a revivin'."

"A revival?" I said.

"Sure."

Virgil took up the story. "So Grandaddy rides on out to 'em in his wheelchair and asks what they doin' all over his property, and they tell 'em they come to save his soul and mend his ways. He asks how they gon' do that, and they say their Preacher Man'll do it for him, all he's gotta do is jus' come to the revivin'. He says he ain't goin' nowhere, that he'd ruther go to hell than sell his soul to a Preacher. He tells 'em don't come back neither, 'less they bring some food with 'em. I guess Grandaddy was hungry that day or somethin'. So them church folk leave a stack a them flyers on a table and go on home. Not long after, them things were blowin' in the wind all over the trailer park. Trash everywhere."

Shaw said, "Well, sure 'nough, would you believe it, them folks come back two weeks later an' setup a whole tent in the middle a the trailers. Ever'body's eager, thinkin' we 'bout to have a feast. Burgers, ribs, beans, coleslaw. Some folks even call their friends and fam'ly. Now, the trailer park had already gone downhill at that point, so nobody was eatin' real good those days. But we didn't see no grill or barbecue pit come out. 'Stead, they put up a platform in that big ol' tent. An' a buncha chairs, not with tables for eatin', but facin' a stage. They setup a big plastic tub they ask us to fill with water."

Virgil said, "The whole thing prolly wouldn'ta even got started if Grandaddy wasn't passed out drunk inside his trailer."

Shaw continued, "'Fore long, they corral us all together under that tent, like we a passel a hogs, and tell us to sit on down.

They start playin' some music, and we think, 'Aw, alright, a little concert 'fore we eat.' They ask us to get up for the music, and some a the church folk stand up front, hands raised an' wavin'. Virg' thought maybe they was on meth. But naw, turned out to be worse'n that. That big ol' guy, Georgia's daddy, I guess - what's his name?"

"Brother Ronny."

"So Brothe–" he stopped. "Hold on. Y'all call 'em *Brother?* Like he's fam'ly?"

"Yeah."

"Naw, I can't call 'em that."

"Call him Ronny, I guess."

"Jus' call 'em Preacher Man," Virgil said.

"So, Preacher Man takes the stage. And at firs', he's real nice, tells us how he used to be not too diff'rent than us. We was all thinkin', maybe he ain't so bad. He's down to earth. Ain't on a high horse or nothin'. So, we get comfy and relax and start to trust 'em. Nex' thing I know, he pulls out a big canvas sack from under the stage, loosens the cinch, and that son of a gun pulls out a live snake, a python prolly eight foot long."

"He ain't lyin'," Virgil said.

Shaw continued, "An' he starts walkin' through the rows a the crowd, puttin' that snake in people's faces, and slidin' the tail 'round on their laps, tellin' 'em the Devil's among 'em, and that they slaves a the Evil One. Next thing I know, an old lady up in the front row name Miss Mattie, she lights a cig'rette. An' Preacher Man charges up to 'er an' grabs that cig'rette out 'er mouth and says, 'Where there's smoke there's fire, folks. I'll show you!" Still holdin' the python under one arm, he holds up the cig'rette and blows on the ash 'til it turns bright and red. He says, "You see it? That's the Lake a Fire right there! An' you suckin' it right down into those lungs a yours!" Then he flicks it into the crowd an' it lands on the lap of ol' Carl, who ain't all there. He jus' looks at it burnin' his leg an' starts hollerin' but don't get up or do nothin'. Then ever'body else starts screamin', 'til finally Prissy his wife come over an' swats it off his lap to the groun' an' stomps on it."

"Then Preacher Man says, 'Hear that folks? That's the sound of a soul perishin' in the fire and sulphur, beggin' for mercy he ain't never gon' get. That's what you can expect, if you don't surrender it all.'

"That's when Virgil's Grandaddy come out," Shaw said. "He wheels on down the ramp from his trailer 'bout a hunnard miles an hour and glides into the tent. 'Who the hell you think you is,' he says, still glidin', 'Wavin' that thing in folk's faces and disrespectin' Miss Mattie! Go 'head, Miss Mattie. Burn one down. Light it up! Go 'head. You alright, Carl? Prissy, you good?' Then he turns to the crowd and says, 'Don't nobody listen to this predator! He the snake, folks! He ain't gon' save your soul, he wants'ta gobble it up.' Now, Grandaddy mighta been in a wheelchair, but he's a big scary fella, 'specially back then. So, the church folk started to shriek a little and back away. But not Preacher Man. Virg' - you wanna tell this part?"

Virgil took up the story, "I ain't never gon' forget what happen next. Preacher Man turns 'bout as red as the Devil hisself, an' he starts shoutin', 'The gates a hell ain't gon' prevail today!' he says, startin' to talk some kinda gibb'rish. Then he starts pointin' an' shoutin' at Grandaddy and says, 'Go on, get! Get thee behind me, thou servant of the Pit!' But Grandaddy don't get behind nobody. He wheels right on up to 'em, just cussin' 'em up an' down. And when he gets close, Preacher Man gets some kinda idea and shouts out, louder'n a gunshot, 'O man who art bound by Satan, be loosed!' An' he sets the snake on the ground, reaches down, and picks Grandaddy up right on outta his wheelchair, and throws him o'er his shoulder like a sack a deer corn, his shriveled ol' legs danglin' down below his big body. An' Preacher Man holds 'em like that for a good ten seconds for ever'body to see. I swear, the whole world was silent. Ain't nobody say a word. Not a crow, not a cricket, not even Grandaddy, who ain't never short on words. I don't like to think a the look on Grandaddy's face. Ain't never seen somebody so 'shamed in my whole life, eyes big and 'fraid like a child, his mouth droopin' in horr'r. Then Preacher Man lifts Grandaddy off his shoulder an' sets 'em up on his feet, an' then let's 'em go.' Course, lame ol' Grandaddy just crumples. When he hits the groun' he cries out like a, like a. . . Shaw what would you call the sound he made?"

"Same one a dog makes when you accident'ly step on his tail."

"Yeah, that sound," Virgil said. "So, I run up to 'em an' - I don't like to think about this neither - poor Grandaddy, he ain't movin' or nothin', just a heap a flesh and bone. We all starin' down at Grandaddy, who's lookin' like roadkill, when all the sudden, *Kaboom!* People scream. Ever'body looks up an' sees Granny outside the tent, a smokin' shotgun in 'er hands. Now you gotta understand, Granny ain't like that. She's sweet as she can be. E'en so, at her feet jus' outside the tent was that eight foot python with his head blowed off, body still writhin' and wigglin'. Granny ejects the first shell then walks past the snake into the tent, pointin' the shotgun at Preacher Man's head. An' she says, 'You sombitch, get your slitherin' self outta here. Now! Don't take nothin' with you 'cept that fork tongue a your'n. Next time I see you on this prop'ty, this 12 gauge a mine'll send you straight back to that Pit you come from."

Virgil continued, "Preacher Man jus' looks at 'er and says,

"Ain't worth throwin' pearls 'fore swine anyway. Dust your feet off, folks, time to go.'

"Then, they gone. Jus' like that. They lef' all their stuff, jus' like Granny said. Hot dogs an' beans - they didn't have no ribs or barbecue or nothin' - the stage, the sound equipment. The headless snake. To this day, the tent's still there. Nice tent, too."

"We don't never talk 'bout that story, 'Lijah," Virgil said, "Don't nobody wanna remin' Grandaddy a that day. But there ain't a soul that don't remember it like yesterdy. Oh, and 'pparently Preacher Man's had the same kinda run-in with other folks like us. Turns out, he likes the trailer parks, where he thinks folks don't know better an' he can o'erpower 'em. Some give in to 'em, but the ones that don't end up payin' for it one way or 'nother."

"So, Elijah, knowin' the story," Shaw said, "I s'pose you can understand why we'd ruther not join you on Sundy."

I didn't know what to say. My neck and shoulders were tense. I wanted to burn or break something, but instead just rubbed my eyes with the palms of my hands. I said, "I don't know how *I* can ever go back to that man's church."

"Why go back to any church?"

"They're not all like that. Besides, for a human being earth without heaven's just as much trouble as heaven without earth. Just the other side of the bayou." They stared at me without speaking. "How come you've never said anything about all that?"

"We thought 'bout it. Figurin' it was Georgia's daddy, we didn't wanna make it no harder for you than it is already with that girl."

"How 'bout this," Virgil said, pausing. "Tomorrah mornin', 'stead a church, how 'bout you come an' meet Grandaddy and Granny. I ain't never wanted for you to meet 'em, for more reasons 'n one, but I s'pose it's time."

"All right. Meet you here?"

"Yeah, mid-mornin' or so."

"Cool."

We were all silent for a while. "Well, 'nough a that," Shaw said, "Let's go find a spot for this fish trap."

Down to Earth

Six

The next morning, I left my house before my parents woke and walked in the woods for a while, thinking about the story of the revival Virgil and Shaw told the day before. I wondered what Brother Ronny's side of it would be.

Around nine o' clock, I met Virgil at the House. Shaw was not there.

"Mornin'," he said. He looked pale, his eyes a little puffy. "You ready?"

"Sure."

"Come on," he said. "Good thing it's Sundy. Granny always cooks a big breakfast on Sundy mornin'." We started walking west. There was a path cut through the brush which gradually cleared as the leafy ground turned loamy and filled with ferns and cypress trees. At a muddy creek we turned and went upstream. "It ain't far, just a few minutes' walk."

"You showed me the place before from a distance."

"Right, from a distance," he said quietly. "You know, bout a hunnard acres a these woods b'longs to Grandaddy. Or did, 'fore they had to mortgage it to get by. Few weeks ago, I heard 'em tell

Granny the bank's gon' take it 'fore year-end. The trailer park ain't the cash cow it used to be, an' I don't think they got the money to make the payments on it." He cleared his throat and spat in the creek. "Won't it be a shame when that day comes."

We jumped the creek and headed up a little ridge, which opened out onto a large field with fifteen or so mobile homes circled around the middle in the shape of a horseshoe. They took up maybe a tenth of the open space. In the middle of them all I could see a giant white tent. Beyond the tent and trailers, the lake glistened in the morning sun. We walked on a worn path through waist-high weeds. Scattered about were old refrigerators and stoves, detached truck beds and rusty tractor parts.

"It didn't used to be like this," Virgil said. "When I was little - I mean 'fore losin' my parents, we had a little grocery and supply store close to the water where 'most the whole lake came an' bought and traded. Granny sold sausage biscuits. Meat pies. Sandwiches and what not. We had 'bout thirty spots on the dock where folks stowed their boats. We had three, four times the number a trailers out here. They liked to party too, 'specially Grandaddy. It didn't get no better. We was proud folk."

"What happened?"

"'Bout ten years ago Grandaddy broke his back divin' in the water on some kinda dare. He was drunk, course. Place like this takes a lotta upkeep. Everything's always breakin'. Ain't nobody with the money or the know-how or the giveadamn to fix it. I try to pitch in, but I ain't good at fixin' and runnin' things. It ain't been fun to watch it all fall 'part. Grandaddy, he don't care no more anyway. He ain't got much left but talk. He got heaps a that though."

As soon as we stepped out of the weeds onto the packed dirt that surrounded the trailers, I saw something darting toward me from the side. I jumped back. "Hey!" yelled Virgil. A giant bird stopped and squawked at him, pecking in his direction. There was another behind it, smaller. He threw a stick and hit the ground in front of the bird. "Go on! That's Elijah! He's alright! That's my friend. He's alright, I said!" The birds ran off a ways and began squawking back and forth to each other. The big one flared its tail and then turned around and showed us its plumage from behind.

"Is that a . . ."

"Peacock. 'Bout all that Granny's got left a the golden age. Used to be lot more. Every Thanksgiving one or two of 'em disappears. Anyway, look out for 'em, they can be nasty. 'Specially the purdy one. He and his girlfriend guard this place better 'n dogs. We got coupla them, too."

We walked around the outside edge of the trailers until we got to one with a wheelchair ramp. "Here we go," taking a deep breath. "Now you'll know why I spen' so much time in the woods."

We climbed the ramp and opened the screen door. The air of the trailer was humid with bacon grease. Stronger than the smell of bacon, though, was the odor of mildew and smoke. "Granny, Grandaddy," Virgil said, "This is my buddy, Elijah."

A woman with short curly hair and bags under her eyes came up and grabbed both my arms. "How are ya, honey?" The skin of her neck wobbled as she welcomed me. "So good to meet'cha. Virgil's been talkin' 'bout you for long time now, like you John the Babdist hisself." She laughed and snorted. "Ger'ld. Ger'ld! We got comp'ny." She walked over to a recliner, muttering to herself. I hadn't noticed at first, but a large man lay back in the recliner, his eyes closed. A blanket lay over his legs. "Ger-ald!" she said, clapping her hands several times in front of his face.

"Woman!" he said, his face angry but eyes still closed. "What is it? I got a hangover that'd keep the Devil hisself in bed."

"We got comp'ny, Ger'ld! Virg' brought a friend."

"Is it that lil' turd Shaw?"

"Naw, it's Elijah," Virgil said.

"Oh, oh. 'Lijah." He opened his eyes a little, pained by the light. "I thought it was Shaw."

He saw me and held out his hand. I couldn't help but notice he was missing two and a half fingers. We shook.

"I know," he said, looking at his hand. "Chainsaw. 'Tween this and my legs, I ain't good for much. But I got it better 'n some. You shoulda seen my sister. She got eatin' up with diabeetus, jus' like our momma. Last ten years a her life, she was losin' limbs right and left. Only one she had lef' when she died was her right arm. Yeah, boy, them doctors carve her up like a side a beef," he laughed. He wiped his forehead with the back of his hand. "Flora! If we got comp'ny, least you could do is turn on the winder unit. 'Specially with all the heat a that stove."

"It's only nine thirty," she said, standing at the stove with her back turned to him. "You chewed me out yesterdy for runnin' it too long. 'Member? Said I was usin' up all your boozin' money."

"That was 'fore we had comp'ny. Dammit, I said turn on the A/C!"

Flora put a cast iron pot and several pans on the table, then she turned on the unit that hung through the window behind me, closing the door. She raised her voice in competition with the rattling hum of the unit. "'Lijah, we got eggs, cheese grits, bacon, biscuits and gravy. An' flapjacks if Ger'ld don't hog 'em. You jus' take as much as you want. Go 'head, get you a plate and let's eat."

"Woman, ain't I the head a this househol'? What 'bout me?" Gerald said.

"I ain't servin' you in that recliner when we got comp'ny.

Wheel on over here and fen' for yourself."

As he was maneuvering himself from the recliner to the wheelchair, Virgil said, "Granny, we should prolly say grace. Outta respect for Elijah."

"Oh, course. He's church goin' folk. Go ahead, Ger'ld. Like you said, you the head of this househol'."

"Grace?!" Gerald said, wheeling up to the table. "Grace ain't somepin' we say. Ain't it all grace? Even my fancy chariot here ain't but a gift."

"Is that what it is? I'll remind you a that next time you whine about it. Jus' shut up and pray, Ger'ld."

Aggravated, he clasped his hands together and closed his eyes. He paused for a moment and then sighed. "Let's see here . . . Lordy, whew, been a while. We ain't got nothin' but these empty, ugly hands to bring to ya. We ain't deserve nothin' but a hangover, but you put this here feast 'fore us. That's mighty good of ya to be so kind to folk like us, who ain't but trash. Oh, and please he'p this young man —" he opened one eye towards his wife.

"'Lijah," she whispered.

"Please he'p 'Lijah feel at home, 'spite a these rough lodgin's. Amen."

We sat at the table and took turns plating our food. As he loaded his plate, Gerald said, "Tell you what. Hah! This is jus' how I like my plate to look. All shades a tan and yellah! 'Minds me a finer times. Feel like a boy at my own Granny's table." He grunted and shifted around in pleasure.

"You came on the right day, 'Lijah," Flora said. "We don't always eat this good. Jus' Sundys, really."

"Rest the week is slim pickin's," Gerald said with a mouthful of steaming grits. "Say, if you come from church goin' folk,

73

what'chu doin' here on a Sundy?"

"Aw," I said. "Hard to know how to put it."

"What, you ain't b'lieve in it all?" Gerald said.

"It's not that. I believe."

"They ain't treat'cha right? You got a grudge?"

"Not against all of them. And I wouldn't call it a grudge. Reckon I just don't belong. The preacher once told me if I was truly born again, I must've come out all wonky-donkey. The runt of the litter or something. They've never known what to do with me, but I don't mind. Actually learned to prefer it that way."

Gerald slapped the table with the palm of his hand, rattling the tableware and making Flora catch her breath. "Boy! Now I know why Virg' here speaks so high a his frien' 'Lijah. There ain't a bit a guile in you! Hah! By the grace a God, you is what'chu is! Y'know'm sayin'?" He poured himself some orange juice. "Yessir, I can tell you a bold son of a gun."

Granny patted my wrist and said, "That means he likes ya."

"I like a man speaks his mind. Sounds like it don't win you no favor with your preacher, but you can stick 'round my house long as you like."

Flora said, "Now, 'Lijah, you got a job?"

"No ma'am," I said.

"Elijah jus' graduated," Virgil said. "Just day 'fore yesterdy."

"More'n you can say for yourself, ain't it Virg?" Gerald said.

"Ger'ld," Flora said.

"What'chu gon' do now that you got a high school diploma? You seem purdy sharp. You goin' to college?"

"Nah, probably to trade school," I said. "I like to work with my hands."

"Elijah welded his own boat."

"No kiddin'. It float?"

74

"Yessir."

"What else you build?" Gerald asked.

"He builds all kinds a things. He's got a dirt bike he built outta junkyard parts."

"It still needs some work. I wouldn't trust it on the highway yet."

"Dadgum, boy. If I had any bones to spare I'd hire you to do some work 'round here. Lordy don't we need it." He belched and slapped his stomach. "Virgil, when you gon' get a job so we can eat like this all week?" He pushed his plate away and began searching in the pockets and crevices of his wheelchair. Finally, from underneath his thigh he pulled a crushed pack of cigarettes. He straightened and lit one and then looked at Flora and said, "Coffee." She huffed and got up and poured him some coffee and then opened a package of powdered sugar donuts and passed it around.

We talked for almost an hour while we ate. I asked a question here and there, which they were always eager to answer. They told me about the glory days of the trailer park, about how it fell apart, about who left and who stayed, about how the bank was threatening to take it all now that they have started defaulting on the mortgage. About the meth heads they'd had to kick out from time to time. They spoke matter of factly about it all, with wistfulness but no apparent shame.

At eleven o' clock, I said, "Sure am glad I got to meet you folks. Thank you. I better get going."

"Elijah's got a lady friend to go see."

"Of course he does," said Granny with a wide smile.

"Come on back, y'hear?" Gerald said. "You're lot better comp'ny than that little inbred Shaw."

"Ger'ld," Flora said.

Virgil walked me out. As we stepped down the ramp, he said, "Sorry, I know they ain't too pleasant to be 'round. There's a reason I ain't ever brought you here."

"I had a great time. I feel more at home here than I do at my own house."

"I will say - they sure treat you better than Shaw. He won't come close to Grandaddy no more." He paused and said, "You'll see. They're a hard pair, him and Granny."

Passing through the circle of trailers, I saw the giant white tent, dirty with a tinge of green, still standing tall. Through the tent I could see the lake, now choppy in the wind. "Maybe so, but in some ways they're not near as hard as my folks."

A couple of dogs came close to us, jumping and barking. Virgil shooed them off. He stopped when we got to the end of the gravel that opened to the paved road, next to the large sign with peeling paint that said, "Lakeside Estates." Underneath it was written on a board, 'Plots ~~Avaleb Avil~~ Open.' "See you 'round, Elijah," Virgil said.

I could have walked through the woods for a shorter route to the church, but the service wouldn't let out for another forty-five minutes. Plus, I wanted some time to think. As I walked the three mile stretch of country road, I replayed the story of the revival in my mind now that I could put Gerald and Flora's faces with it. I thought about the rundown property and their trouble with the bank. No doubt I felt compassion, heartbreaking as it all was, and wanted to help. But there was something else stirring in me. I was surprised by how much I had enjoyed the breakfast conversation, which had affirmed what I already expected. If I had to put words to it, I suppose that, for the first time in my life of exile, I'd found a home.

SEVEN

Two months before my breakfast at Virgil's, when Georgia turned eighteen, she begged her Daddy for a measure of freedom regarding boys. Finally, just a week before when she graduated from homeschool, Brother Ronny made one exception to his rules - after church, a boy could take Georgia out to eat at the diner across the street. It didn't take but a moment to learn why. The whole place was full of his eavesdropping sheep, hungry after a morning of worship. I suppose in his mind, the next best thing to controlling his daughter was spying on her. No doubt an account would be given of every word and touch that took place. Even as I agreed to go, I felt like a catfish being noodled out of its hiding place. I would have at least liked the consolation of seeing the look on his face when he learned it was me that took the bait and came out of the hole.

Although the church hadn't changed much over the last few years, possibly even shrinking a little, Brother Ronny's traveling ministry had grown like a troop of mushrooms. In light of his increasing influence, he was regularly called on to preach throughout the region and to lead revivals and marriage conferences with Mrs. Bonnie. Busy as he was with the Lord's work, Georgia and I found plenty of ways to spend time together beyond his knowledge. I confess, I had not been forthright with the man about my dealings with his daughter, which did bother my conscience some, but I had at least kept my promise to respect Georgia.

I finally arrived at the diner, hot and sweaty after forty-five minutes walking down the vacant road from Virgil's place. I was peering through the windows to see if Georgia was already inside when I felt a pair of cool hands cover my eyes.

Without moving, I said, "I'd gladly stay blind if it meant feeling those soft hands on my face all the time."

Georgia grabbed my hand and pulled me toward the diner. "Come on," she said. No doubt the spies were already taking notes. I was uncomfortable and wary, wondering if we were making a mistake and why she was not being more careful.

The diner was a large, square room, as cold as a refrigerator. On one side was a bar where kids liked to eat. The rest of the walls were lined with windows, parted cafe curtains on the lower halves. I chose a spot in the far corner, reducing the number of listening ears.

"Missed you at the service this morning," she said.

"I know, sorry. I was with Virgil."

"You don't have to apologize to me, but it sure doesn't make Daddy like you more when you're not there."

"I'll keep that in mind."

"No, you won't."

I laughed quietly. "Guess you know me too well. And you also know even if I raise somebody from the dead, your daddy's not gonna like me."

"He'll have to learn," she said, a gleam in her eye.

The waitress approached us. "Anything besides water?"

"Sweet tea for her. Just water for me," I said.

The waitress brought back the drinks and set them on the table. She pulled out her notepad and spoke in a fast monotone, "Special of the day is chicken fried steak, side a mashed potatoes and fried okra; you can substitute the okra for a side salad for an extra $1.50, y'all know what you want?"

Georgia ordered a club sandwich. The waitress looked at me. "Can I just get a can of tuna and a few packets of mayonnaise? I'll just eat it with some of these saltines here." The waitress looked irritated. I smiled and shrugged at her. "I had a big breakfast." She took the menus and walked away.

"Where'd you eat a big breakfast?" Georgia asked.

I told her about my time with Virgil, about Gerald and Flora and the trailer park. I was not yet ready to tell her about the revival Brother Ronny attempted there. "I can't get it all out of my mind, Georgia. It's got me all worked up. It's like finding long lost family or something."

"The way you talk about that place reminds me of the way Daddy talks about his call to ministry."

I recoiled. "No ma'am. Not at all. Matter fact, it's as far from that as can be."

"Then what's it like?"

"Well," I looked out the window. "Hard to say." I watched her sip her tea. "Only two things ever made me feel like this."

"What?" she said.

"The woods, for one."

"What's the second?" she said, gently kicking my leg under the table. "Say it."

"You're bold today. Making me nervous. Where's that meek and mild girl I used to know?"

79

"She's grown up and become a woman."

"Good grief," I said, lowering my voice. "You need to stay a girl a while longer or else you're gonna cause trouble. Don't look now, but every eye and ear in this place are on us. Just 'cause your Daddy let us go on a date doesn't mean we're free." The waitress came and set our plates down. "Anyway," I said when she walked away, "You think I'm crazy about the trailer park?"

She removed a toothpick from one of the quarters of her sandwich. "What do you want to do? Work there? Help them fix the place up?"

"Maybe. I don't have any plans. Definitely want to help. But more than anything, I just feel like I'm supposed to be there." I opened the can of tuna and dumped it onto the saucer, mixing it with the mayonnaise.

"Doesn't sound like they could pay you for your help."

"Nah."

"So, you'd just help for free?"

I shrugged. "At least for now. Maybe they'd put me up in a spare room, work for rent kind of thing." She laughed and shook her head. I opened a package of melba toast and loaded some tuna on it. "What?" I said, "You think I'm nuts, don't you?"

"Yep," she said. "But that's nothing new. You've never cared a lick what people think. Even Daddy, who everybody's afraid of."

"I care what you think."

"So, if I tell you not to do it, you won't?"

"Maybe not. You're about the only person that could make me think twice about it."

She smiled and said, "Let me see. So instead of the plan you've had to go to trade school and get a good paying job to support a family and become a respected member of the community, you want to move down the social ladder into a broke down trailer park owned by a drunkard in a wheelchair, with no promise of pay and no plan for work. And all that based on some kind of instinct you got having breakfast this morning."

"Basically. The instinct has been there for a while though. This morning just confirmed it."

She sipped from her straw and looked around the room. She lowered her voice and said without looking at me, "I wouldn't expect nothing different from the boy who kissed the preacher's daughter the day he got baptized."

"Reckon not."

"That's why I like you. It's like you live upside down," she said. "It won't gain you any favor with Daddy though."

"I know. That's the only thing I worry about. Not him, but you and me. Just tell me this. If it works out, I mean, let's say by some miracle I get his blessing one day to marry you, would you follow me to a broke down trailer park?"

"Whither thou goest, I will go," she said.

"Good to know."

Georgia put down her sandwich and moved the cafe curtain gently back and forth with her finger. Quiet but with eyes full of desire, she said, "Maybe we should just elope."

"I don't like when you say things like that, Georgia. You get me all worked up. It's hard enough already. One of these days I'll take you serious."

"Well," she said, still playing with the curtain.

"Come on," I whispered, looking around at the other tables. "He'll ease up eventually. You're an eighteen-year-old woman now. It's not like he's going to keep you home 'til you're an old maid."

"You don't know Daddy."

"If it's meant to be, it'll work out without having to do a thing like that. That's no way to start a marriage. I'm not crossing a man of God by stealing his daughter."

"You still think he's a man of God?" she said.

I thought of Gerald, lying on the ground under the tent like roadkill. "Doesn't matter I think, still don't want to cross him. There's gotta be another way."

"What if God himself crosses him?" she said.

"I'd be fine with that, but that's none of my business. And don't make it yours either. It'll work out if it's meant to be."

The waitress brought the check. I took it to the counter and paid in cash, then came back to the table. "You ready?" I asked, putting a few dollars on the table. She stood and walked out with me. Half the diner followed us with their eyes without moving their heads. The other half watched us outright with no shame.

I walked her across the street and went past the front and entered the side door of the church, where Brother Ronny's office was. I was going to drop her off and go, but when I started to leave, she said, "Daddy said he wants a word with you." He was meeting with someone, so we sat on the couch in the waiting area outside his door. I kept a wide space between us. After a while, Mrs. Norris, his elderly secretary, came out of the office, smiled at Georgia, and went down the hall to her office.

He saw me through the half-open door. "Elijah! There he is, the Troublemaker of Israel!" he said. "Just picking on you boy, a preacher's joke. Come in." I walked in and shook his bear paw hand, sitting in the stiff chair across from his large desk. He stood and closed his door, leaving Georgia outside, who had lost the color and glow she'd had at the diner.

He sat down and leaned back in his chair, seeming to fill the room. "Good lunch?"

"Yessir."

"What'd you have?"

"Tuna fish."

"Not the special?"

"No sir."

"That chicken fried steak is divine. You missed out."

"I'm sure I did. Maybe next time."

"Huh," he said. Head tilted back, he looked at me down his nose for a while, tapping his fingers on the arm of his chair. Finally, he moved his Bible and the church bulletin to the side and leaned forward, resting his elbows on the desk. A barely audible sound, like the purr of a cat, came from his throat. "I wanted to give this to you personally." He handed me a piece of paper. It was a flyer for the upcoming revival. "Didn't see you last year. Matter fact, haven't seen you in three or four years. Starting to be a little worrisome." I think he wanted me to give some kind of explanation or defense, but I stayed silent. We stared at each other for a while without speaking. "Look forward to having you back with us. The Lord's got something to say to you, Elijah."

"Thanks for letting me know."

"Expect I'll see you there."

"Thank you."

He raised his eyebrows at me, apparently anticipating a confirmation. "You gonna be there or not?"

"No disrespect meant, but it's not likely. I'll be elsewhere next weekend."

"Oh? Worshiping?"

"In a manner of speaking, yes sir."

"Where's that? First Methodist? Church a Christ? Or you sitting under that velvet-mouth Reverend Henry now?"

"Aw, this mountain, that mountain - I thought it was about

spirit and truth?"

"Where you gonna be this weekend, boy?"

"I reckon the Good Shepherd's gonna be leading me through green pastures next to the still waters of Lake Robicheaux."

"The Lord don't lead sheep away from the flock. That's the Devil's work. Sound like he's fooled you into thinking that trashy lakeshore's a replacement for the church."

"Naw, I know there's a difference. I'm sure I'll find a church where I belong one day. Might have to spend some time wandering in the wilderness first though."

He pursed his lips. "Lotta folks get lost in the wilderness. The Devil's Playground, some call it."

"Don't the mountains and hills sing for joy? Even them rocks cry out."

He shook his head and smiled. "You don't know what you're talking about. Those aren't but figures a speech. Your mind's supposed to be set on heavenly things."

"Ain't the earth chock-full of his goodness?"

He gave a quick, high-pitched laugh. "Chock-full, huh? Best definition a worldliness I ever heard. There's no good apart from the Good Lord himself. Afraid you're living according to the things of the flesh."

"Don't the Lord have a body made a flesh?"

He drew back and seemed a little off balance. He had to think for a second. "Course he's got a body, but he's up in heaven, in the New Jerusalem."

"Yeah, but the New Jerusalem descends from heaven down to earth in the end."

He stroked the side of his large face like he'd been hit in the jaw. "You got some impudence in you, son, you know that?" He looked up at the ceiling and sighed and rolled his eyes. Nodding, he said, "You're right, Lord, he don't know. He's just a boy." More at ease now, he said, "I'm not offended. No sir. Brother Ronny takes no offense. A shepherd can't mind the bleat of his ign'ant sheep." He leaned back in his chair and folded his hands in his lap. "Matter fact, I fear for you, Elijah. It might be still waters and green pastures now, but when you go through that valley of the shadow a death, you won't be so insolent. I just pray the Lord breaks that stony heart of yours before it's too late."

"He's never met his match, I reckon," I said. "Thank you for tolerating me and bearing with my ways. That's kind of you. I know I can be trying. There's no sheep more in need of his grace than yours truly."

"Hah!" he hit the desk with his fist, grinning at me. "First true thing you said. I just hope someday, we find out for sure what you are, Elijah. I pray it turns out you're a sheep, indeed, and not a wolf. You know what a shepherd has to do with them wolves."

"I reckon it's kin to what I do with them coyotes."

He leaned forward suddenly, no longer smiling. "What you aiming at, Elijah?"

"Something I said?" I asked. "Afraid I don't understand."

"Your little lunch today." He pointed towards the door.

"Oh, Georgia?"

"That's right."

"I'm fond of her, sir. Grateful for you allowing us to do that."

"No, I said what you aiming at?"

"I'm not sure what you mean."

"What I mean is, I remember what it was like to be a worldly someteen year old."

"Brother Ronny, I promise I'm not aiming to give Georgia nothing but the full respect she deserves as a daughter of the King."

"That's my daughter, too."

"Yes sir, that's right."

"Don't cross me, boy. You hear?"

"I wouldn't dare cross a man of God."

We stared at each other for a while. Without looking, he reached over for his Bible and moved it back on the desk in front of him. "Well," he said leaning back again, "I'll let you go. Appreciate you taking the time. I'm sure a preacher's office is a bit intimidating."

"Aw, not at all. Enjoyed it." I stood and shook his hand. He opened the door for me, and I walked out. "Hope to see you next Sunday, Georgia," I said.

"Come in, daughter of mine. Let's talk," I heard him say from behind me. She passed me as she stepped into his office, looking like a cornered mouse. I left the building.

I suppose I could have made it a bit easier for us if I played by her daddy's rules and told him everything he wanted to hear like everyone else, but I hadn't lived under that man's lordship since I was fourteen, and I wasn't about to submit to it again. What I'd heard the day before about the trailer park revival only confirmed what I'd gathered over the years, that he was not the man he appeared to be.

Even so, I was disturbed as I left that day. Not for myself as much as for Georgia. Alongside her desire to be with me, her courage was growing. She was losing the fear of her father, which is especially troublesome when your daddy is Brother Ronny. That was the first of many times that summer that I felt an approaching doom and wondered how to keep it from falling onto Georgia.

EIGHT

When a teal gets hit with the first cold of fall, the decision to fly south isn't logical but instinctual. I'm sure it's a pain in the rear to fly up and down the globe, but it's in their nature. They don't stay in the cold but seek warmth. And they don't walk but fly. Momma and Daddy didn't like that explanation for why I was moving into the trailer park, but it made sense to me.

My parents and I argued every night that week. Momma told me I was spitting on everything Daddy had worked so hard to give me. Daddy said, "You go and do a thing like that, you're gonna end up like that prodigal son, eating with them pigs."

I said, "But Daddy, this is nothing to do with you and Momma. I'm not turning my back or cursing you. I'm just moving down the road. Besides, that prodigal son came to his senses while he was with the pigs and came out better than everybody."

That was the last straw for Momma. She stood up and put her hands in air and said, "I can't hear no more of these lies, Frank! We got to just hand him on over to his desires. Lord! I'm handing him over to you!" Momma ran to the bedroom and shut the door behind her, continuing to pray out loud for me.

After that, Daddy and I sat staring at each other across the table. "Look what you're doing to your Momma."

"I'm just moving down the road. That's all."

"It's not just that and you know it. Elijah, when you were a boy and you done something foolish, like when you run out to them woods only five years old, we rescued you. But now I hear you saying you want to be a man. All right. Go ahead. Just know, a man don't get rescued. He got to fend for himself. He got to suffer for his own mistakes and learn to pick himself off the ground. So, when you knock on my door a year from now, teeth all black from meth and strung out, asking for money, asking for help, asking to move back in, I'm gonna say, 'Elijah? Elijah who?'"

"Dang, Daddy. That's hard."

"Hard world, son. Best count the cost."

"Tell you what, Momma," I called towards her bedroom. "I give you my word. While I'm there I won't smoke, drink, or chew. Would that ease your mind?"

"And don't date girls that do, neither," Daddy said.

"Done."

I'm sure they were, in part, thinking of my well-being. From their perspective, I don't doubt it was a terrible idea, but there are other forms of well-being they don't account for. Besides that, I'm sure they were also thinking of their reputation. No doubt people would talk. Folks at the church, most of all. I admit, family honor was not a priority at the time, but I had no intention of shaming them.

Having finished with my parents, the only thing left for me to do was talk to Virgil's grandparents. I felt fairly sure they would be up for it, but I knew there might be practical issues. The next morning, a Friday, I walked to the trailer park and found the house with the wheelchair ramp and knocked on the door. Virgil answered, speechless.

"Virgil, honey, who is it?" Flora said from the kitchen.

After a moment he said, "It's 'Lijah, Granny."

"Oh, 'Lijah! Well, ain't you gonna invite 'em in? Ger'ld!" she called. "Ger'ld, we got comp'ny!"

Virgil waved me in. "What'chu doin' here, 'Lijah?"

"Wanted to talk to your Grandaddy about something."

"Ger'ld!" she said, walking to the bedroom at the back of the trailer. "What you doin' on the floor? 'Lijah's here, says he wants'ta talk to you." She came back in the kitchen and said, "He's comin'. Give'm a minute."

After a while, Gerald wheeled slowly down the hall, his skin a little jaundiced and eyes bloodshot.

"'Lijah! Good to see you. 'Fraid we don't have much to feed you this time. Got corn flakes 'n coffee. You like corn flakes?"

"Thank you, I'm all right, Mr. Gerald."

He looked over his shoulder, back at me, and then over his shoulder again. "Who you talkin' to?" I stared at him. He laughed and swatted his hand at me playfully. "I jus' pickin', 'Lijah. Call me Gerald. An' that's Flora. Ain't no Mister and Missus. All right now, go 'head."

"I came thi—"

"No, hang on." He turned to Flora and raised his hand, pointing down at the coffee table. "Coupla coffees," he said. Then, turning back to me, he rubbed his fingers in his eyes and then in his ears and finally nodded and said, "Go 'head."

"I came to see if you got any vacancies."

He raised his eyebrows. "Here at the trailer park?"

"Yes sir."

"Ain't no sirs 'round here neither."

"All right."

"You know somebody needin' a place to live?"

"Yeah, me. I was hoping to move in."

He chuckled quietly to himself, which slowly grew into a bellowing laughter. He swatted the coffee table with the palm of his hand and coughed out a final laugh. "You don't wanna live here, 'Lijah. You got a future. You got a good fam'ly. There ain't nothin' here but a dead end. You don' wanna end up like me. I'd get Virg' outta here tomorrah if I knew how." Flora came and set the mugs down on the table and filled them. "This here coffee's what I call motor o'l black. Good for the liver."

"Gerald, let me ask you something," I said.

"What'cha got, pardner?"

"You ever felt like you needed to do something or go somewhere, but it didn't make much sense on paper? But you were so sure about it, what the paper says doesn't matter?"

He nodded up and down with his eyes closed. "Like a coot flyin' south for winter."

"That's it. So, you do know."

"When I bought the land for this trailer park, thirty, forty years ago, that's how I felt. Didn't I, Flora?"

"Sure did," she said, the loose skin of her neck moving back and forth, "Just like that. I thought you was plum' crazy."

"Only thing is," Gerald said, taking a sip of coffee, "'Fraid I got lost on my way south. Or maybe I got there and forgot the way back. Somepin' like that."

They both looked a little lost in memory. "I saw on your sign out there you had some places open," I said. "Only thing is, I don't have much I can pay at the moment. I was wondering if I could work for rent, at least to start. I like to work with my hands. Maybe I could help out with repairs and upkeep. Sorry, I know it's a lot to ask."

"Listen, bubba. I like you. An' I'd love to have you 'round

long as you can stand us. An' course I'd welcome some he'p fixin' and keepin' everything from fallin' 'part. Only thing is - we got empty plots, but unless you got somepin to park there, won't do you no good. There ain't a single trailer with a open bed here. Ever'body's got a uncle or a frien' or a mistress livin' with 'em. These here trailers are packed tight as my gut after a Sundy breakfast. 'Less you wanna share a bed with that mongrel Shaw, which I wouldn't wish on my worst enemy."

"Ger'ld," Granny said, "What 'bout the Lewises? Ain't they got that lil' Airstream?"

"Their son and his girlfriend moved into it last week. I'm tellin' ya, woman, we ain't got nothin'. Sorry 'Lijah, I really love the idea, wish I could make it work. Come back in a few months, somebody'll prolly die off by then, there'll be somepin' open."

"Huh," I said, sitting back. "Wasn't expecting that. Guess I'll just have to wait." I took a sip of coffee, which was so bitter I could hardly swallow. "Sure seemed like it was right though."

Virgil, who had been forgotten in the conversation, spoke up. "What about the House?" he said. "Shaw and I don't mind handin' it over."

"The Hou'? You mean your lil' play place in the woods?"

"Yeah."

"That's even lower'n this. Might as well sleep underneath an o'erpass with a newspaper."

Virgil shrugged. "Maybe you should let him decide for himself. 'Lijah?"

I set the coffee down and looked at Virgil, then Flora, then Gerald. They were each holding their breath. "Sounds like time to fly south after all." Flora's eyes grew round and moist. Gerald grunted in pleasure and leaned back, shifting around in his wheelchair. I said, "Tell me where to sign."

Down to Earth

NINE

In the time leading up to move-in day, May 1st, Virgil and Shaw fixed up the place for me as best they could, patching holes in the roof, shoring up walls, and re-hanging the door so it would close. They rescued a gently used mattress for the bedroom, added shelves in both rooms and screens on the inside of the windows to keep out the mosquitoes. Lastly, they stocked the cupboard with what seemed like months' worth of food - Wonderbread, peanut butter, jugs of water, flour, Crisco, canned soup and vegetables, and seasonings. Wherever they got it all from, I was grateful.

I figured I'd need some kind of transportation, so while they were busy with repairs and supplies, I worked on my dirt bike. Daddy even helped me with it, more out of compassion for the bike than for me, and not without expressing his disapproval of my purposes for it. The bike didn't look like much, but the engine ran like new once we finished. I didn't have more than a truck bed of things to bring, but on the back of a dirt bike it took about a half dozen trips. Clothes. Guns and ammo. Rods and tackle. A handful of reference books on hunting, fishing, bushcraft and wilderness survival, as well as – to my parent's surprise, I'm sure – a Bible. Besides that, I had two hundred dollars saved up from graduation gifts. I was not yet sure what I'd need it for. Several times Virgil and Shaw brought me housewarming gifts from the neighbors - used kitchenware, odd knickknacks and, my personal favorite, a sign for the door with bullet holes in it that said, "We don't dial 911."

Until I found some way to make money, I'd have to trap and hunt and fish and maybe barter with some of the other tenants. Although I could boil water from the creek for drinking and cooking, I could also walk to the well at the trailer park, which had a hose connected to it. The woods also weren't short on edible plants and mushrooms and tubers, though I'd have to depend on Shaw to help me with what to look for and where. The more I thought about it, the more it seemed like I had been preparing for this my whole life without knowing it.

At the same time, Daddy was right, it was more than just a move down the road. I knew without knowing that this decision would set things in motion that would affect people I loved and determine not only my life but theirs. And I knew if I took this first step, I would not be able to turn back but would have to follow the path to its end, whatever that turned out to be. At the very least, I knew it would involve suffering. It didn't help that I hadn't talked with Georgia in two weeks, since, for reasons I could only guess, she had not shown up to lunch at the café last Sunday.

When everything was complete, Shaw, Virgil and I stood outside the House, admiring the new life given to it. Virgil said, "Some folks might not 'ppreciate a place like this, but I think it's han'some. If I wasn't feelin' so good 'bout havin' you close by, I'd be awful sore 'bout turnin' the keys over to you. It's all your'n now, 'Lijah."

"I don't know what to say. Grateful for you fellas."

"Aw," Shaw said, "You'll be sick of us 'fore long. We gon' be out here ever'day as usual. Only difference is we ain't comin' in the two rooms a the House without knockin'."

"Granny said this evenin', after you get settled in, to come on up for some hot dogs."

"Will do, thank you."

"Welcome home, 'Lijah," Virgil said. They started walking through the woods back to the trailer park.

I stood looking at the House a little longer. It didn't quite feel complete, and I couldn't decide why. I walked around the perimeter and looked through the small paneless windows. I stepped inside and looked at the small table on the left, at the cabinets and shelves of supplies on the right. I ran my fingers along the cast iron stove and the exposed studs of the walls. Something was missing, keeping it from feeling like home. I was no longer a visitor, but a resident, and for some reason that changed things. After I unpacked and sorted everything, I headed up to Virgil's, where Gerald sat in his wheelchair, roasting hot dogs over a fire pit with a cigarette in his mouth. "There he is!" Gerald said. "Come get'chu some grub, neighbor."

When I left the trailer park after supper and stepped out of the moonlit field and descended into the forest, for the first time in my life, I felt lonely in the woods. I've never been afraid of the dark or believed in ghosts. Even so, the path back to the House felt haunted, as if the Devil himself walked next to me with his arm around my shoulder, whispering in my ear like a boon companion. I kept seeing Daddy's red face with his warnings and the tears in Momma's pleading eyes. The church gossip was almost audible, the trees around me distorting into people questioning my sanity, blackening my motivations, clucking their tongues in pity. I had visions of the consequences that would follow, especially of what would become of Georgia. The duck flying south analogy now felt childish and stupid. Why couldn't I, just once, take the normal path? I tried to pray but choked on the words, only groaning.

The doubts pressed me with increasing weight to call the whole thing off, so much so that, by the time I crossed the creek, I figured I'd made a mistake. The compulsion to leave felt urgent, like having a predator on my tail. I decided to grab a few things from the House and head back to my parents', tail between my legs. I could explain it to Virgil and Shaw later. They would understand. They seemed to have their own doubts about whether I'd last anyway.

When I got to the House, there was a brown square package on my doorstep, what I assumed to be another random housewarming gift from the neighbors. It was dark and I didn't have my flashlight with me, so I picked it up and brought it inside, placing it on the kitchen table. I lit a kerosene lantern for the walk to my parents' and hung it from a hook on one of the ceiling rafters while I gathered what I needed. I took the cash from the coffee can and a set of keys from a shelf. Finally, sitting down at the table to write a quick note to Virgil and Shaw, I noticed, written on the brown paper package across from me, *To Elijah, the Troublemaker of Israel.* I tilted my head and stared at it for a while. The compulsion to leave began to weaken, replaced with curiosity. I reached out my hand and grabbed the package, running my fingers across the familiar handwriting. I turned it over and opened it slowly along the seams where it was taped. The paper came off in one piece.

Before my eyes even focused on what I held, I smelled lavender. Then I saw, within a wooden frame, a painting of a belted kingfisher ascending from the water with a fish in his oversized beak. He was turned to the side a little, revealing both his white and chestnut breast, as well as the shaggy crest of his head. The wings and tail of the creature were detailed in a dozen shades of blue, the background a blur of muddy green and brown foliage. Water was falling off his feathers in droplets, and the minnow in his mouth had what seemed like a look of wonder in its eyes. The picture was unsigned, but on the back was written the word *Baptism*.

I shot up from the table and looked through the screen of the kitchen window into the darkness. The woods no longer felt haunted. The dark silhouettes of the trees were themselves again, a midnight blue sky behind them. All the voices had ceased except those of the bullfrogs in the creek. No longer alone, with this addition, the House had become a home, and I was at peace in the woods again. The decision to stay followed naturally.

Taking the lantern into the bedroom, I put it on the shelf next to my bed. On the wall across from the bed I hammered a nail into a stud and hung the painting, my courage growing the longer I observed it. After what may have been a long while, when my doubts were relieved in full, I lay down on the bed across from the painting and turned off the lantern, placing the wrapping paper under my pillow to keep me company through the night. I did not doubt that a cross lay before me, but I was sure again that it was good.

TEN

My daily schedule was fairly simple. Mornings and evenings, being the best time for hunting and fishing, were already reserved. In between the two, my time would be devoted to work at the trailer park. Gerald insisted I didn't have to do that, especially since I was staying in the House, but I wanted to. Plus, everybody was being so generous and kind towards me, I felt indebted.

I sat down with Gerald the first day and asked him to help me make a list of things that needed work around the place. "Aw, 'Lijah," he said, "I don't even much know no more. Go ask the neighbors. They gon' know better'n me. They the ones always complainin'." I set out to go door to door, hoping to be done with the list by lunch time.

"Morning," I said at the first trailer. "I'm Elijah Youngblood. I'm helping Gerald with the upkeep of the property. I was just wondering what you think the biggest needs are."

A short, large woman in a nightgown muttered, "No thank'ye. Cain't hardly 'fford the rent much less pay for a handyman." She began to shut the door.

"No, hang on. There's no charge for it. Gerald sent me to find out what's broken and needs fixing around the trailer park."

"Oh. Oh! Really? No charge? 'Magine that. Sorry young feller, come on in, sit down. I'm Miss Mattie."

It looked like a series of game trails running through the house, one to the kitchen, one to the sitting area, one down the hall. The paths ran through stacks of items. The one next to the couch, for instance, was a stack of National Geographics on top of a VCR, on top of a boxed microwave. "Sorry, I don't get much comp'ny. Just set that box on the other. Have a seat," she said. We sat down across from each other, her on a club chair, me on a couch that smelled faintly like urine. I had to move closer to the middle in order to see her through the stacks of photo albums and cookbooks on the coffee table.

"Miss Mattie, how can I help 'round the park?"

"Well, let's see. Sometimes the water, I'll be tryin' to draw me a bath — funny, when I was a kid Daddy'd fill up a horse trough for a bath once a week, cain't be sure but I think it was on Wednesdys, and each of us kids — there were nine of us — we'd get in the water and Momma'd scrub us down and we'd get so mad at 'er for scrubbin' so hard, but when I think back on it now, course she had to scrub like that, we had a week's worth a dirt caked on us. That way we'd be nice and clean for church — oh, I guess the bath must've been on Saturdy 'cause a church, not Wednesdy. We went to a little Methodist church over in Fuller, that's where I grew up, just outside a Fuller. You know where that is? Anyway, we'd go to church, and you better believe, sure as all the people said Amen, hah, we could not *wait* to get back in that dirt, takin' off to the woods catchin' frogs and crawfish, boys and girls both gettin' wet and muddy. One time, my little brother —"

"Miss Mattie."

"Hmm?"

"I was asking about problems around the trailer park. Were you about to say something about the plumbing?" It took another twenty minutes of stories to find out that some days she had no water pressure in the house.

When I asked if there was anything else wrong with the place, she said, "Yeah, there's a few things. Let's see, what was it? You want some coffee while I think on it?" She stood with some difficulty and walked through the house, leaning forward and putting her hand on each piece of furniture to balance. While the coffee was brewing, she leaned forward on the little two seat kitchen bar and lit a cigarette.

"Open that windah for me, will ya? There's a little piece a wood you can prop it open with." She exhaled a stream of smoke toward the window next to me. "Make yourself comfy, it'll be a sec. I got a new coffee pot somewhere 'round here but I just cain't seem to get rid a this old'n, e'en if it does burn the grounds a bit. Don't perc'late right. Ricky gave it to me for our fifth annivers'ry."

"That your husband?"

She laughed and ashed the cigarette on a little plate on a stack next to her. "We had a good run, Ricky 'n me, 'bout ten years. I wasn't but a girl when we met, long 'fore my hips was all rotted. Ricky loved me good, only person ever told me I was purdy. Made me feel like no one else ever had. It don't take but the love a one to make you feel like you matter - parent, child, hubby - it don't care. Jus' one such'll make you feel worthwhile, like maybe it's worth stickin' 'round this world after all."

"What happened to Ricky?"

"Well, one day, 'bout fi'teen years ago, Gerald come bangin' on my door. Then he busts inside and says, 'Miss Mattie! Miss Mattie!' It's Ricky! Call for he'p and come quick!' So, I go quick as my fat self could go. An' there, next to the mobile home, I saw Ricky's legs stickin' out from under my car, jus' wrigglin'. He'd been changin' the oil for me, an' the jack tumped over. 'Ricky!' I call to 'em. 'Get up, Ricky!' But he don't answer. He was dead long 'fore the amb'lance come." She put out the cigarette on the plate. "Coffee's ready." She poured a cup. "Why don't you come grab yours, save these hips a trip 'cross the room."

We spent another hour talking about Ricky. She showed me an old beard trimmer of his, as well as an alarm clock that was still programmed to his wakeup time. When it was getting close to lunch, I said, "Miss Mattie, you mentioned there were a few other things needing fixed around the park?"

"I did? Oh. No, I cain't really thinka nothin'. I'm content with things the way they are mostly. Don't do too good with change anyway. Hah! Maybe you can tell."

By the time I left, I was hungry. I passed Gerald on the way to the House for lunch, whose wheelchair was parked on the landing outside his door. "How's it goin', 'Lijah?" he said, laughing. "We ain't the most 'fficient folk is we?"

"I spent the whole morning with Miss Mattie."

He nodded. "She got some stories, don't she? Hard life, hard life. She been here since the park opened. Anyway, don't mind me. Take you a long lunch, y'hear? You been workin' too hard, makin' me sweat jus' lookin' at'cha." He leaned back and closed his eyes. "Breezy mornin' like this, I like to bask in the sun like a turtle, 'fore it gets too hot."

I ate a peanut butter sandwich for lunch and came back for the next trailer. "Afternoon," I said.

"Who the hell are you?" a man said, wearing only a sleeveless undershirt and underwear. He looked at me suspiciously. "You one a my son's friends? He send you?" He nodded across the trailer park.

"No, my name's Elijah. Gerald sent me. I'm helping him fix some things around the property."

"Oh. 'Bout fi'teen years too late."

"Better late than never, I guess."

"Fair 'nough. Hang on, lemme get my pants on." He closed the door. Ten minutes later he came out. "I'll show ya few things." We walked away from the trailers into the surrounding field. "'Neath this box here is the septic system. Tell you what, this tank's been overloaded for years. It don't drain right. Ain't nobody maintain it. Gerald spends all his money on booze, so he can't pay no one to service it. So, the three houses on this side a the park, mine an' those two, bein' the closest to the tank, half the time the toilet don' flush, the other half the time we smell what ever'body else been flushin'."

"You think the system needs replacing?"

"Yeah, but that ain't gon' happen. At the very least it needs to be pumped 'fore it explodes. Here's what I think. If you just run some drainage lines from it to some sprinklers out here in the field, you could drain it real quick and efficient, just sprayin' the piss out in the grass. That'd at least take care of the liquids. Solids still need to get pumped, though. Don't look at me like that, sonny, the liquids'd be sanitized by the time they come out. Look it up. 'Septic Irr'gation.'" I scribbled it onto my pad. We walked back to his trailer. He said, "Back when I's in the Navy one a the bases had that kinda system."

"So you were in the Navy, huh?"

"Yeah, what's it to you?"

"Nothing. What was your name again?"

"Call me Monty."

"Good to meet you, Monty."

"Hey, listen. See that trailer over there? Straight 'cross from me? That's my son's house. He lives there with his girlfriend. You see 'em, you tell 'em his daddy still waitin' on that apology. Goin' on five years now, still waitin'. Five years, ain't even seen the face a my grandkids up close." He shut the door before I could respond.

I knocked at Monty's neighbor's. An elderly man opened the door. I told him who I was and what I was doing. He held a shaky hand out to me. "How yoo?" he said. "What's that you said?" I told him again. He looked confused, his head bobbing slightly. "Would love some," he said slowly, "Come on inside."

"Just sit down, you old fart," said an elderly woman, pushing him to the side. She wore an oversized t-shirt over a pair of red shorts. "Can't trust'em for nothin' these days. Let's sit on the porch out here. It's gettin' stuffy inside. You like orange soda?"

"Sure."

"Course you do." She went to the refrigerator and grabbed an orange two-liter bottle and a couple of glasses. Without looking at her husband, she said, "Sittin' outside for a minute. Remote's under the pillah."

We sat in a couple of lawn chairs under a canvas tarp that extended from the roof. "Name's Priscilla, but ever'body calls me Prissy. That no good husband a mine's Carl." She filled our glasses. "Tell me your name again."

"Elijah."

"Yessir. Elijah. Now, what's this you're doin'?"

"Mrs. Prissy, I'm trying to help Gerald some around the property. Just trying to find out what needs work here. So, what problems are you having?"

"Tell you what, Carl won't hardly eat what I make 'em. Jus' this mornin' I make 'em a hot pocket. You ever had them four-cheese ones? They ain't bad at all. Anyway, I set it on a plate an' give it to 'em, an' he says it's too hot. I tell 'em, 'Course it's too hot, it jus' come out the micr'wave. Let it cool.' Thirty min's later I find 'em watchin' *Price is Right*, that hot pocket still sittin' right 'side 'em. I tell 'em, 'It's plenty cool now.' He feels it an' says, 'It ain't cool, it's cold. It's a cold pocket. I can't eat that,' he says. So, I grab it and eat it myself, and I get him a frozen one out the fridge an' toss it in his lap and say, 'You fix it to your own likin.' It sat there in his lap three hours 'fore I threw it back in the freezer. You know what though? If you invite Carl over for food at your house, he'll gobble it up, hot pocket or whatever, don't matter what you fix. God love 'em, I couldn't never live without 'em, but sometimes I wanna cut his throat."

"Prissy," I said, "I was wanting to know about problems around the trailer park. You know, things that need repairing and what not."

"Oh, that. Hmph. Well, somethin' ain't right with the power. For long time, if I'm runnin' the winder unit and turn on the micr'wave, the whole house loses pow'r. I have to be real careful, you know, can't have too many lights on at once, that kinda thing. Tell you what, I wanted to kill Carl last week. I told 'em - loud and clear, mind you - I told 'em, 'I'm 'bout to run the toaster. Don't turn on that TV 'til it's done.' Not a minute later I'm in the bathroom an' all the lights go off. I come out an' there he is sittin' in the dark with the TV remote in his hand. Worst part was, he swears I never said nothin' to 'em 'bout the toaster. Anyway, there's other 'lectrical issues too. When the Lewises 'cross from us run the washer an' dryer, my lights just flicker the whole time. Ask the neighbors, they got same kinda problems."

"Sorry about that, Prissy. I got it written down. I'll see what I can do."

"You ain't touch that orange soda."

"Oh, sorry." I took the drink in my hand.

"Thought you was Carl for a second," she said and laughed without smiling.

I drank the soda and handed her the glass. "Thank you."

After that I decided to call it a day. As I walked toward the House, I found Shaw bending over in the water near where the creek met the lake, checking a crawfish trap.

"How was the first day?"

"I don't have a clue what I'm doing, Shaw."

"Aw, you'll get the hang of it. You're a sharp fella," he said, "I don't care what Virgil says 'bout you." He looked up and smiled at me. "Got a trap fulla crawfish here. You hungry?"

"Starving."

"Get some water boilin'. I'll go steal a few taters and spices from Momma. We gonna eat good tonight."

I went to the House and took a glance at the painting, then went outside to start a fire. There were some embers in the pit from earlier in the day. Tossing some wood shavings and twigs on the coals, I blew on them until they turned bright and caught flame. I added a little more wood and then filled a pot with water from the creek. Sitting on a stump, I stared into the fire and watched the water boil, thinking of the people I'd met that day.

Walking up with the trap in his hand, Shaw said, "You know you don't have to help folks here. Nobody's askin' for it."

"I know."

"Then why you so set on it?" He poured the crawfish into the boiling water then added a handful of small red potatoes and emptied a bag of spice into it.

"I felt - feel - like there's something for me to do here, that's all. Folks have so many needs, can't help but want to do something for them. All the problems Gerald has around the place, I figured I was handy enough, surely I could do some good. Pitch in."

He shrugged. "Maybe you should jus' hunt and fish for a while and see what happens. Enjoy your freedom, 'Lijah."

"Yeah, maybe."

When the crawfish and potatoes were done, Shaw filled a plate and handed it to me, my mouth instantly watering. Without waiting for it all to stop steaming, I cracked and pulled the red tails off one by one and tossed them in my mouth, the spice and steam passing into my sinuses. My eyes watered and ears tingled with the heat. The nicks and cuts on my fingertips increasingly pained me. I took a bite of a potato and felt it burn its way down my throat into my stomach. "Good heavens, Shaw," I said, my face moist. "This is wonderful."

"Good ain't it? Last time Virg' and I had 'em that fresh, his grandaddy said, 'These here crawdads burn better'n a shot a whiskey.' I looked up at him, and that man had tears a joy runnin' down his face."

We laughed together. The heat worked its way throughout my body. "Thanks, Shaw. I needed this. Kinda melts the stress away, don't it?"

"Course. I could tell you was hongry folk tonight."

ELEVEN

The next three days weren't much different. A whole set of different problems were explained and demonstrated to me. The Lewises showed me the foul-smelling place where skunks kept mating under their trailer. Their son and daughter-in-law in the Airstream had no hookups for plumbing and electrical. I approached Shaw's trailer but rather than knocking I just listened to his parents fighting and throwing things against the wall. Each visit took an hour or two, and none of them were very productive. By the end of each day, I was worn out, overwhelmed, and down on myself. I wasn't doubting my decision to move there like the first night, but I finished feeling about the size of a mosquito. I laid in bed a long time, rummaging through all the problems and people and stories. There wasn't a single one I could solve. And now I'd gotten them all looking to me for help.

The next morning, I heard a knock at the door. I hadn't slept well and was irritable, still lying in bed. "Come in."

Another knock. "What?" I raised my voice. "I said *come in!*" Another knock. I rushed to the door and opened it, but there was no one there. I heard a noise around the corner and looked but didn't see anything. I walked around the whole perimeter of the House. Nothing. I peered out into the morning woods. It was either Shaw playing a joke or a woodpecker. Aggravated and still half asleep, I took a deep breath and headed back inside.

"That's no way to greet your girlfriend."

I jumped like a deer with an arrow in his lung. Sitting on the edge of the kitchen table, arms crossed, was Georgia. Her smile faded after a moment. "What's wrong?" she said, standing and hanging her bag on the chair. I shook my head and squeezed the bridge of my nose.

"Want to talk about it?"

"Sure," I said, "You gonna be here a minute?"

She nodded.

"Let me wash up and we can go on a walk," I said. I headed to the creek and washed my face with a bar of soap, brushed my teeth, and changed shirts. A few minutes later I came back, and we started through the woods.

"You get my kingfisher?"

"Yes ma'am, I did. You sure know how to show up at the right moment. Tell you what, though, now that you're here, I'm feeling a little self-conscious. I see it through your eyes all the sudden. I know it must seem strange. I know it's . . . trashy."

"All I see is a man who's wild and free. Alive."

"If you say so," I said. "Anyway, what're you doing here on a - what day is it? Wednesday?"

"It's Friday. I'll tell you about that in a minute, first tell me what's wrong."

I explained the past week to her - all the people and the problems and my complete inability to help. Miss Mattie and the Lewises and Monty and his son and Shaw's folks. Prissy and Carl. I told her about doubting myself and all the questions that had awakened me in the wee hours of the morning. She walked beside me, still and quiet, a look of compassion on her face. After a while, however, I noticed the corner of her mouth begin to lift in a smile.

"Mmhmm," she said when I was done, her face bright with amusement. I waited for more, but she didn't continue.

I stopped walking. "What?"

"I know what's wrong."

"What?"

"You're not content to be a worm anymore," she said, enjoying herself.

"Huh? Something funny?"

"I didn't think you wanted to be a fisher of men."

"I don't."

"Could've fooled me. Seems like exactly what you're doing. You're trying to save this place, to play the hero. Thinking you gotta fix their problems. What happened to being a worm on a hook?"

The trees above swayed a little with the wind. "Keep going," I said, feeling like a child. "I'm listening."

"You came here with a plan or direction or whatever, and it's not working out the way you thought. Well, Elijah, I never heard of a worm with a plan. That's the fisherman's job. He knows when and where the fish are swarming and schooling and how to read the weather and what technique to use for each bait. All the things you've taught me. The fisherman's the one with the plan, and he doesn't tell the worm what it is. The job of the bait is just to let itself be used."

"What you're saying is I'm a worm holding onto a fishing pole." I thought for a second. "Suppose that is silly. That would explain the way I'm feeling. A worm *should* doubt himself if he's trying to be a fisherman, or really anything other than bait.

Maybe that's the next painting you should make for me, a little worm trying to cast a line."

"Besides that, sounds to me like the fisherman's going a different direction than you expected, and it's time for you to hand him the pole and relax. Trust him. Unless you want to be like . . . well, you get the point."

"Go ahead."

"No."

"Might as well say it. I need to hear it."

"Unless you want to be like Daddy."

I felt like I'd been punched in the gut. "Now I'm even more embarrassed. You're right, though."

"We all need help, Elijah. Even you."

"Thank you for putting me in my place. I guess the question is, what *do* I do?"

"This is a dream come true for you. You've wanted to do this since you were five years old. To live in the wild, to depend on nature's bounty, to 'rest on the bosom of Abraham,' remember? This is a gift, Elijah. Don't ruin it by trying to earn it somehow. Receive it. Enjoy it. Go fish, not just for food, but for all the reasons you used to."

"All right boss, ten-four, but what about the people and their problems? Do I just let them be? Leave them as they are?"

"Maybe you should just be a good neighbor and see what happens. Don't try to fix anybody, serve. Just *be* with them. I don't think they need what you think they do, at least not from you. Virgil and Shaw don't want you to solve their problems, they want your friendship. Sounds like Miss Mattie would much rather a listening ear than her water pressure fixed. And Gerald? Hm. He just wants somebody to sit with him in the sun."

I bent down and picked up a stick, snapping it a few times. I tossed the pieces onto the forest floor one by one as I thought and leaned back against a hickory. "You know, we been together a while now. But today I've learned I need you in a different way."

"It's always been the other way around when it comes to this kind of thing. All I'm doing now is reminding you what you taught me these last few years."

We kept walking, finally arriving in silence at our old fishing spot. "Wanna sit?"

"Yes," she said.

We sat at the end of the peninsula, the water surrounding us on three sides. She leaned her head against my shoulder. "So, what are you doing out here on a Friday morning?" I said.

"I got a handful of news, Elijah. Some good, some bad."

"Mmk."

"After our last lunch, when you and Daddy talked, he decided it wasn't a good idea after all for us to meet. He said it was too soon, that he misjudged me, thinking I was mature enough to make wise decisions for myself."

"Figured that was why you didn't show up at lunch the next Sunday. Suppose if it was somebody else. . ."

"That's right, there's a handful of good church boys he'd be fine with. But you? Let's face it, he's not a big fan."

"That's nothing new. And he sure doesn't trust me."

"That's right, and Sunday lunches are over, I'm sure for that reason. Just as soon as they began."

"Not surprised. Probably shouldn't have even done it. No telling where it's gonna lead. From the start I felt like I was baited into the whole thing. Who knew he was so good at setting traps."

"He probably just wanted to see if there was anybody that had feelings for me already. I don't think he suspects everything else." She paused and touched her chin. "Momma, on the other hand, I think she's onto us. She asks some questions every once in a while that make me think she knows about our times together. One time she said, 'You ever see Elijah Youngblood out on your prayer walks? Heard he spends lotta time in the woods.' Another time I told her something you said at youth group and she said, 'Might want to hide that look in your eye if you talk about him in front of Daddy.' But she doesn't ever ask directly about us. If she did and I told her outright, I think she'd feel burdened to tell Daddy. I think it makes her nervous, but I kind of think she's happy for me, too."

I felt the approaching doom again. "So, what's the good news?"

"Well, one more piece of bad news," she said, pausing. "Daddy said he wants to have you over for dinner so he can hear about the trailer park and talk about why you been missing worship."

"Oh, I already knew about that. My parents have been telling me that since I moved out here. I need some time first. I gotta figure some things out. Like what I'm doing here. And what I'm gonna do about us."

"I know. Take your time. You don't have to go at all, you know. Just curious, though — you done with church now that you moved here?"

Peering out at the lake, I saw Brother Ronny throwing Gerald over his shoulder like a sack of deer feed and blowing ash onto Miss Mattie. I heard Carl hollering with a cigarette burning his lap. I said slowly, "If I quit church as a whole, I'd end up no better. Instead of a ghost, I'd be an animal. Either way, less than what a human is meant to be. Done with your daddy's church, for sure though."

She lifted her head and turned to me, studying my face.

"There something you're not telling me?" She knew me too well.

"Nothing that can't wait for later. Come on, now, I need to hear the good news."

"Hm," she said, sitting back again. "Good news is, Momma and Daddy's marriage retreats have really taken off, so they're going to be in Texas and Arkansas every weekend for the rest of the summer. They'll leave early Friday mornings and come back late Saturdays."

"And they're not making you go?"

"Daddy said the conferences would just get me thinking about marriage, and that I'm not ready for it. Said he wants me home, preparing myself for community college in the fall."

"Sounds like you need a tutor."

"You know one?" she smiled.

"Shaw almost got his GED."

She slapped my arm. "You'll do just fine."

"Aw, sure. I got a whole curriculum for you. Marine Biology on the jon boat. Child and Family studies at Shaw's trailer. Theology with Gerald."

"Yeah, yeah," she said.

"Wait, so that starts today? They're gone?"

"Yep. They left this morning, before the sun was even up."

I tossed a rock in the water and watched the circles ripple outward. "We've never had that kind of time together."

"'Til sundown tomorrow."

"Dang," I said, a little shiver of joy running through me.

"What do you want to do? Fish? Swim?"

"Hm," I said. "You ever been on a dirt bike?"

"Course not."

"Come on."

We rode the bike through the woods along the walking paths

I'd cleared the last few years. The bike was only meant for one person, so she had to ride close and wrap her arms around me. For half an hour we hooped and hollered our way through the trees and mud and water. Finally, we rode past the House and up the hill into the field around the trailer park. I did several laps at full speed along the borderline, Georgia's hair flying everywhere. Riding up to Gerald's, we came to a stop, and I turned it off and put the kickstand down. "Watch your leg on the engine there," I said, "It's hot."

"Well now!" said Gerald, from his wheelchair on the landing. "I recognize 'Lijah, and I know that idjit Shaw. But who the hell are you?"

"Gerald, meet Georgia."

"Georgia?" he unparked, wheeled down the ramp, and glided up to her, offering her his sweaty, two and half fingered hand.

"Hi, Gerald," she said.

He turned to me. "You been holdin' out on us, 'Lijah? Where you been hidin' this pearl?"

"She just came this morning. To visit."

"Oh, oh, right, right. What'chall been doin, besides visitin'?" He winked at me.

"Aw, just wandering in the woods, sitting by the water." I looked over at her. "She's been putting me in my place, too."

"Yes sir!" he laughed. "That's it! Every man needs a woman to put 'em in his place. We need our women folk to bring us down to earth, don't we? Huh?" He sat up a little in his wheelchair. "They remin' us we ain't more'n men. But the good'ns - and I 'spect Georgia's a good'n - they remin' us we ain't less'n men neither." He grunted and sat back, pleased with his wisdom. "What'chall doin' the rest a the day?"

"Whole lot of nothing. Fish, swim, cook over the fire. We

don't get to see each other as often as we'd like."

"Oh, right. Well, don't mind us. I'll make sure you're lef' 'lone. You deserve a day off, hard as you been workin'!"

"Actually," Georgia said, "I'd love to meet the neighbors. I heard so many stories from Elijah, I want to get to know y'all, too."

He stroked his unshaven chin. "I'll be damn, 'magine that," he said, looking around at the trailers. "Tell you what. I tell you *what*. Yes sir, yes sir. I'm callin' a potluck tonight. What'chall think? We ain't done one in few years now, and 'Lijah needs a right welcome anyway. 'Sides, I'm sure he wants to show off his rib, here. Ain't that right, 'Lijah!" he batted his hand at me. "I'll let folks know. Potluck under the tent. Six o'clock. BYO*B*!" He turned his wheelchair and went slowly up the ramp, talking to himself. We started back to the House, leaving the dirt bike behind.

"He's something," she said once we got into the woods, "Mr. Gerald."

"Just wait," I said. "They're all something. You don't get characters like this in town. Here, nobody cares what folks think. Nobody's trying to impress each other. And they're not fooling themselves either. They are who they are."

"No wonder you wanted to fly south. This is your kind of place."

"Yeah, they sure do have their share of problems though." When we crossed the creek I said, "Lemme give you a proper tour of the House. Then we can try to catch some fish for the potluck before it gets too hot."

I showed her the repairs Shaw and Virgil made and the supplies they brought, then brought her to the bedroom, where she saw the painting on the wall.

She looked at it briefly and said, "It looks good in here, in this light. Put my heart into that one, you know."

"I know. That's why it ministered to me like it did. And I won't ever be the same for it. I wouldn't have stayed here otherwise."

"I think the place is lovely. Maybe one day I'll get to live in it with you."

"Nah, this is a bachelor pad. You need something a little more fancy, comfy."

"Whatever, doesn't matter to me," she said. "Now, let's go fishing. I got a bathing suit on beneath my clothes. In case we swim."

We walked the creek to where the jon boat was tied up and got in. I paddled us around in a quiet lagoon, me in the back, her in the front. It was a windless day, so I kept us anchored in the shade whenever possible. She asked all kinds of questions about the water and fish, partly out of curiosity, but also, I think, because she knew how much her interest meant to me. I caught a handful of decent sized catfish and perch, kept on a stringer in the water off the side of the boat. When the heat started to get oppressive, I said, "You ready to swim?"

"You're gonna have to wait. I haven't caught a thing." I sat back, pleased with her response. I placed my pole to the side and watched her cast for half an hour, quiet and determined. I rested my eyes a little. Stirring me awake, she jerked her pole back and cried out, "Get the net!" The hook set. Curving her pole, a fish thrashed at the top of the water twenty feet away. After a full five minutes of wrestling, she brought it close to the boat, where I lifted it in the landing net. She reached into the net and, removing the hook, pulled out one of the smallest largemouth bass I'd ever seen. The fierce look she had fighting the fish had turned into a grin. She blew her hair out of her eyes. "Got one," she said, holding out the bass, a little sweat glistening on her forehead.

I stared at her, awed into silence. "That's a lunker right there. Downright heifer."

"Keeper?"

"That's not just a keeper. I'd gladly trade every fish I ever caught for that one," I said.

She laughed. "You're not even looking at it."

"Sure I am," I said. "Hand it to me, I'll put it on the stringer with the others." She passed it to me and sat back in satisfaction.

"All right," she said, "Now we can swim."

"Let me paddle us to our spot. It's not far."

I rowed us out of the lagoon, across a narrow channel of water, and through a forest of half-submerged bald cypress. Arriving at an abandoned deck attached to a clump of trees, I tied us off. Over the last few years, the secluded waters around this half-rotten deck had become our own personal swimming hole. I stepped onto the hot, splintered wood and helped her up. Her blue and red bathing suit beneath, she pulled off her shirt and shorts and dove into the water. Not far behind her, I leapt into the water before she could get too good of a look at my wiry body with its farmer's tan. Even though the water was not cool, it felt refreshing and delicious after fishing in the heat for hours. We jumped and dove off the dock for an hour before finally sitting on the edge of the deck, our legs dangling in the water. Georgia in a bathing suit was almost too much to bear, like looking into the sun, so I kept my eyes mostly elsewhere. We talked until we were dry again, then put our clothes back on and paddled to the peninsula.

I gutted the fish next to the lake while she watched, asking questions. Then we brought it all back to the House, where Virgil and Shaw had a fire going.

"Hey y'all," Georgia said.

"Oh," Virgil said, shaking his head. "Now I get it."

"What?" she said.

"Grandaddy told us, "Lijah's got him a diamon' in the rough down there. Go see the treasure he been hidin'.' I didn't know what he was talkin' 'bout, but now I get it. Good to see you."

"It's been a while," she said, sitting down near the fire. Her hair was still wet. "Good to be back. Hope to come more often."

"Yeah, buddy," Shaw said. "Come on."

"That fire hot enough to cook over?" I asked.

"Sure," Shaw said. "You want me to fillet and fry up that string a fish? For the potluck I reckon?"

"That'd be great. Shaw likes cooking, Georgia. Almost as much as he likes fire." I handed him the stringer. "Let Georgia watch how you fillet them. She wants to learn." I brought the fish fry and a jug of oil out of the House. While Shaw instructed Georgia, Virgil oiled and seasoned a dozen cobs of corn and wrapped them in foil, burying them into the coals of the fire. An hour later, it was time to go to the potluck.

Twelve

We crossed the field and passed through the horseshoe of trailers to the tent, setup in the middle. "Elijah," Georgia said quietly, carrying a pan of fried fish. "Why's this tent got the church logo on it?" My heart dropped a little. I hadn't ever noticed it before, but she was right. On the top side of the tent in gray was the faded logo of Mt. Sinai Community Church, a burning bush. Underneath it, just barely legible now, were the words *The Lord thy God is a consuming fire.* "Surely they didn't steal it?"

"No," I said. "And don't mention that to anyone, trust me. I'll explain later."

As we walked under the tent, two men were laying plywood on top of a sawhorse. Flora put a red and white checkered plastic sheet on top. "Y'all set your food down on the table here," she said. They set up another table while Georgia stared at the roof of the tent.

"Now, who *you* b'long to?" Granny said, grabbing her arm.

"Elijah," Georgia said proudly.

"I knew it! You're his lady friend. Come on inside, you can

he'p me."

Miss Mattie came next, leaning forward and hobbling, a casserole dish in her hands.

"Hey, Miss Mattie," I said.

"Good to see you, 'Lijah. Would you len' me a han' and go close my door? I left it wide open. Cain't quite manage it all. That'll save these hips a trip." She sat down in a chair, breathless. I went and closed it for her and came back. I searched the group for Shaw's parents but did not see anyone I thought could be them.

Prissy came up to me. "Jus' watch," she said without saying hello, "He gon' gobble up Miss Mattie's cass'role, but he won't touch my mac 'n cheese. And it's name brand! He does it to spite me, almost sure of it."

Carl came up to me and smiled and gave me his shaky hand. "How yoo, Jer'miah?" he said.

I noticed a short, stocky lady with white hair coming from the far side of the trailer park, one I had not met so far. She pushed a wheelbarrow in front of her, pausing and setting it down every ten steps to rub her hands. I jogged over to her. "Can I help?" I said.

"Oh, sure. You the new fella?"

"Yes'm."

"You're cute, y'know that? Least compared to what else we got 'round here."

"I like your wheelbarrow ice chest here."

"Thanks. I had to thinka somethin'. I got neurop'thy so bad, I didn't know how to get all these drinks o'er there."

"Neuropathy?"

"My hands. They ache all day long and when I use'm too much they just cramp and lock up like a possum playin' dead."

"I'm sorry to hear that.

"Aw, it's my fault. Drank my way into it. Sober three years now, though. Three years, two months, and . . . eleven days. What's your name, honey?"

"I'm Elijah. You?"

"Samantha, but *you* can call me Sammy."

Once the tent was full and the food and drinks were out, Gerald wheeled to the front of the tent near the stage and called out, "Well! Howdy howdy howdy now! Thanks for comin' ever'body. Got us a special 'ccasion tonight. New blood in town - *Young*blood, y'hear? Y'all give a lil' welcome clap for your new neighbor, Mr. Elijah Youngblood." People applauded casually, looking around the crowd until they spotted me. "We ain't had nobody move in for long time, so y'all treat 'em good. Oh, and he got him a peach with 'em tonight, a Ms. *Georgia* peach. There she is - welcome!" People clapped again. "Now, y'all go 'head and make your plate. Take all you wan', but eat all you take." Everybody started chattering again, making their plates. "Oh, hell! One more thing. We gon' have us a lil' ambyance tonight from our very own - Virgil on vocals and guitar, and Monty on the banjo. We'll let 'em eat 'fore they play. Autographs after, y'know'm sayin'! Aight, go 'head an' eat." He wheeled to the drink table, dipped his cup into the wheelbarrow ice, and poured some cola. Taking a flask from his wheelchair pocket, he added to the drink and stirred it with his finger. He put the cup in his lap between his legs and wheeled to the back of the food line.

I found Georgia, who was glowing. "You look like you're having a good time."

She smiled, but looking over my shoulder, she said suddenly, "Hey, where's Virgil going?"

I turned and saw Virgil heading towards the House. I ran and called to him just before he made it into the woods. He turned to me, pale and sweaty. "You all right?" I asked.

"I didn't even know until ten minutes ago that Grandaddy wanted me to play. Kinda surprised me. I ain't practiced much lately, and it's been ages since I performed. I can't do it, Elijah. Just let me go hide in the woods like a coward."

"You don't want to play?"

"It ain't that. I love playin'. It's just all the people. I can't handle all their eyes on me."

I put my arm around him. "Well, Virg', maybe you shouldn't be playing for those people. Who do you play for when you're by yourself? Who are you singing to? Writing songs for?"

He didn't answer for a while. "When I was seven my daddy gave me an acoustic Baby Taylor he found at a garage sale. I'd make up songs usin' the only four chords I knew. Ever'where I went, I had that guitar strapped to my back, ready to play when the mood struck. So, naturally when things got hard at home, I'd pick up my guitar and start playin'. It was all I knew to do. And often, by the time I was done with my songs, there was peace again in the home. We didn't have a happy home by any means, but those moments I'd play for my parents were the happiest of my life. Maybe they'd say the same. So, to answer your question, I reckon I do it for Momma and Daddy."

"Think you could play for them with a crowd watching?"

He stared in the direction of the tent. "I don't know."

"Who knows, Virg', maybe they can still hear you."

"I guess I'm up for trying." We walked back to the tent together. I noticed a little color had come back into his face. "S'pose once I get up there and get goin' I should be all right. Monty's gon' play with me, too, so that helps."

I made a plate and found an open lawn chair and sat to eat.

There weren't enough chairs for everyone, so Georgia sat on my lap.

"Oh, I see you're taken?" Sammy said from the chair next to us. "That's too bad."

"Yes'm, afraid I'm taken. This is Georgia."

"I'm Sammy," she said, holding out her gnarled hand to Georgia. "You keep hold this boy here. There ain't many eligible bachelors in these parts."

"Yes'm, I sure will."

After Georgia and I talked with Sammy for a while, I heard Virgil's voice come over the speakers. "Thank y'all for havin' us tonight." His voice was shaky, and he was mostly looking down. "We ain't had nothin' to celebrate in a while, so this is a treat havin' my frien' 'Lijah move into town." He paused and took a breath. "As y'all know, name's Virgil. O'er here on the banjo is Monty. Sammy, would love to have you up here like the old days, but, well, you know. Alright, Monty. One. Two. One, two, three."

The first piece they played sounded fine, but Virgil looked stiff, his voice not quite full. In between songs, Georgia brought him some iced tea. He took a swig and rolled his neck a little. "We got any Johnny Cash fans here tonight?"

People cheered. "Cash is king!" somebody yelled.

"This one's called *Country Trash*."

"Who you callin' trash, Virg'!" someone else called out. Virgil smiled and began to strum his chords.

The crowd laughed and hollered in response throughout the song. By the end of it, apparently encouraged by his interactive audience, Virgil said, "Well, guess it's time to share an original with you. This song's 'bout watchin' Grandaddy wrestle an alligator one time when I was a kid. Right off that dock. Y'all 'member that?" Various cheers came up from the crowd. "It's called *Grandaddy Long Legs.*"

People shouted and whistled and patted Gerald on the back. He grunted and cheered and raised his red plastic cup. Virgil tapped his foot and started to loosen up as he and Monty played the intro for a minute. Virgil closed his eyes and smiled while he picked at the strings, beginning to enjoy himself. He sang,

> *Years ago walked a man*
> *Who was married to my Gran*
> *A big fella fulla gall*
> *None brave 'nough to brawl*
> *'Cept once a nasty gator*
> *Come to 'em with a wager*
> *Sayin' "Betcha can't beat me*
> *No way you gon' d'feat me*
> *I'mma stomp you in the swamp*
> *You sorry white chump"*
> *An' without sayin' a thing*
> *That man up and stuck*
> *The crock's head in a lock*
> *"Aw hell!" the lizard says,*
> *And he howls and he begs,*
> *"Mercy, Grandaddy Long Legs!"*

"Hottt doggg!!" Gerald called out above the music. Everybody cheered and began to clap to the beat. Virgil's whole body started moving now as he tapped his foot on the stage.

While he played the transition to the next verse, Georgia leaned over to Sammy and said, "Did I hear Virgil say you used to play?"

"You best believe it, honey," Sammy said over the music, "I was part of a travelin' bluegrass show. We went all over the country. We were big, real big."

"Why'd you stop?"

"Drank too much. Partied too hard. Fun while it lasted. Now my hands can't hardly run the bow 'cross the strings without seizin' up."

"Bow? Does that mean you played-"

"I was the meanest lady fiddler you ever saw," Sammy said. I felt goosebumps raise on Georgia's arm.

The song ended with Virgil and Monty having a duel, back and forth, back and forth, then both at the same time until, finally, Monty's banjo trailed off and Virgil played the outro.

And if you ask what become
Of the alligator scum
Jus' take one gander
At the purdy dark leather
On Grandaddy's long legs.

Over the praise of the crowd, Virgil said, "That'n's for you, Granddaddy."

"True story, y'all!" Gerald said, "He ain't lyin'! Got the boots inside!"

After *Grandaddy Long Legs,* Virgil fully embraced the stage. Seeming to forget the crowd, he gave himself over to the music and began to truly perform. His voice and face and body were no longer his own, but became tuned to the melody and lyrics, synced to the rhythm. The more he played, the harder it became to tell the musician and his music apart. In fact, having entered into his creation, I stopped noticing Virgil at all, being so immersed in the images and stories and emotions that had grown out of the compost of his own life. He sang of the woods and water, of empty cupboards and the small joys of a simple life, of unforgivable regrets and of dreams that could never be - things everyone there knew well. For a brief moment, stepping out from under the spell, I saw Virgil in the fullness of his being, in the height of his powers, and loved him. I was proud to know him, and so was Gerald, apparently, who was weeping so hard by the end that, as the encore started, Flora had to wheel him up to the trailer while he wailed something about Virgil's daddy.

When Virgil finished, he took the strap off his neck and set the guitar aside. He said, "Well, that's all I got. Thanks, ever'body. Let's not wait so long next time." And there he was again, back from whatever blessed place he had gone, a shy, skinny eighteen-year-old with long hair and cut-off sleeves and holes in his shoes. It was clearer than ever in that moment that his music was not his own, being too great to have come from such an unremarkable figure. It was a gift, to him as much as to us.

"Sammy," I said as everyone started to clean up, "Georgia's been trying to learn the fiddle for a while now. Maybe you could give her a few tips."

She looked over at me, her tired eyes wet with emotion. "You don't know what you ask. If I hadn't just watched that performance, I'd say no. But now?" She shrugged. "You caught me at the right time. Come on by. I'll help."

"You sure?"

"I'mma be upset if you don't. Knock on my door, I'm home. Any time. Well, wait 'til ten thirty at least. My hands are mos' stiff in the mornin' and I get irr'table."

I turned to Georgia. "What do you think?"

She nodded. "If it's not too much trouble."

Sammy waved a hand in the air and walked to her wheelbarrow.

I called Shaw. "Could you help Sammy with her wheelbarrow? I have to get Georgia home."

"Sure, boss," he said.

"Come on," I said to Georgia, "We'll take the bike." It was still parked by Gerald's. As we mounted it, I heard loud, incoherent voices from inside the trailer. I started the engine, and Georgia hopped on and held tight. We went through the woods, slower this time and with the headlight on. I stopped a ways before the edge of the church property.

"Want me to pick you up in the morning?"

"No, I'll walk."

"G'night," I said.

I leaned in to kiss her, but she pushed me back. "No," she said. "You're keeping something from me, I can tell. You said you'd tell me why the church tent's there."

"Georgia. It's late. That can wait until tomorrow."

"No, it can't. What are you hiding from me? There's no secrets between one flesh."

"We're not one flesh yet."

"Tell me or I'm not coming tomorrow."

"It's a long story. Let me tell you in the morning."

"You got a curfew? 'Cause I don't." She stared at me, unmoving. "Come on, I'll sit and listen while the stars come out."

I leaned the bike against a tree and we sat near the edge of the field, under the stars and the silhouette of the church steeple. I told her the story of the trailer park revival, about the snake and Miss Mattie's cigarette and Carl getting burned, of the attempted exorcism or healing that left Gerald in a heap on the ground. I thought Georgia would be crying by the end, but instead she sat in silence. In the moonlight I saw her jaw set, her eyes narrowed.

"That why you stopped coming to church?"

"Yeah," I said. "Don't know that I would've kept going much longer anyway."

"Don't blame you," she said. Then she spoke with a firmness that startled me. "Don't ever keep things from me again. No matter how much you think it might hurt." She got up and started walking towards her house.

"You mad?" I called. She didn't answer.

I went home and lay in bed, my thoughts swirling. I turned and looked at the painting of the kingfisher for a while before turning off the lantern. Not fully sure whether Georgia would show up the next morning, I finally fell asleep and had dreams full of music and angst.

THIRTEEN

To my relief, at first light the next morning, through the window over the kitchen table I saw Georgia pass through the brush into the clearing, a bag slung over her shoulder. I waited outside the door. "I'm sorry," I said. "Shouldn't have kept that from you." I'd never seen her so disheveled, like she'd spent the night in a den of wolves.

Without answering, she walked past me and sat on one of the upside-down paint buckets around the fire pit. A hollow, faraway look in her eyes, she stared into the ashes of yesterday's fire and said, "You're not the one I'm mad at, Elijah. A little, but not really."

"Who then?"

"Daddy."

"See, that's why I didn't want to tell you. I didn't want you to hate your own daddy."

"I think I've hated him for a long time. I just realized it last night when you told that story. I've seen him treat folks that way before, plenty of times. Even me and Momma. But he's always giving reasons to justify it, spiritual reasons, you know? And I've always believed him. Last night was the first time I admitted the truth to myself. Finally saw him as he really is. The first half of the night I spent cussing him. The second half I just cried."

"He treats you and your momma like that?"

"Not quite like that, but yeah. That's why we've spent our whole lives trying to keep him happy."

"He ever hurt you?"

"He's never hit me, if that's what you mean. He's got other ways of beating us down and keeping us in our place."

"Like what?"

"Hard to describe, I'm still wrapping my mind around it. There's a whole web that Daddy's spun. A whole system, and it's hard to even know you're in it. Momma and I are both caught in that web. She feels it, I know she does, but I doubt she'll ever admit it to herself."

"Tell me what home's been like for you. You've never said much about it."

"Hm, well," she said, running her fingers through her hair. Standing up from the paint bucket and pacing around the fire pit, she became flushed and spoke rapidly, like a hose full of water that's finally unkinked. "If we say the wrong thing in front of somebody at church, we get humiliated at home for hurting his witness. God forbid we accidentally wear something that shows too much ankle or shoulder. One time I used a little mascara my friend gave me, and he just about drowned me in the kitchen sink washing it off, putting my face in the water and asking how I become a harlot, interrogating me about who I was trying to impress. Just a couple of days ago, he overheard Momma and I discussing whether there's gonna be dogs in heaven, and he laughed so hard and said, 'Y'all so ign'ant! This is why women got to stay silent.' He makes us feel so stupid, like we can't think for ourselves, like we can't know anything apart from him."

"I'm sorry, Georgia. That's so wrong. Shame on *him*, Georgia, not on you."

"If we don't respond right to those things, he'll lock us in our room for a day at a time, nothing to eat or drink, no bathroom. That's what happened after our lunch date. Or he'll shun us for a week at a time, pretending like we don't even exist, until he feels like we're repentant enough. And if we ever, even in the meekest way, push back on any of it, he makes himself all big and red and starts hollering until we're submissive and quiet. Whatever the case, he's always righteous, Elijah, always. And everything and everyone, Momma and I included, we're just tools for his ministry. I swear, that's the only thing we exist for, to serve him. I wouldn't dare try to be my own person around him, have my own dreams and interests and desires. He crushes anything that don't serve him, that don't build up his name."

"Bet you've got a lot of hurt stored up," I said.

"I do, but I didn't even know it until now. The worst part of it all is, he does it all in the name of God. I think that's what makes it so hard to recognize. Even now, it's hard to break free. Even as I'm telling you this, there's a part of me that doubts everything I'm saying. After all, he's done so much good for people. It's got me all tied in knots. I hardly know what I believe anymore. About anything."

"I can't say I'm surprised, but hearing you confirm what I've suspected just about sets me on fire. Thinking of you in that house all these years, a girl whose never been seen by her father, never been pursued as a human being. What kind of dirtbag doesn't take interest in a daughter like you? He's missing out. Holy *smokes*, he's missing out."

"One good thing is - I don't feel tore up about you and me

at all any more after admitting it all to myself. I chose you over him a long time ago, and I know for sure *that* was the right decision. You treat me like an actual person. Not a tool or a hindrance. Makes me want to face him and tell him what I think. Tell him about us, that'll really get him."

"No, don't do that. Not for me, not for us. Promise me you won't say anything about us, Georgia, I don't want to see you hurt no more than you already are. Even though he's not the man of God you thought he was, he's still plenty powerful."

"I hear you," she said. "But it's not going to be easy sitting under his preaching and being in the same house, knowing I'm stuck in a spider's web, getting the life sucked out of me. All I want to do is be out here with you."

"I know," I said. "We'll find a way." I took a deep breath to try and ease some of the anger. I waited to see if there was anything else. "I'll keep listening if you need to say more."

"No, that's enough for now."

"No wonder you couldn't sleep," I said. Seeing her like that, wild-eyed and disoriented, I'd have thrown myself in a fire to make it right. I changed the subject, instead. "What's that you got in the bag?"

"It's my violin case. Fiddle."

"Oh, good. I'll make us some breakfast and if you're not too tired, we'll visit Sammy."

At ten thirty, we went to Sammy's trailer. She invited us in and led us to a pair of recliners. Setting glasses on the side table between us, she filled them from a two-liter leftover from the party. "Should still have some pop to it," she said. Then she went to her room and came back, setting a worn fiddle and bow on the coffee table. "Well, you seen mine. Now show me yours," she said. Georgia took hers out of its case and set it on her lap.

"Good, good. Now. Tell me why you wanna play the fiddle." Georgia told her about her classical lessons and about the man she heard playing at the Cajun festival. She left out who her daddy was but talked about her parents' disapproval. When she mentioned trying to teach herself over the years in secret, Sammy said, "Hah! That a girl."

When Georgia finished, Sammy said, "You know, violin and fiddle actually ain't the same instrument."

"Really? I thought -"

"You know how you tell the diff'rence?"

"How?"

"Nobody cares if you spill beer on a fiddle. Hah! Jus' pickin' with you. Same instrument. Now listen. Nothin' wrong with classical, but I gotta warn you. It mighta ruined you for fiddlin'. All your life you been followin' notes on a page, every jot and tittle, doin' the biddin' of Bach and Mozart. Classical is beautiful, but it's strict as hell. Precise. *Clean.* Some folks like that. They got minds that work that way. But for others, hah, it feels like slavery. 'Cause they like the mess. They need it. Jus' give'm the key an' the beat, but any more'n that an' they feel suffocated. A fiddler plays with their ears, not their eyes. The best kinda fiddlin' is spontaneous, unpredictable. Wild. So, I guess what I'm sayin', Miss Georgia, is if you wanna transform that there violin to a fiddle, you gon' have to break free. An' I'm warnin' you 'head a time, you may not be able to."

"I understand," Georgia said.

"Play for me. Here's the beat," she said, tapping her foot. "Gimme somethin' in the key a D."

Georgia began to play. It was pretty, but I knew it wasn't what it was supposed to be.

"Stop," said Sammy, holding up her hand. "You ain't hardly usin' any open strings. Why you 'fraid to use'm?"

"The open strings?" Georgia said. "Really?"

"Course! You gotta add the open strings that harmonize with the key. The drone strings. Otherwise, you ain't got a fiddle."

"Funny," Georgia said slowly, taking in Sammy's words. "In classical I was taught the opposite, to avoid the open strings since they mess with the sound and dirty up the other notes. I've spent my whole life doing my best not to touch them."

"And that's all true if you're playin' the violin. But in *fiddlin'*, we want the dirt. The beauty is in the mess, honey. Course, it's gotta be mess that harmonizes. Embrace them open strings and let'em ring out, y'hear? That's the heart of what gives the fiddle that earthy sound. Got it?"

"Got it."

"Now, let's start basic. Play me a shuffle."

"Shuffle?" Georgia said.

"Yeah, Nashville shuffle? Georgia shuffle? Synco shuffle? No?" Georgia stared at her blankly. "Oh, boy," Sammy said. "You 'bout as virgin of a violinist as it gets. 'Lijah, you go find you somethin' to do. Georgia and I got some work to do. It's gon' get dirty."

I left and came back after a couple of hours, cracking the door and looking in. They were talking together. "Y'all good?"

Georgia nodded. Sammy said, "I reckon that's enough for one day. We covered a ton. I'm wore out," Sammy said. She looked at me. "I know, I ain't a easy teacher, but don't 'spect me to 'pologize for it. Only way I know to do it."

"I don't take offense," Georgia said. "You're just trying to break me free."

"With that attitude you might just make it. Bye. Come back soon."

"Thank you, Sammy," Georgia said. "I've been hoping for something like this for a long time."

"Your biggest problem's gon' be up here," Sammy said, touching her knobby finger to her temple. "You gotta learn to embrace the mess. Not just the open strings. All of it. Anyway, I'm hungry and need a nap. See you next time."

Down to Earth

138

Fourteen

Despite the rumors, I really can't take credit for what happened next, something people debate and discuss to this day. Having taken Georgia's rebuke to heart, I had committed simply to being a good neighbor. The fact that something remarkable happened on my watch gives me no more credit than is due the soldiers guarding the tomb on Easter.

She was right, though - that was all that people needed from me. I visited with the neighbors and kept my eyes out for any ordinary opportunities to serve or to visit. I pushed Shaw's little sisters on the swingset. I changed the flat tire on Sammy's old Lincoln. I also even had a few awkward dinners with my baffled and disappointed parents. Georgia came on the weekends, taking lessons from Sammy each time. On Sundays I had breakfast with Gerald and Flora. Mostly, I just fished.

As far as work, I did the only thing I felt adequate for, which was to sort through the junk scattered about the field around the trailers. Wanting some company besides the occasional peacocks and dogs, I drafted Shaw to help. Hitching a rusted out jon boat to Gerald's old truck, we loaded the junk into it and dragged it to the side of the road and dumped it. Everyone warned me the local trash service didn't pick up anything that wasn't in a garbage bin, but it turned out not to matter. Other locals passing by on the road saw the junk and threw it in the back of their truck or trailer and hauled it away. Busted dishwashers, blown out tractor tires, rusty car axles - it didn't matter. Before sunset, they were gone. I put everything that seemed worth keeping (or that Gerald told me to take off the trash pile) in a sectioned-off area close to the lake. I would have used the abandoned supply store, but it was so packed with junk already, I could not even step inside. It was also crawling with rats and roaches, so outside storage was fine with me.

On a Monday morning in early June I went to visit Gerald. He was sitting shirtless in the sun, his gray-haired chest shining with sweat.

Without opening his eyes, he said, "Mornin' friend."

I stepped up the ramp to his trailer. "Morning. You sure like to sit out in the sun."

"Yessir. Makes the hangovers more easy passin'. Sweat out them toxins."

I didn't say anything. He opened one eye at me and closed it again. "I see the way you look at me, 'Lijah. You don't say nothin', but I know."

"Look at you? I don't know what you mean."

"Sure you do. I know you don't despise me like some. It ain't that kinda look. But I know you wanna help. Here's the thing, I ain't 'fraid to admit I got a problem. I tried to quit before. Flora gives me hell 'bout it. Ol' Sammy preaches to me 'bout them twelve steps. Listen, I always been a drinker, but back in the day it was for fun. I partied hard, but I wasn't no slave to it. But that changed after the accident. Ever since I been bound to this chair here, I been bound to that bottle. They go han' in han'."

"Well, I'm not here to preach."

"I know it, I know it. Even so, since the firs' time I met'cha, you been one who speaks the truth. You tell it like it is. That's why I like you. Makes me wanna tell it like it is, too. I know you been wond'rin'."

"That's true, I have," I said. When he didn't continue, I said, "So, how'd it happen?"

"You mean how'd I end up in this chariot here?" He slapped the metal on the wheels.

"That's right."

"I'll tell ya the story. We was havin' a good ol' time one night, me an' some frien's. And a buddy a mine from Texas - he's dead now - we was shootin' bull 'bout fishin'. He started talkin' trash 'bout Lake Robicheaux, sayin' it was no good for catchin' fish, sayin' it was so dirty an' dark, e'en the mudcats can't see nothin'. We argue for an hour 'til finally he says, 'Bubba, I'll betcha a hunnard dollars, if I throw this quarter in that water, you couldn't find it in less'n a week.' So, he toss a quarter out. And I's so worked up and defensive 'bout the lake, without thinkin', I hand 'em my beer and dive right on in after that quarter. I didn't e'en think 'bout it only bein' three foot a water. Yessir, went headfirst into the mud. It felt like, like . . . you know how you eat a crawfish? Crack 'em in two and pull the tail off? It felt 'bout like that. Drinkin' and divin', 'Lijah, that's what got me in this fancy chair. They don't mix too good."

"How long ago was it?"

"Oh, I lost count. Ten years I guess."

"Doctors couldn't help?"

"They said them nerves were so black and flatten', ain't no chance I'd ever walk again. Still spent a fortune on surgery though."

"I'm sorry, Gerald."

"Aw, I been plenty sorry for myself, I don't need none from you. Anyway, that's that. You need somepin'? Or you jus' comin' to visit."

"Yeah, so, you know I been clearing the field."

"You keep that fridge like I told you?"

"I kept it. So, I found a whole bunch of wood. It's old, but it's the pressure-treated kind. Not rotten."

"What'cha wanna build?"

"I was thinking about repairing the dock. It's not enough to go to the end, but it'll at least be long enough for people to drive up and park their boat. Or to fish from."

"That's a lotta work. I ain't askin' you to do it, but go right 'head. Them piers and beams should still be good. And somma the boards on top still good, too. Don't go throwin' out every one."

"I won't. Feel free to come supervise if you want."

"I jus' might. And do a little baskin' while I'm at it."

I spent the first half of the week ripping up the rotted boards and was about halfway through the replacement by Friday morning. Georgia was doing lessons with Sammy while Shaw and I worked on the dock under Gerald's supervision. He had parked his wheelchair on the pier not far from us and set the brakes. He sat back, hands folded in his lap, soaking up the sun. He didn't say much to me, but, as usual, he couldn't leave Shaw alone.

Shaw knocked loose an old board and tossed it onto the bank, clearing Gerald's head by no more than a foot.

"Bes' watch out!" Gerald said.

"If you so worried," Shaw said without looking at him, "Maybe you should head on home. Be a shame if someone accidently knocked you in the head."

"That two by four's bigger 'round than you is, Shaw," he said. "I'm jus' doubtin' them scrawny arms can lift it, that's all."

Ten minutes later Gerald said, "Hey boy, ain't that daddy a your'n teach you to swing a hammer?"

"No," Shaw said, "But he taught me to swing a fist."

"Go 'head, hit me, boy! I don't need no legs to put you in a half-nelson."

A little later, Gerald said, "'Lijah done put three nails in to your one, Shaw."

"How you know that? Your eyes ain't even open."

"Don't have to be. I got a pair a ears always open. An' I tell you what else I can hear is you mutterin' under your nasty turd breath 'bout me."

"I ain't mutterin' nothin'. I'll say it to your face." Shaw turned to him.

"Go 'head then!"

"Aight, I'll tell you. I's just thinkin', must be real nice to have a excuse to do nothin', to make ever'body else do the work for you. 'Dock needs fixin', 'Lijah.' 'Trash needs takin' out, Virgil.' 'My crack needs wipin', Flora.' That chair there gives you a excuse for ever'thing. E'en for bein' a lousy no-good drunk."

Gerald bolted upright and unparked his wheelchair. "I'mma crush that lil' inbred head or your'n. Come're!" He grabbed his wheels and rolled them with his full strength toward Shaw. Further up the dock, I leapt to try to get in between them, but I was too late. Shaw stepped aside and Gerald rolled straight off the dock, his right wheel falling first, then his left, twisting him so that by the time he hit the water he was looking straight up at us, his eyes big and fearful, his mouth open in horror. He disappeared underwater, neither calling out nor fighting the water. Shaw started shouting for help. I jumped feet first into the water and felt around until I found Gerald at the bottom, six feet below clinging to his chair, motionless. I planted my feet into the mud and pulled him out of the chair. I couldn't get above the water with him in my arms, so I got underneath and put him over my shoulder, lifting him out of the water. I figured he'd be shouting and cursing Shaw, but he said nothing. I trudged through the mud and water toward the bank, still carrying him, his lifeless legs swinging around in front of me. Shaw's hollering for help had gathered a whole group of people, including Georgia. I laid him down gently on the grass. At first, he looked like a dead, bloated fish, washed up on shore.

"Ger'ld? Ger'ld!" Flora knelt and stroked his head and cheek. He began to blink. Other people started chattering. Shaw stood over him, apologizing over and over.

Gerald stirred a little and his eyes shot open. "Shut up, Shaw! Flora, shut up!" Flora sighed in relief, realizing he was alive.

"I'll go get the chair," I said, but he caught my arm with his hand.

"Hol' tight, 'Lijah. Sit me up." I helped him. He looked down at his bare feet, then around at all the watching people, and then burst into tears.

"It's all right, Ger'ld," Flora kept saying. "It's all right." He leaned onto Flora's chest and wept harder.

"I'm awful sorry," Shaw said again. "I didn't mean what I said. I shouldn't't've provoked you."

Gerald raised loud sobs worth a whole lifetime of grief. Half the trailer park was gathered around him, the same look of helplessness on each of their faces, some wiping their eyes.

"It'll be all right, Ger'ld," Flora said.

"Y'all don't understan', I —"

"We do, we do," she said, stroking his face. "You fell, that's all. But you gon' be jus' fine."

"No. Dammit, lemme talk. These're happy tears."

"What you mean, honey?" she said.

"Look at them lil' piggies go!"

"Ger'ld, you had a fall. You ain't right. Jus' lay back down a while."

"Woman!" he said, slapping the ground with his hand. He pointed at his feet with his two-and-a-half fingers. "Look! Look at 'em go!"

We all looked. And there, down his withered, hairless legs, at the end of his big feet, were two sets of long, ugly toes, moving.

FIFTEEN

Gerald sat like that near the lakeshore for an hour, wiggling his toes in the sun. Flora left briefly, overwhelmed and shaking, and came back with iced lemonade for everyone. The neighbors who were not there for the event gradually came to see, walking up with the same initial look of disbelief that turned into wonder and fear. Gerald retold the story a dozen times, unable to restrain his tears of joy with each telling. He left out no details but also gave no explanation. Inevitably, everyone asked the same question, "How's that possible?" And Gerald answered the same way every time, "All I know's this - I use'ta be lame, and now I ain't. Do what you want with that."

Georgia grabbed my hand and pulled me to the side. "Tell me the truth," she said in my ear, "Was it you? You heal him somehow?"

Still looking at Gerald, I said out of the side of my mouth, "You kidding me? You ever seen a worm do a thing like that?"

She turned toward Gerald again, threading her fingers through mine. "Elijah Youngblood," she said softly, "I love you." My eyes grew round with an even greater wonder and fear.

Virgil was one of the last to appear, having been out on the lake that morning. He saw the crowd huddled around Gerald from afar and came running, but when he got close he slowed down. Hearing the words of the neighbors and seeing the wiggling toes, fell to his knees like he'd been shot and covered his face. He crawled up to Gerald and put his head on his chest. "Grandaddy," he choked out, "Your toes! How they movin'? Them long legs a your'n, Grandaddy, they gon' work again?"

Gerald wrapped his arm around Virgil's neck, putting him in a gentle headlock. "Time to put a new verse in that song a your'n, huh?" After telling the story one last time, Gerald said, "Well, I 'spect I better get on home, so I can convalesce. Don't think I'll be walkin' jus' yet, but it's comin'."

"You sure you don't want me to get the wheelchair?" I asked.

"Hell no! I ain't ever sittin' in that chair a death again. Virg', 'Lijah, lemme put my arms 'round your shoulders. Shaw, where you at? Shaw, follow 'long and open the door an' what not. An' don't throw me off the dock again, you idiot, you blessed idiot. All right, fellas, hoist me up, but not too much. I wanna feel the dirt 'neath my toes."

"I'll go help Flora get the house ready," Georgia said.

We walked with him slowly towards his trailer, about fifty yards away, stopping here and there. He couldn't move his legs, but described everything he felt with his toes. "Crabgrass right there." "You feel that gravel?" "How bout that? Sand 'tween my toes." We rested a while before going up the ramp. Finally making it inside the trailer, we sat him in his recliner, where he propped his legs on the rest. Flora washed his feet with a wet rag. He grunted and squirmed and giggled. "That tickles. Hah! Can you b'lieve? It *tickles*, Flora!"

After he was comfortable, I said, "Well, guess we'll leave you to it. Happy for you, Gerald."

"Ohh! Now wait just a second, Mr. 'Lijah. You ain't gettin' outta here that quick. No sir, I may not be edg'cated, but I ain't dumb. Sit down, son."

I sat across from him and Flora with Georgia next to me. Shaw and Virgil stood behind the couch.

"I didn't wanna say nothin' out there, but I know, y'hear? I know it was you."

"Aw, Gerald, you would've done the same for me."

"I know *you* ain't dumb neither. I ain't talkin' 'bout you jumpin' in an' pullin' me outta the water, which I thank you for." He glared at Shaw for a second. "'Lijah, the second you lif' me outta the water on that scrawny shoulder a your'n, I felt it. Felt a bolt a lightnin' shoot down from my head to my toes. If I wasn't soaked in water, I'da thought my feet were roastin' in a fire. Then, when you lay me down, I knew, even 'fore seein' my toes move, I knew - 'I'mma walk again.'"

"I didn't do anything but pull you out the water, Gerald."

"That's a buncha baloney and you know it," he said, pointing at my face. "You can't tell me the same thing woulda happen if any other neighbor pulled me from the water."

I stared back at him without responding.

"Maybe the Good Lord done it," Shaw said.

We all looked at him in disbelief, not for what he said, but because it was Shaw who said it. Virgil said, "Well this day's jus' fulla surprises. I ain't ever heard a thing like that come outta that dirty mouth a your'n, Shaw."

He shrugged. "Jus' sayin'."

I said to Gerald, "I was just in the right place at the right time, trying to be a good neighbor. That's all."

"You play dumb all you want, Elijah Youngblood, but I

know. I'm on to you."

"Gerald, what'chu gettin' at, honey?" Flora said. "You bein' a little rough on 'em, and he jus' saved you from drownin'."

He shifted his weight and sighed. "Listen, I ain't tryin' to be tough. Not at all. In fact, I ain't ever felt like kissin' a man my whole life 'til you done that for me. I'm fulla thanks. I owe my life to you, boy. Whether you accept it or not, I do. That's what I'm tryin' to say. I'll do anything for ya. You name it. Up to half my kingdom, y'know'm sayin'? What'chu want? Come on, you ain't leavin' 'til you answer. What'chu want from me? I ain't tryin' to pay you back. Jus' wanna show my thanks."

Everyone was staring at me, waiting. Georgia grabbed my hand and squeezed it. I saw Flora do the same to Gerald's hand and suddenly knew what to say. "All right, but you won't like it."

"Spit it out, son!"

"I'm passing to Flora, gonna let her answer for me. Whatever she says, that's what I want from you."

Flora's eyes grew wide as Gerald's face fell. He turned to Flora, afraid. Her head nodded repeatedly, and her lips quivered. She patted his hand and said softly, "I want'cha to quit drinkin', Ger'ld."

"Aw, hell," he said, hanging his head. He glared at me out of the corner of his eye. "That was dirty, 'Lijah."

I shrugged. "Just this morning you said the wheelchair and booze go hand in hand. So unless you want me to go pull that thing out the water —"

"Yeah, yeah, all right. Dadgummit! Get outta my house. Every one of you! I gotta brood and mourn. Flora, 'Lijah, you dirty dogs, you schemin' skunks, you got me good. You got me where it hurts mos'."

"Come on!" Shaw said, "Ain't you thankful? Your legs're

workin' again."

"No thanks to you, you side-steppin' coward! Jus' wait 'til I'm walkin'. I'm gon' —"

"Ger'ld," Flora said.

He looked at his feet and sighed. "Sorry. It's just . . . I didn't expect mercy to burn like hell. I ain't ever been so mixed up in my 'tire life. Y'all go on and lemme laugh and cry a while."

Sixteen

It was evening by the time we left Gerald and Flora, so I brought Georgia to the edge of the woods near her home. We had time, so we walked instead of taking the dirt bike. Sitting against the upturned roots of an oak, we watched the sun go down through the trees. Stunned by the day, neither of us knew what to say. When it was dark, she said, "Sammy wants you to come to my lesson tomorrow. She says I'm close but thinks I might do better with you watching now."

"Sure, be glad to."

"Elijah," she said quietly, staring down at her feet.

"Yeah?"

She hesitated. Unable to look me in the eye, she said, "Lemme stay with you tonight."

Caught off guard, I didn't speak.

"In the House, I mean," she said.

"That's just asking for trouble."

"No, I don't mean it like that. Nothing sinful. Just one time, I want to know what it feels like to sleep next to you. I stay awake a lotta nights wondering what that'd be like."

"Georgia, there's no way. This flesh a mine would be worked up like a swarm a bees. I made a promise a long time ago to respect you. If we made it this far, we can wait a little longer. One day we'll get to nestle like bluebirds every night."

"What if we don't get to? What if I spend the rest of my life lying alone, pretending?"

"I guess that's a risk we gotta take."

She was quiet for a long time.

"I'm sorry," I said. "I'm sure your house is mighty oppressive to go back to."

"Don't be sorry. Suppose I trust you all the more for it. Well then, I better head home." We stood and brushed ourselves off. "Hey," she said, turning my face with her hand. "I'm proud of you. About Gerald, I mean. About Flora."

"Yeah, well. Glad to be of some use, I guess. G'night."

She kissed me on the cheek. "Night."

She walked through the woods and out into the field behind the church. "Georgia," I called. She turned to me smiling, as if she already knew what I was going to say. I thought of the day of my baptism, which now seemed a long time ago. My throat started to constrict, and my breathing became labored. "I reckon I . . . I love you, too."

She put her hand to her mouth and blew me a kiss and walked away. I watched her until she turned the corner around the church to the parsonage. Moseying my way through the darkening woods, I hummed one of Virgil's songs, my heart as full as Lake Robicheaux after a good rain. "Soooooooie!" I called into the night, sharing the news with all my nocturnal friends. I crawled into bed and lay there a long time, replaying the wonders of the day in my mind to make sure they really happened. Gerald walking again, possibly becoming sober? Remarkable, for sure, but I believed it. To be loved in return by a creature like Georgia? That seemed a much greater miracle. Despite no more than a mustard seed of faith, I lay awake for hours in sheer joy and finally fell asleep to the wind rustling the leaves of the trees outside, causing the moonlight to dance on the floor beside me.

When I woke up the next morning, however, it was not without fear. To feel the way I did about Georgia already made me vulnerable, but I trusted her so completely that the risk of being hurt had never bothered me before. For some reason, for us to speak our feelings out loud made me realize how fragile the relationship was, that we could lose such a thing for reasons beyond us, no matter how much love and trust there may be between us.

Georgia didn't come until late that morning. We had both slept in, exhausted from the day before. After eating a bowl of oatmeal, we headed up to check on Gerald. Flora was outside beating the dust out of a floor mat. "Mornin', you two," she said.

"How's Gerald doing?"

"Oh, he ain't feelin' too good. I told 'em he needs to go to one a them detox places, that it ain't safe to jus' up an' quit like that with no he'p. He says to me, 'Hush, woman, you got your wish. I'mma do this my way. An' if I die, I die.' I think he'll be all right, might jus' wanna keep your distance for a few days. He gon' be sore in more ways'n one. Good thing is them toes still wigglin'." She laughed softly to herself. "Oh, an' I was gon' pour out all his liquor but ol' Wally, Shaw's daddy, he gimme a wad a cash for it."

"That's good, Flora. You need anything else?"

"Keep your eye out for a pair a crutches. He's gon' need 'em 'fore long."

"Sure will," I said.

We walked to Sammy's, who opened the door, gripping her hands. "Hey," she said curtly and motioned us inside with her head.

"You feeling OK, Sammy?" I said.

"Same ol'." She hardly looked at me.

"Neuropathy?" I said.

"Yeah."

"Would it help if Elijah rubbed them?" Georgia asked.

"My hands?" she said.

"Yeah."

She glanced at me for a moment then back at Georgia. "Sure! Long as it don't make you jealous."

"Course not," Georgia said.

I massaged Sammy's cold hands and knobby fingers while we discussed Gerald. I felt the tension in her hands begin to ease, and then she began to tell me about Georgia. "I tell you, it ain't the technical ability she's missin'. We been able to get that down purdy easy. She been workin' hard, a real good student, in some ways *too* good a student, does exactly what I tell her but don't have a mind a her own, which you gotta have for fiddlin'. Somethin' ain't clickin' upstairs. We ain't talkin' bout strokin' the instrument a lil' different. It takes a whole change a mind. Georgia here, she's like a fine mare that can run beautifully with a bit an' bridle in her mouth but can't run for nothin' on her own." I glanced at Georgia to see how she took Sammy's words. She seemed fine. "She's got the mechanics down. She can shuffle, roll, cut, bend the strings. Double stops, you name it. An' she knows her chords and scales better'n me. But she ain't been able to bring it all together. She waitin' on JS Bach to tell her what to do instead a playin' her own music. Fiddler's got to play with her ear, to improvise and harmonize with what she hears. Like I told her from the start, she may never be able to do it after all the years with Vivaldi in the saddle."

"So how are you gonna teach her all that?"

"Beats the hell outta me," she said, raising her hands. "First time I ever given lessons. But she ain't quittin'. An' she's gettin' closer, she really is. That's why yesterday I tell her, 'Bring 'Lijah in tomorrah.' Partly jus' wanna see that sweet face a yours, hah, but more'n that, thought you might be the one to help 'er gallop on 'er own, without a ridin' crop on her rear and spur in her side."

"I gotcha. Don't know what to do but just sit and listen."

"That's all I'm askin', honey. Anymore'n that and you'll be in my way. You can stop rubbin' my hands now. They ain't throbbin' so bad no more." She winked at me and turned to Georgia. "Now, come on. Put that thing up to your chin. Let's see if you holdin' a violin or a fiddle today. One, two," she started tapping the ground with her feet.

Georgia played for a minute, looking at Sammy the whole time. I thought she sounded fine, but Sammy held up her hand.

"When you gon' stop lookin' for notes, huh? Quit *lookin'* at me like I'm a sheet a music. Again. This time, play with your ears not your eyes."

After thirty seconds of listening, Sammy said, "Stop! You jus' playin' the same thing over and over again. I wanna hear somethin' I ain't heard before. I wanna hear some improv'. *Feel* the music, y'hear?" she said, giving the beat.

They went back and forth like this for half an hour. Finally, when Sammy stopped her, Georgia let out a huff, clearly irritated. "Hang on, Sammy," I said. "Georgia, you OK?"

"I'm good, 'Lijah," she said, her green eyes hardened with determination.

Sammy said, "Mmk, let's try again. You gotta take your hand off the wheel, girl. Your grip's too tight on the music, you're suffocatin' it. It's alive, you hear? Let it breathe."

Georgia sighed and hung her head, then she lifted her eyes to me for help. I would've plucked out an eye to have a good word for her just then.

"I think I better try again tomorrow," she said, patting her on the shoulder.

"Takes time. I think you'll get there," Sammy said.

Georgia tucked the instrument under her arm, and I opened the door for her. Stepping off the stairs onto the dirt, I thought of putting my arm around her to comfort her, but I could tell she was prickly. A mourning dove cooed from the power line, answered by a cardinal on top of a nearby trailer. Unsure how to encourage her, I just said what came to mind. "Funny thing about birds, most of the time they don't even have a reason to sing. It's not work or anything important, it's just for fun. They're like Gerald, they just like hearing themselves talk."

Georgia stopped walking and looked up suddenly at the clear blue sky as if a bolt of lightning had struck. Her lips moved silently.

"Huh?"

"Like the Dawn Chorus."

"Oh, sure. Best time a day to be in the woods."

Georgia whipped around and went back up the stairs, entering without knocking. "One last time, Sammy."

"Well, hell, I just got comfy." She glanced at me, and I mouthed *just once more* to her. Turning to Georgia, she said, "Last shot for the day. I'm beat." She got in place and began to tap her foot one last time. "One, two . . ."

The instrument and bow by her side, Georgia didn't play

immediately this time but looked out the window over our heads towards the woods, then closed her eyes. She lifted and tilted her head as if listening to a far-off sound, the way I might listen for the footsteps of an animal. She hummed softly, starting to sway, and put the instrument up to her chin. Swinging to and fro a while, her hair fell down over her face, strand by strand. Then, tapping her foot along with Sammy, she began to play. Her grip on the bow in her fingers relaxed as she ran it back and forth over the strings, twisting, cutting, jerking. The notes were no longer formulaic and predictable but rang with a rough energy that even I knew did not belong in the orchestra halls of Europe. Instead of precise, sophisticated notes, a mess of sounds converged together, carrying us away to the hills of Appalachia. Through a part in her hair, I saw the joy on her face and knew, for the first time in Georgia's austere life, music was not a duty or a lesson or a chore but play.

Sammy let her keep going for a full ten minutes, glancing over at me occasionally with a nod and a grin. We watched in awe as the bit and bridle of her classical training fell to the side, allowing her to run wild and free. Georgia finally stopped on her own, no longer holding a violin, but a fiddle. "'Magine that," Sammy said, "You did it. You fine woman, you bucked Mozart right off an' broke free." Georgia pulled her hair back from her face and tucked it behind her ears, beaming.

"Amazing," I said.

"No, 'Lijah, hold on now," Sammy said. "Don't get ahead of yourself. It was fiddlin' for sure. She proved she could do it. But it wasn't amazin'. It was passin'. She's got a lot to learn. Georgia, you keep practicin' like that. Often as you can. Come back here anytime. More'n anything, play 'long with some music. Or with Virgil. But don't let doe-eyed boy here tell you you're amazin'.

Then you won't learn no more."

Georgia said, "Sammy, I don't know how to thank you."

"Girl, just seein' another lady fiddler come up in the ranks behin' me is all I need. I ain't had this much fun since I was on the road, playin' myself. Now go on, get. I'm like a dog in front of a fire, wore out and happy."

We left the trailer and stepped down to the dirt.

"Well, what'd you think?" she said.

"I'm glad I got to witness that, to see you come into yourself like that. Afraid I don't have words for what I just saw."

"You sure seem to have the right words when you need them."

"Only when I'm not trying."

Georgia and I walked out onto the mostly repaired dock. It was hot, but there was a breeze coming across the lake. We sat in a spot where we could cool our feet off in the water. I passed her one of the bagged ham sandwiches Miss Mattie had given me earlier. "Elijah," she said, "I got something to share."

"All right. Don't sound good."

"Daddy got a job offer in Louisville, Kentucky. Big church. Apparently, these marriage conferences got him noticed." She opened the bag and looked down at her sandwich. "He said he's gonna take the job." The water sloshed up on our legs. "We're moving at the end of the summer. I don't know what to do."

I didn't speak, trying to think.

"Say something," she said.

"I reckon it's time to take your daddy up on his offer to join y'all for dinner."

"Oh, Elijah, how would that help? Can't we just ride off in the middle of the night, me and you? Just find some cabin up in

Arkansas and disappear?"

"No, I need to face him. Trust me, I'm uneasy about it. I don't want to do it any more than you. No telling what'll come of it. Afraid for you, afraid for us, but it's the only way. I'm not spending the rest of my life and marriage hiding like we have been." A handful of ducks swam near the dock, chattering. "Come on, you can't tell me you expected for things to stay like this forever. I've always known this day was coming, didn't you?" I tore off some of the crust from my sandwich and threw it to the ducks.

"I know. I agree, we can't stay like this forever. We have to get the ball rolling at some point, somehow. Especially with Daddy wanting to move us to Kentucky at the end of summer. I just think facing him is going to make it worse."

"Maybe, maybe not."

"What are you planning? Face him how? Wouldn't it be easier to just elope? Every other way is too risky. Just say the word and I'll go. Let's go tonight. Let's go now."

I watched a boat drive by, someone skiing behind. "Go where? At best we'd have to cram into some little hut like the House."

"Fine with me."

"A little old shack like that?"

"Sure, as long as you're in it with me."

"Well, anyway, we can't do that kind of thing. It's not right."

"Even against a man like Daddy? You really think he deserves better?"

"It's not about what he deserves. It's about what you deserve. I'm not willing to poison what I got with you. Stealing a man's daughter? Don't think that's the best way to start a marriage. There's lots of ways we could do this, but most of them are cursed.

Only one way that's not, and that's to face him. What comes after that, who knows? But it's the only way."

"So, what's your plan? You going to ask him for my hand, for his blessing? You going to stand up to him? What?"

I threw the last bit of my sandwich to the ducks and brushed the crumbs off my hands. "Don't got a plan. Somebody once told me worms like me don't get to make plans or even know them. I'm telling you, Georgia, I know this is the right next step. I'm handing over the pole, you know? Just playing the worm. And I'm trusting that, when the moment comes, I'll know what to do. As soon as you head home today, I'll use Monty's phone to call and make dinner reservations with the preacher."

SEVENTEEN

On Tuesday Miss Mattie gave me a haircut, then the Lewises let me use their washing machine to do a load of clothes. On Wednesday at 5:30, I put on the only collared shirt I owned and a pair of blue jeans, then hopped on the dirt bike. Heavy with dread, I rode through the trailer park and turned onto the highway, arriving at the parsonage next to the church a few minutes early. After cutting off the engine, I lingered on the bike in front of the house, looking at the upstairs window on the right, Georgia's bedroom. The church stood just a stone's throw away, towering over the house. I had forgotten how tall the steeple was, higher than most trees in the woods. It seemed a little top-heavy to me, too big for the chapel below it.

I walked to the door and knocked. Not long after, Mrs. Bonnie opened the door. "Well, Elijah! So good to see you. Come on in. Georgia's still upstairs getting ready. Ronny's around here somewhere. Ronny? Elijah's here. Ron?"

I heard the creak of a leather chair and heavy footsteps on the floor. Then, through a door at the end of the dim hallway, stepped Brother Ronny. He took up the entire frame of the door, a wide smile on his face. "Elijah the Tishbite, sojourner of Gilead. Been a while!" He wet his lips with his tongue. "Been wondering when you were gonna show."

"Yes sir, good to see you." I walked down the hall and shook his hand.

"Dinner should be ready soon," he said. "I'm hungry. Powerful hungry. Step on into my office and we can have a little chat while we wait." I followed him into the wood-paneled room, feeling the wariness of a bobcat nearing a trap. "Sit," he said. I sat and surveyed the office, which was almost entirely made of stained wood. Dark shelves lined the walls behind him, floor to ceiling, matching the large, polished desk before him.

"Beautiful desk," I said.

"Thank you.

"Maple, I believe."

"Oak."

"Oh?" I said, running my hand along the edge. "That closed wood grain sure looks like maple. Oak's got a open grain."

He eyed my hand on his desk with discomfort, as if I were defiling it. "That ain't maple," he said, rapping his knuckles on it. "You hear that? Oak. I'd know, I had it custom-made."

"My mistake." It was certainly maple. I turned to my left, where there was a giant picture of Bonnie. Next to it was a smaller picture of Georgia, posing with her violin at graduation, a strange smile on her face I'd never seen before. "Beautiful office you got here."

"Thank you. Lotta the Lord's work been done in this room over the years. Lotta the Devil's work undone, too. Speaking of, been wanting to check on you for the last month or two. You know, a shepherd's accountable for the welfare of his sheep." He smiled. "Haven't seen you at worship. I ask your folks one Sunday and they tell me, "Elijah's moved out on his own."

"Yes sir, that's right."

"I hear you're living at that trailer park just outside city limits."

"Yes sir."

"Dangerous folk there."

"Course. Dangerous folk anywhere you go."

He paused. "I thought you were going to trade school."

"Someday I might. For now, this seemed like the right next step."

"How's that?"

"Hard to explain."

"Imagine so. Your daddy told me you said you was 'flying south for winter'! I said, 'I didn't know you had a migratory fowl for a son! Hah! That what you are?"

"In a manner of speaking."

His smile disappeared. "Lotta them get shot flying south."

"Course. I shot some myself last winter. I'm sure it's possible I could run into trouble. It's risky, but I trust it'll be worth it in the end. Sure beats staying in the cold."

"What are you doing at a place like that? You mixed up in drinking? Drugs?"

"No sir, haven't touched either one since I been there."

"Matter of time, I suspect. So why you there? The only good reason for living at a place like that is winning souls for the Lord. But them folks are hard-hearted as it gets. I'm afraid you're throwing pearls before swine, Elijah."

"Aw, I don't know about that." I glanced out the window to the right, distracted by a hummingbird.

"You telling me you been winning souls?"

I turned back to him. "Nah, nothing like that. I leave that to the professionals like you."

"No, didn't think you would be. Don't know how you could. Blind leading the blind."

"Don't know why I'd throw pearls before anybody, swine or man. Kind of a strange saying. Tell you the truth, I haven't met any swine there so far, except the shoat somebody traded Flora a couple weeks ago. There's hard folk there for sure, and they got hard lives. But they're tender on the inside. Like a red-eared slider."

"Red-ear what?"

"A turtle."

He rolled his eyes and shook his head. "If you're not winning souls, what's the point? Why you there?"

"I reckon I'm just learning to be a good neighbor. You know, getting to know folks, enjoying each other's company. Serving them best I can. They take good care of me, too."

"It's not worth a heap of beans if the Lord's not part of it. 'Filthy rags,' as the Good Book says. Where's he in it all?"

"I done a lot a thinking about that. I don't know about your life, but in mine, the Lord don't often work through hurricane winds and earthquakes and fire. Most times he's still and quiet, like a fine mist that you don't even know is falling, but before long you look down and your shirt's soaking wet. That's how I think of the trailer park. First glance you might think the Lord's nowhere. But if you pay attention, you'll see he's getting mixed into everything, everywhere."

"'Nowhere and everywhere!'" he leaned his head back and laughed. "That's the same kind of nonsense Reverend Henry down the road talks about. I can't make up my mind what you are, Elijah. You some kind of liberal? Tree-hugging hippy? Or maybe just ign'ant trailer trash. 'Nowhere and everywhere!'" he laughed again.

"Don't matter to me what name you put on it."

"It's true, don't make sense no matter how you say it. Go on, try again. I'm listening." He leaned forward with his hand on his chin, as if entertained.

"Well," I said, thinking. Once again, I noticed Georgia's fake smile in the picture. "Some folk's religion is like cheap, thick icing smeared on top of dry bread. Pretty to look at, decorated and all. But I'd rather the Lord be mixed and baked into a plain moist cake, worked all the way through instead of a sticky sweet layer on top."

"That what you think the Lord is? Hah! Some kind of baking ingredient?"

"Sure, like a pinch a leaven."

He stopped smiling and stroked his jaw. "Leaven's for bread, not cake. Anyway, I think you're mistaking self-denial for dry bread. If you don't deny that flesh of yours in this life and learn to like that dry bread, don't count on any cake in the next life."

"I know more than you might think about self-denial. That's why I gave up that sweet icing. Now that I think about it, I reckon that's why I'm living in a trailer park. Besides, I like to think there's a way to have my cake and eat it, too." I smiled at him. "The kingdom's at hand, Brother Ronny. Already among us. Ain't that's what the Good Book says?"

"Dadgum, boy," he said, shaking his head and leaning back in his chair. "You're worse off than I even expected. Your daddy told me you were caught up in the cares of the world, but I didn't know you were this far gone."

"I confess, I've strayed from your teaching, I'm afraid."

He swiveled his chair and leaned back, turning his attention to the picture of Georgia. He rested his large palm on his maple desk. "You know what them shepherds used to do to a sheep that wouldn't quit running off into trouble?"

"What's that?"

"First time he runs off, shepherd's gentle. Second time, gentle. Third time? *Still*, gentle. After a while though, lots of patience and longsuffering, that shepherd's got no choice but to break one of the legs of that little lamb and carry it around for a while by the scruff of its neck. Only way it learns not to stray again, assuming it survives. Sometimes love's got to be severe, Elijah."

"What if it's not a lamb straying but a wild goat?"

"Shepherd's not that dumb."

"Wouldn't a sheep know the voice of his shepherd? Maybe he won't listen 'cause it's a stranger. Maybe the lamb's not straying from a shepherd but running from a thief. Or a wolf."

Anger flashed into Brother Ronny's eyes. He leaned forward and reached his long arm across the desk, pointing at me. "Takes one to know one. Now. I got a question for you. There something you want to tell me? Hm? Something I should know?"

"Daddy, supper's ready," said a quiet voice I didn't recognize. We both turned. Georgia stood in the doorway behind me. I had forgotten what she looked like in a dress. Pretty as she was, she did not have the usual color in her face or the light in her eyes. She looked faint, almost like a different person. "You and Elijah get caught up?" she said in a soft monotone.

I could feel Brother Ronny staring at the back of my head, but I kept studying Georgia's face. "Reckon so," he said. I heard him breathe in deeply through his nostrils. "That pot roast's got my mouth watering." He came around his desk and gripped my shoulder with his large hand. "Come on, let's eat."

We sat down at the table in the dining room, plates and silverware already on the table. Mrs. Bonnie brought the food to the table - pot roast, sweet potatoes, corn casserole, green beans. When we all sat down, nobody spoke or moved. Georgia and Mrs. Bonnie were looking at Ronny, at the head of the table, who was looking at me. "Ron, you going to ask the blessing, honey?"

"I thought I might extend the honor to Elijah here."

"Aw, I don't want to impose on the head of the household."

"That so? Coulda fooled me."

"Ronny," Bonnie said.

"You aren't gonna pray?" he said to me.

"Sure, I'll pray. Just making sure. Appreciate the honor." We bowed our heads. I took a deep, quiet breath. "Aw, Father, sure is good to sit before a bounty such as this. We don't deserve nothing but dry bread, but you load our plate with this heavenly food. We're chock-full of sin, but you're more full of grace than we ever knew. Everybody at this table's nothing but dirt, but you good enough to put that holy breath of yours in us. Thank you for the patience you show us while we walk the lonesome path of this life. Protect us, we're not but helpless sheep in a world full of wolves and thieves. Amen."

"Amen," echoed Bonnie and Georgia. Brother Ronny cleared his throat. We started to plate our food. "What a sweet prayer, Elijah. I'll be sure to tell your mother about that prayer."

"Thank you, Mrs. Bonnie."

After a pause she said, "You still see your parents after moving out?"

"Oh sure, yes ma'am. About once a week I try to eat dinner with them. Certainly miss my momma's food." I took a bite from my plate. "Mm, aw, wow. Good as her cooking is - and keep this between you and me - I'm afraid it can't shake a stick at this corn casserole. Mrs. Bonnie, this is wonderful."

Mrs. Bonnie giggled. "That is so sweet. Secret's safe with me," she said, avoiding her husband's gaze.

Brother Ronny shoved a large forkful of pot roast in his mouth and said, "Tell Georgia what you been up to at that trailer park. Y'all know he's living in a trailer park now, don't you?"

"That's right, Lakeside Estates."

"*Estates*!" he said with a snort. "That's one word for it. Tell us about it, son."

"Aw, there's not much to it. Just learning to be a good neighbor. Lot harder than I suspected. Not 'cause of them, though. At first, I thought I was supposed to rescue the place. Instead, more often I feel like it's rescuing me. I thought it was my job to fix the place up, but a wise friend put me in my place, told me that's not what they need from me."

"What they need from you?" Brother Ronny said. "Hm?"

I paused. "Now that I think about it, I reckon they don't need me at all."

"I reckon not. Not less you're doing the Lord's work there."

"Naw, I could never do the kind of things you do, Brother Ronny."

"I heard a healing took place," Georgia said with a gleam in her eyes, the only time that night I saw the girl I knew.

Ronny's fork clanged on his plate. "What's that?"

"A healing," she repeated quietly, turning to her plate. "And something about a redneck prophet."

"Where you hear that from?" he said, his brow furrowed.

"Oh, you know, just the grapevine."

"There's no grapevine in town that reaches far as that place. Who told you that, Georgia?"

Mrs. Bonnie said, "Ron, why're you talking to her like —"

"Bonnie," he said, pointing a fork at her, "Don't." She shrunk back into her chair.

"I don't remember how I heard it, Daddy."

"That true, Elijah? There been a healing?"

"A healing? Hm, hard to know what to call it. Nobody knows how it happened. As the man himself said, 'All I know's this - I used to be lame, and now I ain't. Do what you want with that.'"

"You have anything to do with it?" Georgia asked without looking up.

"Well, I was there when the man fell off the dock into the lake, wheelchair and all. All I did was pull him out the water. When I laid him down on the ground, he didn't need that wheelchair any more." I shrugged.

"Wheelchair, huh? It's not that big ugly fella that runs the place, is it? Drunkard? Don't hardly speak English?"

"That's him. Old Mr. Gerald. He's not a drunkard any more though. Why? You know him?"

"Oh, heavens, no. Don't know Mr. Gerald from Adam. Just heard about him."

"Through the grapevine?" I said.

He raised his eyebrows at me and set his silverware down. "Traveling evangelists know all kinds of things most folks don't."

"But Ron, honey, I thought I remember you doing a revival there a while back," Mrs. Bonnie said.

He glanced at her, agitated. "That place? If I did, I don't remember. Lotta revivals under my belt, you know. Wouldn't remember a little place like that."

"Now that you mention it," I said, "There's a big white tent there. Would you believe it, it's got the church logo on it, the burning bush. I've been wondering how it got there. Figured it must've been left there after a revival."

"Trust me, there's been no revival there. Those folks are like Capernaum. Nazareth. Too hard-hearted for a revival to take place. If they got a church tent, they probably stole it. That's all right though, the Lord taught me a long time ago to turn the other cheek."

Feeling the tension peaking, for everyone's sake, I changed the subject. "My folks told me y'all been doing marriage conferences all over Texas?"

That set off a half hour of updates from Brother Ronny and Mrs. Bonnie. They talked about the itinerary of the retreats and all the places they had gone in Louisiana and Texas and Arkansas, about the prominent church leaders they had met and dined with. They spoke with assurance of the many evidences of God's hand on the work.

As her parents carried on about the fruits of their ministry, Georgia didn't say a word but stared down, moving the food around on her plate and sitting with her hands folded in her lap. She resembled a porcelain doll, beautiful and prim, but so spiritless and diminished next to her father she was hardly recognizable as the girl I had seen flourish into a woman over the last few years. She seemed more like a decorative fixture in their home than a person. Sure, they were mightily proud of her, but as they were of the relics from the Holy Land on the shelf, not as a human being. I saw more clearly than ever what her childhood must have been like, languishing under the inhumane piety of her father, existing only for his glory, and I felt a new compassion towards her. I finally understood why she was interested in a rough character like me who offered her a chance to spread her wings. I thought back to the last three years we'd spent sneaking around in the woods and had no regrets. For her sake now as much as mine, I was glad. I did not arrive that night expecting my feelings towards Georgia to grow, but they did. Enfolded into everything else I had always felt towards her, there was now a new kind of love, one that filled and cleansed the others, a love that no longer cared so much what became of me, even of us, as long as she was free to braid her hair and paint from her heart and play her fiddle.

"Elijah," Brother Ronny said, clinking his glass with his fork. "Son!" he said.

"Yes sir?"

"You listening?"

"Reckon I'm just in awe of all that a man of God like yourself has done over the years." He tilted his head back and glared at me down the bridge of his nose. "Mrs. Bonnie, can I help you clear the table?"

"That's sweet, sure, that'd be fine."

"I'm not done with my plate yet," Ronnie said. "Big appetite tonight."

After I cleared the table, Georgia went upstairs and Mrs. Bonnie walked into the kitchen beside her husband and said, "I'll take it from here, thank you so much, Elijah."

"Yes'm, thank you again."

"Getting late," Brother Ronny said, "I'll walk you out."

"All right," I said, walking with him from the kitchen down the hall to the door. He opened the door for me and stepped out onto the porch, closing it behind us.

Standing close, towering over me, he said, "Something you want to tell me?"

I peered into the dark woods beyond the field around the parsonage where the sun had just set, leaving a streak of orange like a gash in the purple sky. I glanced up and noticed the hungry look in his eyes, the one Shaw described as 'a cat danglin' a mouse.' And somehow, I knew that he knew. Not everything. He did not yet have a good enough shot to pull the trigger, but I had no doubt he had caught the scent and was on the hunt, that he would not stop until he had his prey. I saw visions of what would happen after I left if I did not intercede, of Georgia being interrogated until she broke, of the discipline she would have to endure after she told him everything. Finally, I remembered Georgia sitting at the dinner table, like a body with no soul, and my compassion warmed toward her once again. The moment had come, and I knew what was being asked of me. No, not honesty, but sacrifice. To spare her the pain myself. "Yes sir, I reckon I got some confessing to do."

"I'm listening," he said, straightening and lifting his chin.

"I'm afraid I haven't been honest with you. Over the last few years, I've been sneaking around with Georgia. Not often, just when you went out of town. I know it's mighty dishonest of me. What's worse, not only was it behind your back, it was against her will. See, she don't give a fig about me, but I . . . I wouldn't take no for an answer. I was manipulative. Persuasive. She's a good girl, *godly* girl. I had to use all kind of tricks to keep her from telling you. Now, she maintained her purity. She wouldn't let me lay a finger on her, in spite of my fleshly desires. Matter fact, just last week I tried to get her to stay the night with me, but she flat out refused. When I found out y'all were moving to Kentucky, I even asked her to run off with me and elope, but she'd had enough. In the end, her loyalty to you won out. She chose you over me and told me it's over, and if I didn't come here and confess then she would, and that's not fair to her. Not a bit of it is her fault, Brother Ronny, it's all mine. Never been more than a worm. Let the hand of judgment fall on my head, not hers."

I don't know what I expected from him, but it certainly

wasn't the wave of relief that passed over his face. He leaned down toward me. I could smell the pot roast gravy on his breath. "You know, for the past few years, I've gone back and forth about you. And it bothered me. That Elijah - what is he? A sheep? A wolf? Or some kind of —" he laughed, "No, I won't say it out loud. Clearly not. And now judgment's come and revealed the truth, and now we all know who's who. Now I can say what you are. And it ain't a worm. You're nothing but a *snake*." His face became tense and red, and he placed his hand on the back of my neck. "Far as Georgia, I had my suspicions ever since your little lunch date. And you just confirmed every bit of what I started to piece together the last week or two. Least I know now where to place the blame." As the last word left his lips, he threw me off the steps of the porch like a sack of garbage. I landed on my chest and laid in the dirt with the wind knocked out of me. "Look at you, on your belly eating dust, just like the prophecy says. You remember what else was said to that serpent in the Garden, don't you? 'Bruise my heel, I'll crush your head.' You're going to know what that means before long. Even a man of God can't always be gentle. Love is strong as death, boy, jealousy's cruel as the grave." He dusted off his hands and turned to walk inside. "Take care of that soul of yours while there's still time, Elijah," he said over his shoulder, "The Lord's a lot harder judge than me."

I brushed off my jeans and walked to the dirt bike, swinging my leg over the seat. Looking up at the house one last time, I saw a figure sitting in the open window of the second-floor bedroom. The lamp light shone from behind, leaving only a silhouette. I could not see her face in the shadows but could hear her stifled cry and knew that she had heard every word. A hand over her mouth, the figure waved, and I nodded, neither of us knowing whether we would ever see each other again.

EIGHTEEN

I kickstarted the dirt bike and headed toward the woods, the bike feeling light and unbalanced. I passed the place on the edge of the field where I sat after my baptism. Speeding down the silent walking trails, I rode alongside the dark lakeshore where my jon boat was parked, beyond which was the abandoned swimming deck. Arriving at the House, I skidded to a stop and turned off the bike, only the sound of crickets around me. Heading inside, without lighting the lantern to see, I turned her painting around so that it faced the wall, only the word *Baptism* showing on the back.

Lying down, I drifted in and out of sleep. Dreaming I was fishing on the peninsula, I watched her cast a line toward a fish that had struck topwater. She was trying to tell me something, but there were geese honking overhead and I didn't understand. Waking at dawn, I remembered what I'd done and tried to fall back asleep and dream again. Instead, a robin came and perched on the windowsill, filling the bedroom with a song that was unbearably happy.

"You did what?" Shaw said later that morning, bewildered. I

was sitting up with a pillow behind me, Virgil and Shaw at the foot of the bed. "What'chu go and do a stupid thing like that for?"

"It was the only way," I said.

"Bubba, I can think of a bunch a other ways," he said.

"It was the only way to spare her from her daddy's wrath."

"Why would he even believe you? You jus' confessed to lyin' and deceivin'. You think he really believed she was an innocent victim in it all?"

"His ego would much rather pin it all on me. The thought of a daughter that hates his guts and wants to elope? He doesn't want to believe it. His pride won't let him."

"You don't think he's gon' mistreat 'er even still?"

"Course he is, but no more than he has the last eighteen years. He's going to see her as an ignorant lamb that got seduced by a wolf in sheep's clothing. But as long as he's the savior and I'm the devil, she'll be all right. He'll be satisfied. It fits too perfectly with everything he already tells himself."

"Lemme take'm out," Shaw said. "Jus' a twenty-two bullet in the head one night when he's takin' out the trash. I'd go to jail for you, 'Lijah. Matter fact, I'd feel like I finally done somethin' worthwhile. Come on, my life's cheap. I'll do it."

"Quit playin', Shaw," Virgil said.

Shaw shrugged. "I ain't jokin'."

"If I wanted to go about it the wrong way, I would've done so a long time ago. And in less violent ways, Shaw."

"You and them scruples," he said. "Gonna end up costin' you the love a your life."

Virgil had a faraway look in his eyes. "I don't know, Shaw. We'll see. Wouldn't be the first time 'Lijah surprised us. Unusual things happen 'round this fella."

"Speakin' a scruples," Shaw said, "You didn't seem too

bothered by lyin' to the man's face. You deceived him 'bout your deceivin'! How's that any better?"

"It's not so much about right and wrong, it's about what's best for Georgia. I couldn't just leave and let her Daddy eat her alive. I wasn't aiming for honesty. I was trying to take a bullet for her." Shaw shook his head at me, disappointed and baffled. "I don't know Shaw, don't ask me any more questions. I'm doubting everything now. Let's discuss something else, I don't even want to say her name. I'm sick over it all."

"How 'bout we jus' go fishin'?" Virgil said.

"Y'all go on without me. I'm going to lay back down a while."

"Naw, we ain't lettin' you mope. Come on."

We took my jon boat out and baited a trot line. Although Virgil and Shaw had made me come with them, they didn't make me talk or ask anything else of me. After the line was baited, they started to fish while I sat in the front of the boat, watching the water pass as we trolled quietly along. They caught a load of fish. "Sure you don't wanna join?" Virgil said. "Brought an extra rod for you."

"I'm good. I just need to look and listen for a while."

A few days later, Virgil told me Gerald wanted to see me, so I paid him a late morning visit. "'Lijah!" he called when I was still far off. "Hot dog, looka me, boy! I'm standin'!" He was leaning on the rusty barbecue pit just outside his house. "Lookout, worl'! Grandaddy up on two feet!"

"You've come a long way in a week," I said, coming near.

"You done the heavy liftin' for me. This here physical ther'py's nothin'." He lowered his voice, "Don't tell Flora, but quittin' that fire water has put some fresh life in me, too." He raised his voice again. "Yessir, standin' up today, climbin' Ev'rest tomorrah, y'know'm sayin'?"

I tried my best to smile.

"Hey," he said, "What'chu lookin' like that for? All hangdog. Horse face an' all. Somepin' wrong?"

"Hard week, Gerald."

"Come're, have a seat in my office." He motioned with his head towards one of the lawn chairs across from the barbecue pit. I sat down. He said, "I hear I ain't the only one who lost a fight with the devil."

"Huh?"

"Preacher Man."

"Oh. Virgil told you?"

"Course. I always stay curr'nt on my frien' 'Lijah. Virgil told me he's worried 'bout you. I says to 'em, 'Virg', a lil' sufferin' never hurt nobody.' An' he says, 'No, Grandaddy, this ain't a lil' flesh wound, this'un cut deep.' So I says, 'Sometimes surgery got to go deep.' Then Virg' says, 'What if he ain't strong 'nough to recover from it?' And I says to him, 'If these here legs taught me anythin', it's that it ain't about bein' strong. Let 'em grieve, boy, but he'p 'em do it with hope.' He says, 'Hope in what, Grandaddy?' And I tell 'em, 'If the lame can walk, hell, anything can happen!" He grunted and shifted around on the barbecue pit.

"There's no guarantees, Gerald."

"That ain't right, an' you know it. True, plenty a things ain't guaranteed, but some things you can take to the bank."

"What guarantees do I have?"

"I ain't gon' say. Wouldn' help none if I did. You got to figure that out yourself. All I'll say's this. Don't be like me, 'Lijah. Don't waste your suff'rin'."

"All right, Gerald."

"Y'know'm sayin'?"

"I hear you."

"'Lijah."

"Yeah."

"Look at me," he said. I lifted my head. "Naw, up here, eyes on mine." I looked him in his clear, sober eyes. "You done good, 'Lijah. Some folks - like that lil' punk Shaw - may not understand what'chu done. But I'm proud of you, boy. You may feel like a runover dog, but you a bigger man than anybody I ever knowed. Weep an' howl if you want, I don't care, but don't you dare hang that head a your'n."

"I got you."

"'Lijah."

"Yeah?"

"Make sure you do weep an' howl, though, y'hear? If I woulda admitted to myself how bad I was hurtin' long time ago, I wouldn't've needed to drink so bad. Don't nobody like feelin' pain, 'specially yours truly, I like to have a good ol' time. But avoidin' an' numbin' that pain ain't gon' take you nowhere good."

"Yessir."

"Ain't no 'sir' here but you, Mr. Youngblood. My good man, I salute you. Don't worry, we gon' help you. We gon' see you through."

"Thanks, Gerald."

"Now. My dogs're tired a standin' up. Get Virgil out here an' y'all he'p me inside. Oh, and hey, 'member that fridge I made you keep? I traded it with a fella down the road for some more wood for the dock. Don't feel like you have to, but if you want somepin' to do, feel free. To keep your mind busy, I mean."

Early one morning two weeks later, I was working farther out on the dock, ripping out old boards. Around one of the trailers came a shirtless, tattooed man with a trucker hat. I felt the thud of his boots on the dock as he walked toward me. Before he introduced himself, I knew who it was.

"You 'Lijah?"

"That's me." I shook his hand.

"Name's Wally. I'm Shaw's daddy."

"I figured, y'all look just the same."

"Yeah, guess so. Say, you hear the news?"

"News? No. If it's not good I'm not sure I want to hear it."

His bloodshot eyes got even redder. He sniffed and twitched his mouth. His voice cracked. "It's Shaw."

My heart sank, bracing for a blow. "What happened? What's wrong?"

He sniffed again and took a breath. "Shaw got him a job."

"A job?"

"That's right," he said, a proud look in his watery eyes.

"Well, that's not bad news."

"Naw, not at all."

"What's he doing? I haven't heard a word about that."

"That boy's fightin' fires. You believe 'at? Yesterdy a man come knock on the door sayin' he was the local fire chief. He says we entered into a drought now, and they gon' need some extra he'p puttin' out fires, enforcin' bans and what not. I says to him, 'Well, thanks, but we ain't interested.' Just as I start closin' the door, Shaw jump up off the couch an' tell the man, 'I'll do it!' I say, 'Shaw, you don't know nothin' 'bout fightin' fire.' An' he says, 'No, Deddy, but don't nobody love fire like me!'"

We both laughed, and I said, "Makes sense when you put it that way. I reckon he'll be good at it."

"It ain't even volunteer. It's for pay! Seasonal, but still, could become permanent."

"No telling what he's gonna do with that money."

"That's right, no tellin'!" he laughed again. "That's good. Anyway," he said, looking down, "You know, I ain't ever been too good a daddy. Tell the truth, I been purdy rotten. He woulda been better off raised by wolves. But this makes me feel like there's hope for the boy, spite a what I done. Like maybe somma my wrongs can be undone somehow. Seems like there's a word for that, but I ain't smart 'nough to know it."

"Yeah."

After a pause he said, "Anyway, I don't know why I'm tellin' you all this. I jus' saw you out here, and I know you been a good friend to 'em. He's got a lotta respect for you, said he wants to he'p folks like you done 'round here. Seems like maybe you inspired 'em. Thought you might wanna know."

"Thanks, Wally. It's good to finally meet you. Heard a lot about you."

"I'm sure ain't none of what you heard been good." He spat tobacco juice into the lake and pulled up his jeans. "Say, you need some he'p with this here dock? I got nothin' to do."

"Sure," I said. Wally and I spent the rest of the morning working side by side. He talked most of the time, telling me stories of his rowdy past. No doubt most of it was exaggerated if not made up, and not all of it made sense. Even so, the tall tales were entertaining and hilarious, making the morning pass quickly. He was just like Shaw. He used the same mixed-up figures of speech and had the same spastic mannerisms. And it was often hard to know whether he was joking. The only obvious difference I saw between the two was the self-hatred Wally had for himself, no doubt from a lifetime of regrets. By the time we broke for lunch, Wally and I were friends. He told me to come knock on his door next time I worked on the dock, and he would help me again, as long as it was before five.

When we parted I headed to Sammy's, who had invited me over for lunch. I knocked at the door. She opened it and invited me in.

We sat down to a table of sandwich fixings and fruit, and she said, "I been lookin' forward to our date all week, 'Lijah."

"Yes'm. Thanks for having me."

"Where's that girlfriend a yours? I ain't seen her in weeks."

"You don't know?"

"Know what?"

"Never mind."

"Oh!" she said, "You single again?"

"Yeah," I said, "Sorta."

"Sorta? Come on, gimme the juice. What's goin' on?"

"Nah. That's all right. Tell me about some of your touring days."

"Nah, sorry. Boring. Talk to me."

"There's not much to say."

"That ain't right. You know I'm invested in you and that girl as much as anybody. I got a right to know. What's up? Where y'at?"

I sighed. "Her daddy's a preacher."

"So? Nothin' wrong with that."

"You know the white tent over there? He's *that* preacher."

She sat back in her chair and squeezed her hands. "Oh," she said. "Well, damn."

"Long story short, because of her daddy, our relationship's always been a secret, and . . . well, now it's not, and it's done. And now I probably won't ever . . . now I have to try to move on."

"You jus' gonna give up like that?"

I shrugged. "What else am I supposed to do?"

"What's this?" She copied me, shrugging her shoulders. "Huh? What good does this do?" She rolled her shoulders again. "I can't tell you what to do, but it can't be that. That's what a wimp does when he's given up. I know you, an' you ain't a wimp."

"I'm stuck, Sammy, if you really want to know. On one side, hope's too painful. It's too hard to sit and wait and hope on some miracle to bring us back together. At the same time, I'm not ready to say goodbye to it all, to her and all we had together. I don't know how I'd survive it."

"Listen," she said, "I know somethin' 'bout hope and pain and grief. Would you know, 'fore you and that girlfriend came 'long, I hadn't listened to music since I got sober. D'you know that? For three plus years, I been mopin' 'round. Sober, but doin' a lotta this," she shrugged her shoulders. "For a few reasons, I think. Deprivin' myself a music, I felt like I's payin' for somma my mistakes. But more'n that, rememberin' the past hurt too damn bad. Listenin' to music jus' reminded me a what I lost when these hands stopped workin'. So, three years, no music. Three years, two months - blah blah blah - bein' sober. Sober, but not really livin' no more. Kinda dead inside. And *bored!* An' then, Gerald invites me to this potluck concert. I almost didn't go, but I heard there was a new young neighbor gon' be there who's easy on the eyes, so I go. An' when I'm all nostalgic and vulnerable after watchin' Virgil play, that young fella asks me to teach his girlfriend the fiddle. Hell! But hey, you know what? I been listenin' to music again ever since. Does it feel like hell to remember the old days? Better believe it. Is it painful to have my hands tied while I watch that girl learn to play? Sure it is. But guess what? Now, 'stead a goin' 'round shruggin' my shoulders, I'm livin' again. Joy and pain all jumbled up together."

I sighed. "I hear you, Sammy. I'm glad to hear that, thank you. Same time, I'm just not ready to revisit it all, whether hoping or grieving. Even this conversation has me wanting to go hide in a foxhole. Most of my days now are spent trying to stay busy, to keep my mind on other things. I'm stuck. I'm not ready."

"I know, I know." Her face softened. "Look, I'm sorry. I warned you 'fore, I ain't the most gentle teacher. Take your time, 'Lijah. Jus' don't take three plus years, y'hear?"

"Yes'm."

"Now, you think you can rub these hands a mine before we eat? Feel like a bear with a thorn in 'er paw today."

"Sure," I said. She reached her hands across the table, and I massaged them while she told me about her touring days.

A week later, Shaw and Virgil came and visited one afternoon. Shaw had spent the week at the fire station and came back full of stories of wildfires and dangerous rescues, most of them highly unlikely, given that he was still in training. He had the next few days off.

"What'chu wanna do with your time off, Shaw?" Virgil asked.

"Well, workin' as hard as I been, I reckon I earned myself a lil' R an' R." He put his hands behind his head and closed his eyes.

"Wish there was some huntin' we could do this time a year," Virgil said. "Dove season opens end a August, don't it?"

"I've been hearing a feral hog rooting around at night," I said. "Can't get a good shot on her 'cause it's so dark, but she's a big old girl. You could hunt her."

"Or we could trap 'er." Shaw said, suddenly alert. "Where you seen that hog?"

"Well, sometimes over by the creek or even here by the fire pit. Mainly, though, it's on the other side, near that little game trail. Where I toss my leftovers and pour out my grease."

Virgil looked over at Shaw. "You still got that shebear trap somewhere?"

"Yeah, it's too bad we ain't ever caught that bobcat. Guess she's too smart for it. I'll go get it. 'Lijah, you jus' show me where you dump them leftovers, an' I'll set it up there. Jus' don't put that foot a your'n in it."

"I ain't that dumb."

"Lemme go get it. I'll be back," Shaw said, standing up. "Gimme five minutes."

"I thought you needed some R an' R after all that hard work?"

"Shut up, Virgil," Shaw said, walking off. "You know I didn't do nothin' but sit in a classroom all week."

"That's what I thought," Virgil said. "I'm sure you'll get to do your share a fightin' fires 'fore long, dry as it's gettin'."

NINETEEN

The robin kept coming back to the House. At first, she only dropped by to sing through my window for a few minutes at dawn. Before long, she started using the windowsill for a collection of debris from the forest floor, which she soon began shaping into a nest. Disappearing for a while, she would return with a twig or dry grass in her mouth. She'd hop around, tilting her head to examine her project, until she found the perfect place to weave the new piece. After folding it in, she would try the nest out for a moment and then fly off again. She completed her task in less than a week, apparently comfortable and unthreatened by me. I named her Dorothy and spoke to her in the mornings while lying in bed.

One morning she was especially chatty. "Morning, Dorothy," I croaked, my eyes still closed. "What you know good?"

Tuk tuk. Zeeeup. Tuk tuk.

A few minutes later I said, "Rain coming any time soon?"

Cheerio, cheerio.

"You ever gonna let me sleep in?"

Teacheach. Cheerio. Zeeeup.

After a few minutes of endless chatter, I said, "Dorothy, you ever sing outside the window of a girl named Georgia?"

Silence.

I wished I hadn't asked. That was the first time I'd said her name out loud since the day after my confession. Dorothy's lack of response kept the name echoing in the room. I looked at the frame on the wall, hanging backwards from its string. *Baptism.* I got up and made a small fire and some oatmeal. Looking down at the bowl of food, I lost my appetite and threw it back into the fire, smothering it.

Not wanting to be around anyone, I decided to walk along some of the old trails. Too lost in my hazy, dulled mind to realize where I was heading, I lifted my head and saw that my feet had taken me to the old fishing spot.

"Sheesh, this is the last place I want to be," I said. I intended to turn around but found myself stepping out onto the peninsula instead, drawn in by the striking changes of the place. I sat amongst the cypress knees, my back against the tree. The lake was several feet lower due to the drought, the shoreline trees drooping and faded. The water was not only still but stagnant and filled with alligator weed and flowerless hyacinth, more like a swamp than a lake. It was too quiet, as if all the native creatures had migrated elsewhere to escape the heat. Noticing all the differences from before and after the drought, I accidentally stirred old memories awake. I saw her wrinkling her nose in frustration the first time she tried to cast a line. I smelled her lavender-scented head on my shoulder, listening as I pretended to be an expert about the woods and water. I saw her pulling a baby largemouth bass out of a net, blowing her hair out of her face with a grin. Realizing what was happening, I tried to shut off the memories just as I had over the last month, but it was too late.

The dam had broken, and the pain that had been sealed away now flooded over the banks of the rest of my life.

I got up, hoping a change of scenery might put the nostalgia to rest, but that only raised the tide. Everywhere I wandered that morning her ghost followed, torturing me with the most wonderful words and glances and touches, haunting me with visions of a life without them. I felt like a catfish being gutted alive, my insides being hollowed out of everything I held most dear.

Even the House was not safe. Passing the fire pit, I thought of her holding her own against Shaw the first time they met. I opened the door and saw her likeness sitting at the table nonchalantly. The memories pursued me like bloodhounds after a fox, at my heels until I grew weary and finally gave myself up.

I flipped the painting around again. Dorothy started chirping in the window. Reaching out my finger, I felt the layered colors of paint on the kingfisher's wings and the texture of the water below it. The eyes of the fish looked familiar somehow. I put my forehead on the picture and closed my own eyes. By some trick of the mind, I heard the cry of a fiddle in the distance and felt my face get ugly with grief. My chest contracted a few times like I was going to be sick. Collapsing onto the bed, I covered my face with a blanket and wept until it was dark. Having let myself remember her in all of her goodness and beauty, I was finally able to say goodbye to her and even to wish her well without me in Kentucky, praying and hoping she would somehow flourish despite being entangled in her father's web.

By the time the tears ran dry, I was exhausted but relieved, assured I would not descend any lower. I got up and grabbed a bar of soap and washed my face in the creek, feeling a little more like myself. Watching the trees for a while, swaying in the night breeze, I felt somewhat renewed, like there was room for hope again. I came back inside and satisfied the little appetite that had returned with some deer jerky. Saying goodnight to Dorothy, she shifted around and fluttered her wings, giving me a glimpse of the five bright blue eggs beneath her.

TWENTY

The next morning Virgil came to the House and let me know I had a visitor up at the trailer park. "Your daddy," he said nervously. I followed him up the path and saw Daddy in the gravel drive, arms crossed, sitting back on the hood of one of his classic muscle cars.

"Daddy, hey. Sorry I haven't visited in a while. It's been a hard few weeks."

"I bet," he said without looking at me.

"I see you finished restoring the Chevelle."

"Let's take a drive. Get in."

I got in the car with him, which smelled of leather polish with a faint smell of cigarettes from the previous owner that he had not been able to remove. He cranked the engine and drove down the gravel drive onto the main road, turning right - away from town.

He didn't say anything for a few minutes, so I said, "Well, I can tell you got some concerns you want to share with me. I'm listening."

"I don't have concerns, I got outrage. What's the matter with you? Huh? First, you go and embarrass us by moving into that broke down dump full of meth heads. And if that's not enough to break your momma's heart, next thing I hear, you been messing around with the preacher's daughter. Son! Who you think you are?"

"I'm nobody, Daddy. Everything's gone wrong."

"You best believe it has. I about fell over dead of shame two weeks ago at church. I hear Brother Ronny say from the pulpit, 'We got us a trial on hand, folks, a case of church discipline.' Little did I know what's coming next. He said, 'We gonna have to do some excommunicating today, concerning Mr. Elijah Youngblood.' And he told us about you sneaking around all these years, messing with that innocent little girl of his. Said you forced her to have relations with you. Elijah! Assault!? That how we raised you? To treat a woman like that? Like a object to use for your own wicked desires? You could be in jail, Elijah! You best be glad Brother Ronny's a forgiving man. No doubt a less godly man would already have you in the clink."

"Assaulted? Relations? Daddy, no, that's not —"

"We had no choice but to excommunicate you. Even your Momma and I voted for it."

"Does that mean —"

"That means I shouldn't even be having this conversation with you. I'm supposed to be shunning you. My own blood! How could you do this, Elijah? Especially to Momma? She ain't hardly left the house."

"I'd try to defend myself, but I know it won't do any good. He's already given the word." I shook my head. "That Brother Ronny's got him some power, don't he?"

"Leave that man alone, Elijah! Haven't you done enough to that suffering servant and his family? What defense could you even make? That poor girl's so humiliated, she hasn't shown her face one time since the news broke."

"I didn't mean for any of this to fall on you and Momma. Especially not on Georgia."

"Shut up, son, that ain't the half of it."

"All right."

"That blessed man and his wife, you know they got that marriage ministry of theirs? They had a tour booked all around the country, several years' worth of conferences lined up. The Lord's hand of blessing clearly on it. Well, word started spreading about what happened with his daughter. Folks that don't know better started saying, 'If Brother Ronny can't protect his own family, why're we gonna listen to what he has to say? What kind of shepherd can't protect his own daughter from wolves?' Then, one after another, churches start pulling out of his marriage conferences, canceling on him. Two weeks of gossip and slander, and now there's not one left, son! Not a *one*!"

"That's what you call a backfire."

"Don't you see what you done? You'll have to answer to God one day for this. Tearing down his kingdom, doing the work of the Devil!"

"Tearing down whose kingdom?"

"Who else? The Lord's! Kinda question is that? And I'll tell you what else. Brother Ronny had him a job offer up in Kentucky. After all these years of humble service in a little town like this, finally getting the recognition he's due. Big pulpit, thousands of members. TV, radio broadcast. But then, all 'cause of you, Elijah, all 'cause of you and the despicable things you done to his daughter, they called him a few days ago and told him they offered somebody else the position. They said he ain't fit! Can you believe it? That man, anointed and called by God, responsible for the salvation of thousands - them fools said he ain't fit!"

I covered my mouth and looked out the side window at the blur of trees passing by.

"And now," he said, "The whole church's in a uproar. People are asking questions about the marriage conferences, and even a couple of deacons are up in arms 'cause they found out he's been using the church's money to fund the conferences. What does it matter how his servant spends it? That's God's money, not theirs! Other folks are saying they feel betrayed that he was thinking about leaving for Kentucky. Questions, accusations, people meeting behind his back. Worship attendance is down. Tithes are down. I see it all and you know what I say to myself?"

"What's that?"

"I say to myself, 'Look what that no good son of mine has done.'"

"Daddy."

"What!?"

"I got something to say to you."

"There ain't nothing you can say. I just wanted you to know what you done. You're lucky I'm not throttling you right now."

"Ten-four, boss. I'll keep it to myself."

"No, go ahead. But if it's not an apology out of the depths of that wicked heart of yours, I don't want to hear it."

"That's the thing, Daddy. I'm awful sorry to see this hurting you and Momma. That hurts me, too. And most of all I hate hearing how Georgia's been shamed along with me. But, as far as Brother Ronny . . ."

"What? Say it!"

"I ain't sorry."

He slammed on the brakes and pulled to the side of the highway. Turning and grabbing me by the shirt, he pulled me close to his purple face. "I should've shunned you like I was told.

I've never been so ashamed of you in my life!" He let go of my shirt and threw me back against the seat. "Now get your redneck self out of my dadgum car." I opened the door and stepped out. He sped off without another word. Through the dust of his tires, I saw he'd added a sticker to the chrome bumper of his car that said, *Where are you going? Heaven or Hell?* I wasn't so sure at that moment but felt fairly certain how Daddy would have answered for me.

I started walking in the other direction, back towards the trailer park. He zoomed past me back to town about ten minutes later. As far as we had driven, I would be walking for hours, until well past lunch, but I had plenty to think about.

When I got home that afternoon, sweating heavily and thirsty, I came down the gravel road and saw Gerald outside his trailer. He was pushing a walker, wheels in front, tennis balls in the back.

"Dadgum boy, you look *hot!*" He twisted his head toward the trailer. "Flora!" he yelled. "Woman! Get out here and get our frien' some ice water. Flora! You hear me?"

"Shh, I hear you," a voice said through one of the screened windows. "Quit hollerin'."

Flora brought me a glass of ice water. She smiled at me and made a face at Gerald. "'Lijah," he said. "I got somepin' to tell you."

I sipped the cold water. "What's up, Gerald?"

"Well, hold on a second! You got a little life back in them eyes a your'n. Looka that! Either Flora slipped some spirits in that water or you found yourself a little hope. Huh? Which is it?"

"No, you first. What were you about to say?"

"You better tell me after I tell you." He cleared his throat.

"Listen, I've decided. Once I get to walkin' on my own, I'mma re-open the place. Jus' like it used to be. Yessir! Grocery an' supply store. Get the dock finished an' the marina runnin'. Flora's gon' start sellin her ham sammiches and sausage biscuits. Virgil even said he'd manage the store for me, like we was father and son. Those are his words! 'Like father and son,' he said! Keep it all secret for now though."

"That's great, Gerald. Only question is —"

"I know, how'm I gonna afford all that? It'll take a lil' time. But you know how much money I save not drinkin'? I's drinkin' 'bout a fifth a whiskey a day, spendin' bout twenty dollar a day. So, I reckon I'm savin' . . ." He counted on his two and a half fingers. "'Bout two-, three-hundred dollars a month. Yessir! Won't take long 'fore this place is back to its former glory. Yesterday I paid the mortgage note for the firs' time in months. Soon, I'mma start payin' you for all your hard work. Back pay, too, hoss!"

"Nah, Gerald."

"Now, your turn. What'chu got that's makin' the corners of that mouth lift up? Huh?" He inched toward me with his walker. "What them eyes lit up for? You got you some good news?"

"Mix of good and bad, not sure what to think of it all. But I'll tell you what, the gates of hell aren't prevailing."

"You tellin' me the Devil ain't winnin' after all?"

"That's what it seems. We'll see."

"Bet'chu had somepin' to do with it?"

"In a way. Accidently."

"Yeah, jus' like you accidently got me walkin'. Well, bes' watch out. Only thing more dangerous than a cornered snake is a wounded one. Don't worry, if he gon' touch you, he gotta get through Grandaddy Long Legs first, y'know'm sayin'?"

"He'll end up like that gator."

"That's right! But you know what else? I wouldn't lay a finger on 'Lijah Youngblood. I'm scared a you, boy! I'd be back in that wheelchair 'fore the curse even lef' my lips. Sure am glad to be on your side, young fella."

Down to Earth

TWENTY-ONE

The drought continued into August, July passing without another word from Daddy or anybody from the church. As far as I knew, Brother Ronny had regained control and righted the ship, and things were back to normal. Gerald was now walking, slowly, with only a cane. Flora thought he was rushing it, especially after he fell a few times, but he was dedicated and wouldn't let anyone deter him.

With the lack of rain, the water level of the lake dropped so much that part of Gerald's wheelchair, alongside a grocery cart and other long-lost and forgotten items, were now visible. He found it hilarious. At least once a day he pointed his cane out towards the water and said, "Somebody plunder that sunken ship a mine and bring me my cigarettes."

One sweltering afternoon, Virgil handed me a piece of yellow construction paper.

"What's this?" I said.

"From Grandaddy. Read it."

Written in magic marker, the sign said, "This Fridy - potLUCK consurt feat. Virgil & Co. Important ~~Anunce Anowns~~

News TBA!"

Virgil said, "Grandaddy wants to celebrate. He says he wants to tell ever'body 'bout the reopenin' of the place in the comin' days. 'A lil' pre-party,' he called it. He told me, 'An' make sure our frien' 'Lijah comes. *Dadgum* I love that boy.'"

"I'm sure it'll be a hoot, I'll be there. You want some lunch? Got a pot of canned soup on the fire."

"Sure, I'll take some. You doin' good? You seem a lil' better." He came and sat on a cinder block near the fire.

"I'm good, I guess. Still getting used to life without her, you know?" I stirred the soup with the ladle. "Sometimes, I hear a twig snap or something, and I catch myself searching out the window for her, expecting to see her walking through the woods. Or I start wondering what fishing tackle I should put on her line next time we go out on the lake. Would you believe, last Friday morning I made her a plate of hotcakes? Wasn't 'til her plate got cold that I remembered. That's always the worst part, when it hits me - 'She's gone, and she's not coming back.' And my heart gets broken all over again. But it's almost worth it, Virg', just for the few seconds where I've forgotten, and I'm living in a world where she's still here, where she's coming."

"Sounds worthy of a song."

"Go ahead, write one. A long ballad with a sorrowful ending."

"Well, we don't know how it's gonna end just yet."

"I feel pretty sure I know, and it's not a fairy tale. I might just have to get used to living with a heart that's not whole. But you know what? At least I have no regrets. It doesn't have to have a happy ending to be a good story. We had us a good run."

He nodded and didn't speak for a while. The pot of soup started to bubble. "Gene and Candy," he said.

I looked up at him. "Huh?"

"My parents. That was their names. Gene and Candy. Sometimes I say 'em out loud. I don't really like to, it's like reopenin' the wound, but I think it helps, gives it some fresh air, keeps it from gettin' infected, y'know? I can remember their faces again when I say their names. You should try it."

"All right," I said. I swallowed. "Georgia. Me and Georgia had us a good run."

"Takes a lot of courage to mourn, don't it?" Virgil said. I took the soup off the fire, and he said, "You notice the creek's dryin' up?"

"Yeah," I said, "Worst drought I can remember."

"Ain't gon' be no more crawfish for a while. It's August anyhow."

"Maybe that hog'll turn up."

"Yeah, maybe," Virgil said. "Dang, I can't wait 'til October. I feel like I ain't tasted venison in ages. I'm tired a corn dogs."

"We'll get some dove at the end of August. Here, have some soup. Vegetable beef. I'll grab another spoon. We can just eat out the pot."

"Shaw ever lecture you 'bout this fire? 'Cause a the burn ban and all?"

"He does, but he doesn't mean it. He may fight fires at work but the first thing he does on his days off is come down here and light one."

Virgil laughed. "Figured."

Early Friday morning I helped Gerald and Flora setup for the party. They wanted to get things in place early to avoid the midday heat. While Virgil and Monty checked the microphones for the concert, I put out the sawhorse tables and chairs. Gerald asked me to go door to door and make sure everybody was coming.

At seven o' clock that evening, people started gathering, setting their various dishes on the tables. Grandaddy had thawed some catfish from the freezer and fried it in addition to a twenty-pound lunker Virgil caught on a limb line. Miss Mattie brought her late husband's favorite jalapeño cornbread.

Carl came up and shook my hand. "Hey Daniel," he said slowly, "Been a while. How yoo?"

"Hi Carl, I'm not so bad. How're you?"

"Aw, you know, I —"

Prissy moved between us and said, "Looks like you can hear jus' fine, huh, Carl? Jus' go sit down." He slowly eased into a chair, and she turned to me. "That man won't hardly speak to me. He act like he deaf in my househol'. Then he sees you, or whoever, an' turns out ain't nothin' wrong with his ears. I swear I'mma choke'm, God love'm." Laughing without smiling, she walked past me and clanged a pan of blueberry muffins onto the table. "Bet he won't touch them muffins neither."

Wally came up and patted me on the shoulder. "Evenin', 'Lijah. Want'cha to meet somebody." I turned. "This here's Shaw's momma." I shook her hand.

"Hi," she said, "Darlene." Wearing a tank top, she was rail thin and a little hunched over. At first glance, she seemed young enough to be his sister, but then, no longer smiling, she could have passed for his grandmother. Her two daughters were carrying plates of saran-wrapped rice krispie treats.

"Say, you hear 'bout Shaw?" Wally said. "That boy rescued a whole mess a kids from a orphanage that was burnin' down. Whole thing collapsed not a second after he got the last'n out." Virgil, unrolling an audio cord just a few feet away, shook his head.

"You must be a proud pops," I said.

"I ain't jus' proud, I'm humbled. Don't know where he gets it from. It ain't from his daddy, tell you that."

I saw Monty walk away from the tent between two trailers. I figured he was taking a smoke break, but he just stood unmoving, facing the lake. I went to him and said, "You good, Monty?"

He wiped his eyes and cleared his throat. Without turning he said, "See that tall fella over there behin' me?"

"Yeah, think so. Young lady and a coupla kids next to him?

"That's my son an' his wife. An' my . . . my grandkids."

"I heard you mention them a long time ago. Seen him pushing his kids on the tire swing before, never met him though. He's been pretty scarce."

"Well, he been a stranger to me, too. As you know, he lives across the lot from me. Five years, not a word, ain't seen his face in *five* years. An' jus' few minutes ago . . . he walk up to me like we fam'ly again and said, 'Thought I'd come hear you play tonight, Pops, if that's alright. Sorry I been scarce these last years.' I been waitin' for that moment, so I could cuss 'im, but instead, I's lost for words. I jus' put my arm 'round his dadgum neck and held 'em tight. Then he let me meet my grandkids for the first time. Names're Tommy and Daisy."

"Aw, I'm happy for you, Monty."

"Been a long five years. Jus' like that, we talkin' again. He comin' to hear me play with Virgil, said he heard the last one was really somethin'. Ah, well, better go warm up."

I went to Sammy's and helped her with her wheelbarrow and drinks. As we walked from her house to the tent she said, "You thinkin' what I'm thinkin', 'Lijah?"

"What's that?"

"Wish we had a lady fiddler playin' 'longside these two fellas tonight."

"I was trying not to think about that. But I'm with you."

She patted my arm. "You quit shruggin' them shoulders yet? You let them tears roll?"

"I reckon so."

She put her arm through mine. "Well, I can't replace what's been lost, but least you got some friends to make things more easy passin'."

"That's right," I said.

Just after we got to the tent, Shaw arrived in his fireman's uniform, his buzzed head glistening with sweat. "How y'like that? They let me off for the party," he said. "On call, though."

"Heard about that orphanage," I said with a smirk.

"Huh?" he said.

"Never mind."

"Well! Howdy howdy howdy now!" said Grandaddy, raising his cane in the air. I'd never realized how tall he was. Wearing his alligator boots, at his full stature he was a head above most of the crowd, as tall as Brother Ronny. "Y'all a fine lookin' group, know that? Sure is good to see you from above, up here on two feet. Monty, I forgot how bald you is, boy! An' Miss Mattie, you the purdiest widow I ever saw. Anyway, listen up folks, times is a changin' 'round here. I got news. Big news. We gon' be proud folk again."

"You gon' be a great grandaddy?" Shaw called out, "Virgil get a girl pregnant?"

"Shut up, Shaw. No! We gon' reopen this place. Marina, grocery and supply store. We got the dock restored already, been workin' on the store last week or two. My side rib Mrs. Flora's gonna get her some more exotic animals like she used to have. An we e'en gon' have us a lil' gas pump! Virgil an' me gon' work side by side, like father an' son - ain't that right Virg'!"

Virgil nodded and the crowd started chattering.

"We gon' have us a concert every Friday night, that's right, Virgil gon' have him a record label this time next year, y'all know'm sayin'! We gon' be proud folk, I tell you, but not in a mean way. No, I'm talkin' 'bout dignity. I don't know 'bout y'all, but these lean years a sufferin' with a lil' drop a mercy at jus' the right time, it done somepin' to me. If you can b'lieve, it took the mean outta me." He got teary-eyed and his voice cracked a little. "Hot dog, I love y'all. I could kiss ever'one a you. Even you, Shaw." People laughed. "Well, thank y'all for comin' to this lil' pre-party here. Tonight, we gon' celebrate what's already come in hopes a what's comin' next, y'hear? Gimme few months, an' we gon' reopen an' have an even bigger party. OK, I'll shut up." He pumped his cane in the air a few times. "Let's eat!" People clapped and whistled.

We made our plates and visited. I was watching the path towards the woods until Virgil came up and said in my ear, "Don't worry, I ain't runnin' away this time." I smiled and made my plate of food. After fifteen minutes or so, I heard Virgil's voice over the speakers. "Evenin', folks. Thank y'all for havin' me tonight. I got a good setlist for us. Some of 'em you heard before, some you ain't. Hope you enjoy."

Virgil and Monty played for a while without vocals. He seemed a little stiff at first but seemed to loosen up before it was done. Then, just when he started to sing his first word, Shaw stood up, shouting and waving his hands in front of the stage. "Stop the music!" he called out. Thinking he was joking, Virgil and Monty kept playing. But Shaw continued shouting and waving.

"What is it, Shaw?" Virgil said, irritated.

"Stop the music!" he called out again, pointing behind us.

"We got us a fire!" We turned around to see dark smoke billowing out of the windows of Gerald's trailer, which was glowing inside.

"Grandaddy!" Virgil called into the microphone, looking wildly around the crowd. "Where's Granny?"

Twenty-Two

Shaw was the first to get to Gerald's trailer, tying a bandanna around his face on the way. He tried to open the door but burned himself on the knob and cursed. Using his shirt tail, he opened the door and ran inside. By the time Gerald to the ramp, Shaw had Granny out the door, coughing and shaking but apparently unharmed. "Flora!" Gerald cried out. "Flora, honey! You alive? You breathin'?"

"Y'all gotta get away," Shaw yelled. "This trailer's a goner. Get movin'!"

I helped Gerald move down the ramp quickly. "Hang on!" he said, sniffing the air. "Hold on a minute! That ain't no grease fire." He sniffed again. "I smell diesel!" He swung his head around. "*Who* the *hell* set my trailer on fire?"

As we moved back toward the tent, we saw there were new fires. Next door to Gerald's, Miss Mattie's trailer was engulfed, too. "Ricky!! Oh, God, Ricky!!" she called out, hobbling towards the fire, where all her collections and stacks of nostalgia were being incinerated. Wally held her back. Closer to the lake, the top of the old supply store was blazing in the dark, like a pillar of fire, its rusted metal roof already caved in. We moved away from it all, keeping to the center of the park, some walking up the gravel drive. Even from a hundred yards away, we could feel the heat from Gerald's and Miss Mattie's trailers.

"I rang the fire station," Prissy said. "They comin'."

Monty ran up to us, breathless. "I stopped a fire at my place just in time."

"Ever'body!" Gerald roared out. "We got a terr'rist afoot! Go check your homes! Somebody's settin' fires. Virgil! Fetch me my shotgun outta the shed."

Shaw pulled a flashlight from his pocket and began running from home to home, checking for fire.

I turned in circles. So far only Gerald's and Miss Mattie's and the supply store had visible fires. There were so many helpless, wailing neighbors, I didn't know what to do. I stood alone, rooted to the ground. Just as I saw the blue and red lights of the fire trucks and police coming down the highway, another light caught my eye, this time beyond the trailers and in the woods, in the direction of the House. I walked towards it slowly until I realized that the light was growing brighter. Another fire. Without a word, I took off through the field and down the wooded trail, across the creek to the House. By the time I got there, I could hardly stand within thirty feet of it. The House, dry as kindling, would not last long. I stood as close as I could to it, just past the empty creek bed. A handful of explosions, probably from ammunition, sent some of the tin roof flying into the air. In my mind I started sorting through everything I had inside. Clothes, books, fishing poles, food, guns and . . . the painting. I ran towards the house, not even feeling the heat, but as I reached for the door, someone blindsided me, tackling me to the ground. Shaw. He tried to drag me away from the fire, but I resisted, pulling him toward the House. He kicked me in my side and cursed at me and finally dragged me away by the back of my shirt.

"The painting, Shaw," I cried. "It's all I got left of her."

"You ain't gonna have nothin' left to *you* if you don't let it burn." He held onto me until I stopped fighting. I laid my head back in the dirt. "No time for tears, we gotta get outta here, 'Lijah. Whole forest is gon' be on fire 'fore long, dry as it is." He pulled me to my feet and put his arm around my shoulder. "You gon' be fine." We started to walk away when he stopped abruptly. His face was orange in the glow of the House. "You hear that?" he said.

I listened. "All I hear are sirens and screams, Shaw. And crackling pine."

"No," he said quietly, "Sound to me like we finally caught that feral hog."

"Shaw it's not the time. I thought you said –"

He whispered. "It ain't no hog, 'Lijah. We got even bigger game this time. C'mere. Quiet."

The heat on our backs, we stepped through the woods in slow motion like we were stalking a turkey. Arriving at the little game trail, Shaw stopped and held up his hand. "Looky here," he whispered, pulling back the brush silently. "Just as I thought. We trapped ourselves a terr'rist."

There before us, was the red-rimmed silhouette of a man, so tall and broad-shouldered that it could only have belonged to one person. "That's no terrorist, Shaw," I whispered, "That's Preacher Man."

"What's the difference?" he said, quietly.

Watching him through the brush trying to free his leg from the trap, the overwhelming grief from a moment before evaporated and became concentrated and hushed, like the moment a deer steps into the crosshairs. Nothing else existed in the world but me and Brother Ronny, and it was time to pull the trigger. My blood began to boil. I *wanted* to pull the trigger.

I grabbed Shaw's flashlight and said, "I got this, stay out here," and stepped through the brush.

"That you, Brother Ronny?" I said casually. "Been a while. What are you doing out here?"

He turned and lunged at me, stopping short, the teeth of the foothold ripping a little further into his pants and ankle. Standing just outside the range of his arms, I was safe. The trap, not anchored to the ground but to the root of a tree, was going nowhere.

"How'd you get yourself trapped? Must've mistaken this game trail for a walking path. I'd let you go, but I see you got yourself a couple cans of diesel there. Can't help but wonder if you were the one setting fire to all these poor folks' homes. But surely not, I don't see how a man of God could do such a thing."

"Take this thing off my leg right now, boy, before I get myself out and put your head in it."

"You light a dozen families' homes on fire, and you think I'm just gonna let you go? Go ahead, admit it. Confess what you've done."

"I'm doing the Lord's will. Something you've never known about."

"And what's his will?"

"Judgment!"

"And how do you know that?"

He stood tall and looked over the brush toward the House. Dancing in his eyes was the light of the fire that was consuming all I held most dear. "The day cometh," he said, "That shall burn as an oven; and all the proud, yea, and all that do wickedly, shall be stubble. Thus saith the Lord of hosts, that it shall leave them neither root nor branch."

It took everything in me not to find a stick and beat him with it. "Only problem is - you're not the judge. Good grief, you've fooled yourself for so long you've forgotten who you are. You've lost your mind entirely. You'll be eating grass on all fours before you know it. Judge? Anointed? Fisher of men? There's only one of them, Brother Ronny. And it's not me, and it sure ain't you."

"Pot calling the kettle black! Mr. Redneck Prophet!"

"Your words, not mine. I'd never claim a title like that."

"I'm here to hasten the Day and prepare the way of the Lord. He'll never come when the land's filled with Devil worshiping Canaanites."

"But don't you know? You dig a pit for somebody, you'll fall right in it yourself. Violence boomerangs, brother."

He reached down and started fumbling with the trap.

As he searched for the release, my thoughts went to Georgia. Imagining what she had been going through the last few months with a father this deranged, my anger started to burn hot. "You know why I think you're really here? 'Cause that house of cards you call a ministry is falling down. The conferences, your church, your family - you lost control of it all. Admit it, this has nothing to do with the Lord. You needed somebody to blame, to punish, because the last thing you'll do is admit fault. And you were . . . I can't believe it, you're jealous, aren't you? Jealous of a little old trailer park that's been blessed with some mercy and dignity. You couldn't stand it and had to destroy it. Don't sound to me like the Lord's work. Sounds like the opposite."

"You got some nerve to talk about my family," he said, without glancing up from the trap.

I knelt down across from him. "Speaking of, I heard you

embellished my confession. Said I took advantage of Georgia. Assaulted her."

"Might as well have, much as you corrupted her. Just wait, after all this, I'm pressing charges. I'll make sure she gets up on that stand and testifies against you."

"Nope, not gonna happen. You lied, Preacher, just to get everybody to hate me as much as you do. I wouldn't care that much if it was only me you threw under the bus, but you tossed Georgia under there with me. You shamed your own daughter, sacrificed her right on the altar of your own ministry. And now it's all backfiring on you."

"What you know about sacrifice, boy?"

"How's Georgia?"

Silent, he started to dig around the root of the trap.

"Tell me how Georgia's doing."

Finally giving up on the trap, he leapt at me again, only inches from my face. The teeth of the trap sunk deeper into his ankle. "She's locked up. She and her momma got in the Lord's way."

"Locked up where? At home?"

"Somewhere safe from wolves."

I heard voices in the distance and turned. Flashlights were coming down the path towards the smoldering House. "Tell you what, Brother Ronny. I'll give you a choice. You got two options. Number one, I give you over to whoever's coming down that hill. Probably Granny with her shotgun - you remember her? I'm sure the police are right behind her. Option number two, I let your ankle out the trap and set you free, giving you into the Lord's hands. And we'll let him be the judge."

Shaw cried out from the bushes, "You kiddin' me? Hold up!"

"Shaw, it's not your call," I said over my shoulder. "OK, Brother Ronny, what'll it be? The judgment of God? Or the judgment of man?'"

"Set. My ankle. Free," he said, baring his teeth, a little foam forming at the corner of his mouth. Flaring his nostrils with ragged breaths, he put his hand on the tree and tore at the bark. His hair, normally slicked back, had leaves in it and had fallen over his dilated eyes. He neither looked nor sounded human. At the sight, my anger toward him began to cool and, for the first time in my life, I felt compassion for the man. "Ronny," I said gently. "Come on, 'fess up to the police. Just this once, quit fooling yourself."

He looked over my shoulder, where the flashlights and voices were getting close. "I know where I stand with the Lord. I'll let him judge between you and me any day. Now take it off."

"Naw, 'Lijah!" Shaw said from behind me.

"Hush, Shaw," I said over my shoulder. "Vengeance don't belong to me."

Slowly, I stepped close and knelt down at the trap, the flashlight between my teeth. His pant leg was torn and soaked with blood which ran down his massive foot. "You know Ronny, that's the thing. It's not me you'll be judged against." I put my thumbs on the base of the trap and pushed down the levers on the side as hard as I could with my fingers. The jaws opened, and he pulled his foot out. In a flash, his good foot swung and struck the side of my face.

"Told you I was gonna crush your head," he said as I hit the ground. He limped away quickly down the game trail. Shaw knelt beside me, yelling curses after him. Everything went quiet and dark.

When I opened my eyes again a few minutes later, I was staring up from the ground into the starless, cloudy sky above the trees. Looking down at me were Gerald, Granny, Shaw, and

Virgil, asking if I was all right. Shaw was fumbling with his words, trying to explain the situation to them but making no sense. I felt something fall on my face. Ash? I touched it, trying to understand. No, not that. I rubbed it between my fingers. Blood? No. I felt it a third time and knew what it was. I bolted upright and looked each of them in the face. "Y'all better find shelter," I said. "A hard rain's a gonna fall."

Twenty-Three

The rain began to trickle.

"I'll be damn," Gerald said, lifting his head to the night sky. I walked toward the embers that stood in place of the House, circling to the back, where the bedroom used to be. Knowing the painting was long gone, I scanned the ashes anyway. Nothing but charred wood. The trickle increased and steadied into a true rain, the drops sizzling on the coals. A small ring of fire was slowly moving out from the House.

"Hey boy, where you goin'?" Gerald said.

"It's not over yet," I said, jumping onto the dirt bike, which was hot but unharmed, leaning against a tree opposite the House. "I gotta make sure that fool doesn't hurt Georgia. He's lost his mind, Gerald." I kick-started the bike.

"You safe to drive that thing?" he called over the sound of the engine. "And what're we supposed to tell the police?"

"Tell them what you want. Afraid it won't matter before long." The raindrops increased in size and number. I shifted into gear and sped up the path to the trailer park, where firemen were at work with their hoses. Blue and red lights flashed onto people huddled in small groups, talking to police. The rain was falling in sheets before I made it to the end of the gravel drive, and the sky flashed and rumbled in the distance.

I put the bike in its highest gear and sped down the highway toward town but quickly had to shift down and curb my speed. I could hardly see. It was like trying to drive while being sprayed in the face with a hose. I passed cars with flashing hazard lights who had pulled over to wait out the storm. The ditches alongside the highway began to overflow onto the road, causing the bike to lose grip and hydroplane a few times. I cut my speed even further but continued, driving blind half the time. After twenty minutes, I saw the steeple of the church through the trees ahead, illuminated by a floodlight beneath it. Next to the church was the parsonage with its lights on. I drove up to the front steps of the house and ran to the door. Locked. Yelling up at Georgia's bedroom window, I could hardly get my voice above the roar of the rain. I banged on the door again. A stone's throw away, the lights of the church chapel came on, shining through the windows. I pounded at the front door one last time, then stood back and looked through the rain to her bedroom window again. No response.

Running to the church, I peered into one of the front windows through the foyer into the sanctuary. Down the aisle that I had walked six times for baptism, up on the stage, behind his huge wooden pulpit, was Ronny, preaching. To whom? I didn't know. At least from the window, I could see no one in the pews. In the bright lights of the pulpit, he looked even less sane than he had in the woods. I tried one of the double doors, but it was locked. Releasing the handle, my hand suddenly went numb. Running from my fingers to the rest of my body, my skin began to tingle, my hair standing on end. Taking a step away from the church, I heard the sound of fish frying and then, like a gunshot from heaven, a noise so loud I collapsed to the ground in fear and trembling, the earth quaking beneath me. It was daylight for a moment, and then dark again, everything silent except for what sounded like the whine of a mosquito. Catching my breath, I saw fire running in lines down the scorched steeple.

The rain lessened to a steady downpour. I headed to the rear of the parsonage and found the back door unlocked. The lights were all off now, the power having been knocked out by the lightning strike. My hearing was slowly returning. I went inside and called out for Georgia. No answer. I called out for Mrs. Bonnie. No answer. Passing through the empty kitchen into the hall, I saw Ronny's office on the right with its huge maple desk. Heading up the stairs at the front of the house, I stepped into Georgia's bedroom, catching her scent, but she was not there. Her fiddle was out of its case at the foot of her bed. Through the window to my left, I saw for the first time the view Georgia had grown up with, the steeple of the church towering over her bedroom. I stepped closer to the window, surprised and in awe at how much the fire had advanced in spite of the rain. The eaves over the covered landing where I had stood a moment before had already collapsed. Bright lights no longer shone out of the chapel, only dancing red shadows. An explosion suddenly blew out a few of the chapel windows, rattling Georgia's bedroom. And then, only slightly at first, the steeple began to shift in the wind and rain. Beginning to buckle at its base, it tilted toward the parking lot for a moment, and then, as if pushed by the wind, it fell backwards, crashing onto the center of the pitched roof of the chapel, plumes of smoke and ash shooting out the hole and shattering the rest of the windows. Eyes wide, I thought of Ronny at his pulpit. Then, far more alarming, I wondered if maybe the sanctuary was not empty. Maybe, as they had every

Sunday for eighteen years, Mrs. Bonnie and Georgia were dutifully sitting in their place, the first pew on the right, listening to their husband and father preach his sermon. Images flashed through my mind. I hauled it downstairs and picked up the phone on Ronny's desk to report the lightning and the fire. No dial tone. I sprinted out the back of the house.

The side door of the church was unlocked. The wind slammed it closed behind me after I walked through. Although the foyer was dark and smelled of smoke, the fire had not yet reached that wing of the church. The only light came from the red emergency exit sign over the door. Passing the waiting area where I'd sat with Georgia long ago, I heard a rapid knock coming from Ronny's office. I stopped and turned, approaching the door slowly. "Hello?"

"Elijah!"

"Georgia, is that you?" I tried the door and put my ear to it.

"It's Momma and me both! Daddy locked us in a couple hours ago. And now the lights are out."

"Georgia, the church is on fire. We gotta get y'all out."

I heard a voice from within the office. Then she said, "Momma said Mrs. Norris should have a key in her office down the hall. Hanging on a peg behind the door."

I sprinted down the hall in the dark, running my hand along the wall until I felt the door frame of the secretary's office. I tried the handle. Unlocked. I went to the other side of the door and felt along the wall, eventually bumping into a little set of jingling keys. I grabbed them and ran back, the smoke now visible in the glow of the exit sign.

"Got them," I said, trying one key after another in the lock. Finally, one slid into the keyhole, allowing the latch to go down, and I swung open the door.

They both exhaled in relief. Mrs. Bonnie emerged first without a word. Georgia came out behind her and fumbled for my hand in the dark.

"Come on," I said, leading them outside.

When we stepped out the door and got away from the building, Georgia glanced over her shoulder and gasped. "Oh, Momma, look!"

We all stopped and gazed at the hole in the sky where the steeple used to be. Mrs. Bonnie's face glowed with the fire, and the rain fell on her cheeks. She resembled Georgia.

"Ronny!" she screamed.

"Georgia," I said, "I think he's still in there. I gotta see if I can help." Georgia stared at me helplessly.

I started toward the church, when Mrs. Bonnie said, "Elijah!" I turned to her. Her lips were trembling, and it took her a moment to speak. "He ain't right."

"I know," I said, running back to the door.

Twenty-Four

I re-entered the side door of the church and took a right down a row of classrooms, rain pelting the darkened windows. Passing the prayer room and a couple of bathrooms, I finally got to the chapel entrance. I tried the push bar of the heavy door and immediately drew back, feeling like I'd grabbed a hot cast iron skillet. I cooled my hands on my wet shirt and kicked it open with my shoe. Stepping into the chapel, my eyes immediately stung in the fumes and heat. The wooden floors and carpet runners looked like a giant bed of coals. Burning fragments fell from the roof onto the pews below, which crackled and smoldered. Straight down the middle of the roof was the long, jagged hole where the steeple had fallen, cutting the chapel in two. The steeple was now unrecognizable except as a roaring bonfire. A sermon Ronny once preached on Sodom and Gomorrah came to mind. Hearing a cry, I turned to the stage and saw Ronny pinned to the ground under his giant wooden pulpit, which was also on fire. I put my shirt up over my nose and mouth and ran to him, trying to avoid the debris dropping from above.

"Ronny!" I called.

"How you like these tongues a fire, Elijah!" he said with a strange laugh, his lower half under the fire and wood. There was no way I could lift the pulpit off him with the tip of the steeple weighing it down. I took one of the heavy deacon's chairs from behind his head and propped it against the mass and pushed. Nothing. "You can't stop a consuming fire!" he yelled, trying to push me away. Pausing to cough, I glanced through the hole in the ceiling and took a breath, then got lower and pushed harder. Smelling my hair begin to singe, I felt the pulpit lift an inch.

"See if you can get out now," I cried, starting to gag.

"Leave me be! I'm not the first martyr by fire!"

"You're no martyr, Ronny," I said. My shirt and pants began to steam, my skin stinging beneath. I did my best to wedge the chair at an angle to keep the pulpit propped for a moment, then went and grabbed him underneath his huge arms and pulled him out from the fire. He clawed and screamed at me. For a few seconds after he was out, what was left of his legs were bright red like a hot cattle brand before fading. Howling in pain, he said, "You always fancied yourself a prophet. Here you go, Elijah! Here's your chariot of fire!"

I felt the stage shake underneath and saw the door I'd entered through now buried in rubble. The door on the opposite end was not even visible. Fire pressed in on all three sides in front of us, backing us up to the wall at the back of the stage. The moisture in my clothes had fully evaporated, and my skin began to feel like it was being seared in a pan. In the pain, the thought crossed my mind of just diving into the flames to get it all over with. No wonder Ronny didn't want my help. He was ready to die. "You and me, boy!" he cried, "Back where we started. Baptism by fire!"

I turned suddenly and looked up behind me. The baptistry. I grabbed him under the arms. "Forgive me, Preacher, this won't feel too good." I dragged him to the side of the stage while he struggled against me. When we got to the stairs, he caught hold of my shirt and tried to pull my head down to the ground. I had no choice but to swing back at him, landing a right uppercut to the jaw. I'd be lying if I said it didn't feel good. He let go, limp and surrendered.

Opening the narrow door of the baptistry, I heaved his big body up one stair at a time and then down into the baptismal waters. His legs sizzled as they went under. I placed him on the steps on one side and sat across from him. The water was warm, not frigid like the other six times I'd been in it. Even so, it was cool in comparison to the air, like jumping into a lake on a hot summer day. My mind began to level. My mind slowed down and the irrational thoughts faded. Ronny, hardly moving, rested his head on the step behind him. Eyes closed, his breathing steadied.

After a few minutes soaking in silence, no longer feeling like a pork rind in hot oil, I lifted up and looked through the little opening at the burning sanctuary. The flames were creeping up the stage toward us. I was thankful at least for the hole in the roof, letting some of the smoke and heat out. Doubting we would survive, I knew I had done everything that could be expected of a worm. Whatever happened next was out of my hands.

"It was lightning, wasn't it?" Ronny said, eyes still closed. "That started the fire."

"Yep, struck the steeple."

He was silent for a while. He tried to move and contorted his face in pain. "Hey, come here."

"Why?"

"Move me up a step, so I can get one last look at the sanctuary. Before I die."

"I think I'll keep my distance."

"I'm done swinging," he sighed. "Truly."

Suspicious, half-expecting him to try to drown me, I went to him through the water. Standing behind him, I grabbed him under the arms and moved him up a step, leaning him against the back wall.

I could tell it was painful but, to his credit, he did not swing or holler. "Thank you," he said. I sat back in my spot across from him, glad for the relief of the water. "Look at this place, Elijah."

"Hell on earth, if you ask me."

"It's not just that, it's hell in the house of God. Judgment on the house of God. I don't understand, how could that be? A kingdom divided against itself don't stand. A king don't tear down his own kingdom. Judgment on the house of God?" He pushed his hair back out of his face, a new, contemplative look on his face. I kept an eye on him, unsure of where his mind was going on the brink of death, watching the destruction of his church. "No, that's not right, it's judgment on . . ." The firelight flickering in his eyes, a wave of grief crossed his face. "With what judgment ye judge, ye shall be judged." He shook his head back and forth and turned toward me. "What a fool I been. You should've just let me burn. What'd you go and draw me out the flames for? You're a fool, yourself, Elijah, you know that? You can't thwart the hand of justice."

"You ever heard of this thing called grace?"

"What are you giving grace to me for? Now you got yourself damned along with me. What are you doing here? Surely my death would've been a dream come true for you. With me out the way, you could run around with Georgia all you wanted. Why'd you try to save me?"

"It's not out of love for you, I'll tell you that."

"Then why?"

"Can we just go out in peace and quiet?"

As the heat intensified, Ronny eased down a step further into the water and narrowed his eyes at me. "Your confession," he said. "You lied to me."

I splashed my face to cool it. "We already discussed that, Ronny. That was the point of the confession."

"No, that's not what I mean. You weren't sincere. You didn't mean it. It was phony! A phony confession."

I shook my head. "This really what you want to talk about? Here at the end?"

"She loves you, don't she? Georgia." He moved himself down to the last step of the baptistry.

"What?"

"Your confession. 'She don't give a fig about me.' That's what you said. Why'd you lie about that? Hm? Tell me, boy."

I shook my head. "You wouldn't understand." Smoke hovered over the water like fog. Off the steps entirely now, we both descended as far as we could without going under, like a pair of alligators, fully submerged except for our faces.

"It's me she don't give a fig for," he said. "I can see that now. She won't care if I die in here, will she?"

"You ain't right, Ronny."

"Know what?" he said, sitting up suddenly, looking at me through the smoke. "I've never been righter in my life."

I didn't respond. The fires crept closer, the baptistry now feeling like a hot tub. I could smell some kind of chemical in the air. "Let me just go out in silence, please, thinking of fonder things," I said. "You've lost your mind. You've gone insane."

"No, listen, I've never been saner. Mind's clear as this here water. Come on," he coughed. "Before I die. Just tell me. Why'd you lie for her? Why'd you make that phony confession?"

I thought for a moment whether I wanted to use my final breaths on this discussion. "Part of it was true, Ronny - I *was* sneaking around with her. As for the rest, the part I made up, I reckon I wanted to take the heat for her. Confess her part as if I'd done it myself. Didn't want you to hurt her any more than you already had. Even if I never got to see her again, I thought maybe if I took the bullet from you myself, there was a chance she'd find a way to live, in spite of that death grip you always had on her."

He nodded again and again, then rubbed his eyes. "Now I see. Now I know why you came in here for me. You love that girl, don't you?" Without waiting on a response, he closed his eyes solemnly and leaned back, taking a deep breath, and disappeared beneath the water. He was under so long, I began to wonder if he was coming back up. When he finally re-emerged, his eyes were easy and gentle, fixed on me. I'd never realized until then where Georgia got her green eyes. "I reckon you're a better man than me, Elijah Youngblood."

"Aw, neither one of us is much of anything."

The baptistry began to shake violently, sloshing waves against the walls. A loud roar came from the chapel. Sure that we were about to be buried alive, I covered my head and ducked underwater, which did not muffle but magnified the sounds of destruction and gave them an alien tone. For a full minute, I stayed under, waiting to die. When I could hold my breath no longer, the rumbling finally stopped. I rose, gasping for air, truly surprised to be unharmed, neither drowned nor buried nor burned. I looked out of the opening as the dust settled. The roof had completely collapsed and much of the walls with it, the rain now pouring in. The smoke in the chapel and the baptistry began to whirl out into the cloudy night sky. The wailing siren of a fire truck drew near, the red lights flashing on the wall behind us.

Before long, there were voices and the blast of a fire hose. Steam and smoke rose into the heavens from everywhere.

When the firemen advanced into the building, I called out from the baptistry window and waved to them for help. They waved and spoke to one another, continuing to hose down the fire.

"Elijah," said Ronny, who had not moved.

"Yeah?" I said, watching one of the firemen coming toward us through the wreckage.

"Look at me, young man, I got one last thing to say." I turned to him. Just as he opened his mouth, the door opened at the top of the steps behind him. It was Shaw.

"'Lijah! Dadgum, it's you! You're alive! You OK?"

"I'm good. He's hurt bad though," I said, nodding towards Ronny.

Noticing Ronny for the first time, Shaw fell back. "The hell?" he said.

"It's OK." I glanced at Ronny, who nodded at me. "He's all right. He can't walk, though. You'll have to get some help to get him out of here." I stepped up the stairs past Ronny, next to Shaw, water pouring off me. A hand around my shoulder, he helped me through the wet, charred floor of the chapel. When we got out, he went to talk to the paramedics. A crowd had begun to form in the parking lot in front of the church, huddled together under umbrellas. Through the rain, someone burst from the crowd and leapt on me.

Georgia and I held each other for a long while without speaking. She would not stop shaking. "Been a long summer, huh?" I said.

Pulling back to look at my face, she said, "I thought you were dead."

"Nah," I said.

"I was *sure* you were dead."

"Yet, here I am, alive and well. Back from the dead, I guess. Except I think these eyebrows of mine might've perished in the fire."

"What about Daddy? You find him?"

"He's alive, but his legs got burnt pretty bad, Georgia. I don't know if he's ever gonna walk again. Same time, believe it or not, we might've struck a truce."

She wrinkled her forehead in unbelief. The paramedics came by, carrying Ronny on a stretcher, a blanket over his lower half. Georgia gasped, and Mrs. Bonnie cried out and ran to him from the crowd. The paramedics stopped a moment while she stroked his head and cried and kissed him. He motioned for her to move closer to him. Bending down, she turned her ear toward him while he spoke. She pulled away, perplexed, then stepped back so they could carry him to the ambulance. The crowd, mostly made of church members, cried out in shock when they saw him go by on the stretcher, murmuring to each other. Georgia and I walked up to Mrs. Bonnie.

"Is he OK?" Georgia said.

Mrs. Bonnie nodded slowly.

"Are you OK?" Georgia asked.

"No," she said. "But thankful he's alive."

"What'd he tell you?" Georgia asked.

"He told me . . . he said, 'Bonnie, I'm gonna have to confess what I've done. Forgive me. For everything. Tell Georgia I'm sorry, and I love her. And in case I don't make it, tell Elijah . . .'" Mrs. Bonnie paused and stared at me in disbelief. "Tell Elijah he has my blessing.'"

Twenty-Five

"What on earth did you do?" Georgia said, wide-eyed.

I shrugged. "I just pulled him out the fire."

"Then what happened? What'd he say?"

"Listen, I'll tell you the rest of the story later. I gotta find somewhere to sit before I talk anymore. I'm about to fall over."

"Let him get home, honey," Mrs. Bonnie said, "He's exhausted. He can come by tomorrow morning. I can't thank you enough, Elijah, for saving Ronny. And us. Truly, thank you."

"Yes ma'am," I said. I thought about the House and the trailer park and my parents.

"Momma," Georgia said, watching me closely. "He doesn't have a home anymore."

Mrs. Bonnie closed her eyes painfully. An ambulance pulled away, sounding its siren and flashing its lights against her face. A different paramedic approached us, saying she needed to look me over. Mrs. Bonnie said, "You can stay with us tonight. Once they make sure you're all right."

I followed the paramedic to her vehicle, where she checked my vitals and examined me, pressing my reddened arms and legs.

"Well, you're a lucky son of a gun. Mostly just first-degree burns. Should be better in a week."

"I reckon it helped I was soaked to the bone going in there, huh?"

"Reckon so," she said, placing a tube of medicine in my hand. "Rub this on the burned areas a few times a day and stay out the sun. Oh, and, if you didn't notice, there's not a strand of hair on your arms and legs. Or face, for that matter. You're going to look like a newborn babe for a couple of months."

"More like a scalded pig, I'd bet."

She smiled.

"Thank you, ma'am."

She told me I needed to go see a doctor and gave me some instructions and warnings about the smoke I'd inhaled, but, having locked eyes with Georgia across the parking lot, I stopped listening. The paramedic let me go.

I walked with Georgia and Mrs. Bonnie to the door at the back of the house, which was still without power. When we got inside, Mrs. Bonnie said wearily, "Georgia, make Elijah a sandwich while I go get him some clothes. Pour him a glass of cold water. Should be a candle and matches in that first drawer."

"Thank you, Mrs. Bonnie," I said.

Walking off, she said in a tired voice, "Just call me Bonnie."

I sat at the kitchen bar while Georgia lit a candle and set it between us. She took some ham and cheese out of the dark refrigerator and made a sandwich in the dim candlelight. She sliced an orange and put it on a plate next to it. Sliding the plate in front of me, she watched me eat in silence. A few minutes later, Bonnie came in with a handful of dry clothes. "Hope these'll work. They'll be a little big." She turned to Georgia and hugged her. "I'm heading to the hospital. Thank you again, Elijah. I'm sorry for everything. We'll make it right."

"Momma," Georgia said, "You scared for Daddy?"

"Yes, but he'll be OK. Just glad he's alive. Now I'm just plain exhausted. Like waking up after a long nightmare. I better go," she said, leaving the kitchen.

"Where's Elijah supposed to sleep?" Georgia called to her.

"Wherever he wants," Bonnie said from down the hallway, sounding half-dead. "I'm sure I'll spend the night at the hospital. See y'all tomorrow." The front door closed behind her.

Georgia raised her eyebrows. "Things sure are changing quick. You still hungry?"

"You could smoke me a whole rack of hog ribs, and I'd still be hungry. But that's all right, I can eat more tomorrow."

"At least have some more water."

I emptied the second glass and set it on the counter. "You know what I want more than anything in the world?"

"What?" she said.

"To sit with you and talk for a while. Maybe next to a window where I can see the woods."

She smiled. "I can manage that," she said. "There's a spot in the living room. Go shower and change. Bathroom's at the top of the stairs on the right. Take the candle."

Ten minutes later, after I showered, Georgia covered her mouth when I descended the stairs, dressed in her father's shirt and sweatpants. "What?" I said.

"Nothing."

"Aw, I see. The clothes? Like David in Saul's armor, huh?"

She laughed. "Something like that. Come on." She led me to the living room at the back of the house, where she had turned a couch to face a large, paneled window. Tall, heavy curtains had been drawn back behind hooks on either side. She sat on one end and patted her lap. "Lay your head down. I'll give it a rub while you tell me about tonight."

"I was hoping to hear how your summer went, first."

"No, tell me about tonight."

I lay across the couch and rested my head on her warm legs. "Careful," I said, "The other side of my head's pretty banged up." She began to stroke my hair. I'd forgotten what her touch did to my heart rate. Looking out across her backyard into the woods where we'd spent our entire relationship, I started to tell the story of the night, beginning with the preparations for the celebration party that morning. She stopped me and asked what we were celebrating, so I told her about Gerald deciding to re-open the marina. Each step forward in the story brought questions, and I had to go back two steps and explain. Before I knew it, I had not only told Georgia about all that had happened that night with her daddy but about the entire summer since our separation.

After a while I said, "Well, I've been running my mouth for hours now. Enough about me, tell me what's happened with you."

"Wait, I got one last question. About Daddy."

"I'm listening."

"Why do you think he changed his mind?"

"About us?"

"About everything - you, me, even himself."

"You know, earlier today I heard Gerald say that mercy had taken the mean out of him. I reckon it's something like that."

"You think he's really changed?"

"No telling, but everything else in his life just got turned upside down. Maybe he has, too. Now, come on, I've done enough talking. Tell me about you."

"My life hasn't been near as exciting as yours."

"Tell me anyway."

She yawned. "Another time. I don't want to spoil this. I've dreamed of sitting with you like this, watching the sunrise, since I was fourteen. Look, Elijah, the sky's already getting lighter."

We stared and watched the light of dawn begin to show itself above the trees. "You tired?" I asked after a moment.

"Not at all. You?"

"Naw," I said.

We were both asleep before the sun made it over the horizon.

.

TWENTY-SIX

While Gerald waited to hear back from the insurance company, he and Flora stayed with various neighbors, undeterred in his plans for the grand re-opening. The trailer park residents pulled together to help those whose homes had been damaged and had lost belongings in the fire. Although not free of stress and conflict, in many ways it turned into a never-ending party.

Gerald was staying at Monty's the day he received the long-awaited letter from the insurance company. Opening it, he hollered, "Flora! Get in here, woman!" Hearing a thud, she rushed in and found him lying on the floor, his eyes staring blankly at the ceiling. Shaking him violently, she was afraid he was dead, but he turned to her and said, "Look, Flora. Look!" He handed her the letter from the insurance agent. "Grandaddy fin'lly bring home the bacon, baby." He sat up against the wall, his eyes large with visions of the future. "We gon' eat like it's Sunday ever'day. We gon' get'chu som'more peacocks, sugar. A whole passel a peafowl. Kang'roo, g'rilla, anything you want. An' we gon' make sure nobody in this here trailer park strugglin'. For the firs' time in our life, we gon' get to be gen'rous."

Reading the letter carefully, Flora said, "Ger'ld, what'chu talkin' 'bout, honey? Did you even read what this says? All you did was look at the coverage amount. But arson ain't covered, though. If this was a flood or tornader, we'd be in good shape. But honey, we worse off than ever."

"Say what? Where you read that?" he said. She knelt down and showed him.

"Too many dadgum rednecks commitin' insurance fraud, I bet, so they don't put it in the policy for folks like us. Dammit, Flora, what we gon' do?"

"I don't know," she said, sitting on the floor next to him and taking his hand. "We still got each other, though."

A week later, Gerald was outside working on the septic system with Monty when an eighteen-wheeler pulled off the highway onto the gravel drive. "Huh?" Gerald said. He walked to the drive and waved the truck over. "You truckers always think you can use my property to turn your loads 'round, an' I'm right tired of it, y'hear? I ain't havin' it. We got enough damage done here lately. Just back on out and find yourself a depot to turn 'round."

"I ain't here to turn around," the driver said through the window. "I'm makin' a delivery. This is Lakeside Estates, ain't it?"

"Sure is, but I ain't order nothin'."

The driver handed him a clipboard with a delivery receipt on it. "A double-wide?" he stepped back and looked at the trailer. "That what you haulin' under that cover?"

"Yessir, half of it, anyway."

"That for Miss Mattie?"

"Delivery address don't say nothin' about a Miss Mattie. It's for a Gerald somethin'. Says in the top right corner. You got a

Gerald 'round here?"

"Yours truly, pardner. Some kinda mistake though. I didn't order this and can't afford nothin' like it anyway."

"Invoice says it's already paid. Buyer is listed on the invoice. Second page."

Gerald turned the page. "Mt. Sinai Community Church? What the hell is goin' on? I ain't ever been so confused in my life."

"Reckon you can figure that out later. Show me where you want the trailer. I'll bring the other half this afternoon."

A few days after they had moved into the new mobile home, I came to visit.

"There he is! C'mere friend," Gerald said.

"New trailer's fancy," I said, observing the place.

"I know, the Lord's spoilin' me rotten, ain't he? Huh!" He laughed and batted his hand at me. "Tell you what, I won't never say 'nother foul word 'bout church folk. After they righted the wrongs a that preacher, I ain't got no business keepin' a grudge 'gainst 'em. S'posedly the whole church chipped in, an' they ain't even rebuilt their chapel yet. They workin' on somethin' for Miss Mattie, too. Ain't that somethin'?" A serious look came over his face. "Hey, listen here, Mr. Elijah Youngblood. Let's have us a lil' chat. Man to man. Sit on down." I sat on the couch next to his recliner.

"What's up?" I said.

"Ain't no way to say this but straight. You listenin'?"

I nodded.

"I want'cha to be my pardner. I'mma give you a quarter share in the trailer park. Course, only if you wanna spend your life with folk like us."

I laughed uncomfortably. "Gerald, you can't give me that.

Just hire me as a caretaker or something."

"Don't tell me what to do. I give what I want to who I want. I don't need permission a nobody, certainly not you."

"This place belongs to you and your family."

"My fam'ly wouldn't have nothin' left if it wasn't for you. The bank woulda taken this place by the end a the year. Plus, this ain't just fam'ly owned no more. Miss Mattie's a quarter owner now."

"Miss Mattie?"

"Turns out she been hoardin' more than jus' junk. She come up to me yesterdy and says she wants to invest a hunnard thousand in the place. A hunnard thousand, boy! 'Pparently that woman been sittin' on a nest egg after Ricky died, but she ain't ever wanna use it. You know how she is. But she said now that she lost ever'thing else a Ricky's in the fire, might as well do somepin' with his money. Yeah baby, we got cold hard cash in the bank now. Grand reopenin' just got a lot closer! Anyway, I want you to have a quarter share in the place."

"I'll think about it."

"The hell you will. Oh, an' I got somepin' else for ya." He nodded at me. "That's right, hoss, grace 'pon grace." He leaned over and grabbed an envelope from the side table and handed it to me. I held it in my hand. "Go on, open it," he said.

I paused. "What is it?"

"Jus' open the damn thing!" he said. I'd never seen him so eager before. I opened it. It was a thousand dollars cash.

"Nah," I said, tossing it onto the side table.

"'Scuse me?" he said, throwing the envelope at my face.

"Gerald," I said. "Use it for the reopening. I don't need it."

"You actin' like proud folk all sudden, like you don't know how to receive nothin'. I thought you was differen'. I thought you was down to earth. 'Sides," he said with a little happy grunt, "You ain't even ask me why I'm givin' it to you."

I paused and sighed. "Ok, why?"

"Thanks for askin'. Num'er one," he held up his thumb. "I tol' you I was gon' give you back pay for all that work you did. Num'er two," he held up his pointer finger, "I b'lieve you lost a few things in that fire, too. Huh? And num'er three," he said, holding up the stub of his middle finger, "It's time for you to put a ring on that finger, boy! Hot dog!" he said, slapping me on the back. "Now take that money and get outta my face. Go get you that Georgia peach 'fore she finds out you a redneck." I smiled and sat shaking my head until he said, "Go on, get!" I stood and went to the door when he shouted, "Hey! Wait, wait, wait. Hang on." He got up on his feet and walked to me, taking my hand in his and not letting it go. "I jus' wanna know one thing."

"What's that?" I said.

He leaned close and eyed me suspiciously. "You make a lame man walk. Not bad. You raise a brokedown trailer park from the dead. All right, I'm impressed. But how the *hell* did you get a blessin' from the hand a the Devil? That there change a heart's a bigger mir'cle than all of it put together."

"Aw, Gerald," I said, laughing. "I'm as surprised as you. Turns out he's not the Devil after all. Just a man like you and me who lost his way. Lil' grace at the right time can change a fella."

"Firs' time in that man's life, he got himself a revival! Y'know'm sayin'? Hah!" He elbowed me in the side. "Now go get yourself a woman!"

The next week I took Georgia fishing. When we got to the old spot, I noticed the water had risen since it had begun raining again, the levels almost back to normal. September now, the weather had finally begun to cool a little. We were sitting side by side at the end of the peninsula, her long brown hair moving in the breeze. "Hey, listen," I said. "I had something fancy prepared but . . . I'm too dang nervous." I opened Shaw's tackle box and reached in. I held a shaky hand out to her, the ring flat on my palm. "What do you think?" I said.

"You proposing to me, Elijah Youngblood?"

"Suppose I am," I said, my voice quivering.

She smiled and said, "I've never in my life met a man like you."

"I'd appreciate an answer before I keel over."

She took the ring and put it on her finger and kissed me.

"That a yes?"

"Yes."

"Well, that's a relief," I said. "I'd feel bad having to return that ring. Shaw donated a kidney to help me pay for it."

"Oh, hush," she said, holding out her hand to look at the ring, a simple gold band with a diamond no bigger than a mustard seed, about the size of a flea.

"One day our kids are gonna ask us about the story of how we got married. And you'll have to tell them about me handing you a ring from a tackle box full of dried worm guts. Sorry, I know I'm not too good at romance."

She put her arm through mine and leaned her soft head against me, looking out at the water, rippling in the wind. "Like everything else, you're pretty good at it when you're not trying so hard. Plus, we've got a story to tell them. Good one, too."

Twenty-Seven

With no reason to wait, we set the wedding for a month later, the last week of October. Since there was no longer a chapel to hold a service in, we decided to have it at the trailer park. And to save Bonnie the money, we would have a potluck reception, with Virgil & Co. providing the entertainment. Come to find out, in his time in the Navy, Monty had been a chaplain, which was news to everyone. He offered to step out of retirement to officiate the wedding, which we gladly accepted. Bonnie invited the entire church to come. Georgia and I wondered how many would be willing to associate with the rumored scandal of it all.

Thankfully, Bonnie had cleared up things with my parents, telling them what happened shortly after the fire. Although there was much my parents would never understand about me and could not approve, they decided they could claim me as their son again. For the first time in my life, Daddy apologized to me, saying he had been too quick to judge.

We invited Ronny, who had gone through multiple surgeries and was awaiting his sentencing in the local jail after pleading guilty. Speaking to the sheriff and warden, we requested a furlough so he could attend the wedding, which was granted with the condition of a police officer escort. Ronny agreed to come as long as Gerald approved. Although Shaw was staunchly opposed when he heard, Gerald said, "Fine with me, jus' tell 'em to leave his python at home this time."

The day of the wedding arrived. That morning, Virgil and Shaw, my best men, helped me set up what must have been close to a hundred lawn and camping chairs in front of the dock, with an aisle up the middle. The ceremony would take place at sunset with the lake behind us.

That afternoon, Virgil and Monty started preparing the sound stage under the tent. A half dozen grills appeared and were prepared for various meats. Gerald danced and bobbed his head to the rehearsal music while he smoked a barbecue brisket, a cigarette hanging out his mouth. Granny kept a close eye on him, making sure he didn't slip back into old ways in his merriment.

The ceremony was set to begin at five thirty. By four thirty in the afternoon, I still had not seen Georgia. I went to Gerald's trailer to shower and get dressed. Although he was probably joking, Shaw brought me a pair of overalls and insisted I wear them. I put on an old tuxedo of Daddy's instead and compromised with Shaw by wearing a camouflage bow tie. Close to five o' clock, I was about to leave when Gerald came inside. He looked at me in disgust and said, "You gettin' married like that?"

"Yeah?"

"Naw! There ain't never gon' be 'nother day like this. It's gotta be fancy! Hang on," he said, disappearing to his bedroom. He came back with a pair of dark, knobby, leather boots. "Put these beauties on."

"Those your gator boots? They survived the fire?"

"Nothin' survived that fire, but I was wearin' 'em that night, 'member? Go 'head, put 'em on." I took off my shoes and put on the boots. They were at least three sizes too big.

Virgil shook his head. Shaw covered his mouth, holding back laughter. Gerald stepped back so he could look at me from head to toe. Eyeing me like a prize-winning buck, he said, "Bubba, you 'bout the most han'some redneck I ever saw."

I went outside to greet the guests who had arrived. The trailer park residents were already sitting in the chairs by the lake. Most of them had on the same wardrobe as usual. A few, like Wally, felt like they were dressed up simply for wearing a shirt and shoes. And then some, like Miss Mattie, who brought a date with her named Allen, were truly well-dressed. Seeing my neighbors in all their splendor, I loved them.

A surprising number of church members came. They were a little stiff and awkward when they approached, greeting me, not with coldness as much as fear. I smiled and directed them to the chairs by the lake. Daddy and Momma arrived in his turquoise 1951 Studebaker. They each gave me a hug, congratulating me. Passing under the tent, they stopped short when they saw the church logo, bewildered, and hurried to find a familiar face.

At five thirty, I took my place next to Monty in front of the dock. "You don't look so good, fella," Monty said. "You good?"

"Just ready to get this part over." I wiped my palms on my pants.

"Don't worry, I'll make it quick. I ain't long-winded." After a moment he said, "Didn't know you were one for nerves."

"Most time, I'm not." I took a deep breath. "This girl has a way with me though."

"What'chu worried 'bout? That she won't show?"

"More worried that she will."

From somewhere beyond the chairs, Virgil's guitar began to play an instrumental prelude, which mellowed my nerves a little. The crowd hushed. Before long, Bonnie walked down the aisle escorted by Carl, who shuffled along, proud and slow. He led her to a chair and took a seat next to Prissy, who took his hand and smiled a little, momentarily proud of her husband. Next came Virgil, still playing his guitar, strapped around his neck. A girl I remembered from youth group walked beside him, her arm resting on his as he played. She took her place across from me, and Virgil stood behind me, continuing the prelude. Shaw swaggered down the aisle next, wearing his firefighter's uniform, a cousin of Georgia's on his arm. Wally whistled from somewhere in the crowd. Lastly, Mrs. Flora came, tossing red and orange flowers on the grass. A peacock followed behind her, eating the petals as quickly as she dropped them. When they got to the front, she untied a string from the bird's neck and handed a ring to Shaw.

The prelude stopped, and Virgil began playing *Just as I Am*, the first time I'd ever heard him sing a hymn. Knowing there was only one person left in the procession, I felt like I was going to pass out, but Shaw came and put an arm around my shoulder. He leaned toward me and said in my ear, "Can see you're nervous, friend. Tell you what. I'll marry her if you ain't man enough." I laughed and felt a little better.

Everyone stood and turned to look down the aisle. As I waited, my eyes blurred with visions of the past. A shy fourteen-year-old girl at a revival, peeking at me across the aisle during her father's prayer. A young lady playing with the cafe curtains at the diner, her eyes full of desire, asking me to elope. Sitting in a windowsill, the silhouette of someone I loved who I doubted I'd ever see again. And then, no longer a vision, a full-grown woman walked down the aisle toward me in a simple white dress. Rather than a veil, she wore a long braid with flowers woven in. She had emeralds in her newly pierced ears, a string of pearls around her neck and the slightest hint of blush on her sun-tanned cheeks. Seeing such a creature proceed down the aisle - towards me of all people - I still had a hard time believing it was true. Yet, if the summer had taught me anything, it was that blessings too good to be true do happen, and typically to the unlikeliest of folks. Thus, beholding my bride, I received her and gave thanks.

Holding her hand as she walked was Ronny, pushed along in a wheelchair by a police officer. His eyes shone as he looked around at the crowd, nodding to his former congregants. He wore a navy button-down shirt with a pair of khakis, which flapped in the wind below the knee. The music stopped shortly after they got to the front. Monty asked, "Who gives this woman to be wed in marriage?"

Ronny glanced at Bonnie, then up at Georgia, and then finally at me. He didn't say anything for an awfully long while but sniffed and pursed his lips a few times. He rubbed his jaw a moment, in the very place, I couldn't help but notice, my uppercut had landed. He reached over and grabbed Bonnie's free hand with his left. "Her momma and me," he said, nodding and putting Georgia's hand in mine. I saw Gerald standing in the back, shaking his head and wiping his eyes.

We turned towards Monty, the lake behind him, and listened while he gave a five-minute sermon about how two become one by "leavin' and cleavin'." I was prepared for Shaw to pretend to not have the ring, but for once, he didn't joke. We exchanged rings and made our vows. Declaring us husband and wife, Shaw swatted me on the rear, and Gerald called out from the crowd, "Go 'head, 'Lijah! Kiss that woman!" And so, I did. And just like the first time, it was very good.

TWENTY-EIGHT

With the ceremony over, Monty set his Navy-issued Bible down and took up his banjo, playing alongside Virgil who led the bridal party over to the tent. As they took the stage and kept playing, Georgia clapped along with the music and laughed happily. Seeing her full of life and without fear, I wondered at what had come to be. Having forgotten myself in my bride, I was no longer anxious but relaxed and able to celebrate.

She greeted the guests with poise and grace as they came under the tent, encouraging them to go ahead and plate their food. Ronny and Bonnie remained by the lake, enjoying the rare moment they had to talk outside of the jail. Gerald put on an apron and began to slice his brisket. "Looka the crust on that girl!" he kept saying, placing a piece of meat on their plate. A few people later, "Dadgum, you ever seen a smoke ring like that? Half inch, easy!"

Virgil said, "Any Doc Watson fans here tonight?" The trailer park residents cheered and a few church members clapped hesitantly, glancing around to see who was watching. "This one's called *Tennessee Stud.*" Virgil was completely at ease on stage. It was not, as in the past, that he played without minding the crowd. Instead, he engaged with them, inviting them to participate in the music and unashamed to have their eyes on him.

Hoots and cheers followed Virgil's conclusion of the song. "All right, folks," Virgil said over the speakers, wetting his lips with a sip of water. "Got an original for you. It's called *Visions*." Not everyone was listening, but Georgia and I were locked in. He began to sing,

> *Purdy pony just a puppet of a power-hungry child*
> *A thoroughbred, well-mannered, brown beauty undefiled*
> *Never galloped in the field, only stabled, meek and mild*
> *Come're, he said, I'll show ya visions of the wild*
>
> *Coupla coons out in the woods, creatures of neglect*
> *Diggin' in the garbage, as trash what you expect*
> *Livin' for themselves, life's direction indirect*
> *Come're, he said, I'll show ya visions of respect*
>
> *Crazy cussin' catfish, a bottom dwellin' slug*
> *Drownin' out his problems, mournin' like a dove*
> *Hateful as a gator gar, punch-drunk in his love*
> *Come're, he said, I'll show ya visions from above*
>
> *Slith'rin' through the grass, fork tongue from his face*
> *Venomous and crafty, preyin' while he prays*
> *Huntin' down the weak, fell on his belly in disgrace*
> *Come're, he said, I'll show ya visions of his grace*

While Virgil played a bridge to the last verse, Georgia leaned over and said, "Your own song, Elijah."

"Nah," I said, "Virgil knows better." He continued,

Flyin' solo in the heavens, shiverin' in the north
Bird's eye view of new land, only olive leaves' worth
Hidin' with his hen, a drake denied his double birth
Come 're, he said, I'll show ya visions of the earth

"See," I said. "I'm just like the rest." She squeezed my hand.

When it was over, Virgil bowed his head towards me, his long hair falling forward. "Wooo doggy!" Gerald shouted from behind us. "That's my boy up there, y'all!"

With a break in the flow of guests, I made Georgia a plate of food. After listening to another song, Sammy came up and hugged Georgia. "Sure missed you, honey. Tell you what, my whole life, ain't never seen somebody as lonesome and tore up as this fella while you were gone. He ain't himself without you, just slinks around like a skunk, shruggin' his shoulders like he don't know up from down. He come alive when he's with you, jus' like you come alive when you play that fiddle. Speakin' of," she turned around and grabbed something from the edge of the stage. "Here," she said, handing her fiddle and bow to Georgia. "Thought you might wanna borrow mine."

"Borrow? For what?" Georgia said, tilting her head.

"What else? To make your debut!"

"Oh, no, I don't think so. On my wedding day?" She turned to me, biting her lip. "I don't know. Elijah, what do you think?"

Sammy raised her eyebrows a couple of times. I said, "Don't ask me. You're a free woman now, remember? No more bit and bridle. It's up to you." Both pleased and irritated with my response, she narrowed her eyes and took the instrument from Sammy. Without even waiting on the next song, she stepped on stage next to Virgil. Sammy put her arm through mine, and we watched as Georgia closed her eyes and began to sway in her white dress. Without bending down, she took off her heels and began tapping her bare foot. When she was sufficiently submerged in the music, she began to play. The whole crowd ceased talking and eating and turned to see the bride on her fiddle. Virgil laughed in surprise and nodded, continuing to sing. Her bow jerked and skipped across the strings, producing a mess of unpredictable sounds that dovetailed into something so wonderful even the church members began to dance. I cannot imagine a soul without awe as the preacher's daughter made her long-awaited debut into the world.

As the band transitioned seamlessly into another song, I saw Ronny, finally arriving from the lakeside, wheel slowly next to the stage. As breathtaking as Georgia was, I could not help but fix my eyes on Ronny as he saw his daughter for the first time in his life. The longer he watched, the further his mouth fell and the rounder his green eyes grew with astonishment. After Georgia played an improvised solo followed by a roar of cheers and applause, tears began to run freely down his face, which he did not try to hide. After one final song, she set the fiddle down and bowed in response to the crowd's praise, stepping gingerly off the stage with her shoes in her hand. Ronny rolled his wheelchair to her and held out his arms. Unprepared, she stopped abruptly in front of him like a fox in a spotlight. The band continued to play.

"All these years," he said over the music, dropping his hands to his lap, "And I haven't even known you, baby. We're not but strangers! I kept you under lock and key, like some kind of trophy, only there to make me look good and no more. How blind I been! All these years, never even noticed how beautiful you were!"

She stood before him, torn between love and anger toward her father, no doubt thinking of all the years he'd stolen from her. "I would say it's all right," she said, "But that'd be a lie."

"No, don't say that, it's not all right, not at all. I wasted my life making a name for myself, building my own kingdom, and lost my only chance to know you. And look, there I go, making it about me. It's not about me and what I lost, is it? That's the point. It's about what I took from you. It's about the things I never gave to you, things every daughter ought to have from her father."

"Shame on you, Daddy, for waiting until my wedding day to say these things. Eighteen years I've waited for you to call me beautiful. The kind of father you've been, you don't even deserve for me to call you 'Daddy,' 'cause you've never been anything but a Preacher."

He wept like a child into his hands, only nodding. Seeing Bonnie across the tent, he reached down to roll his wheelchair away. Having finally said her piece, her face softened, and she stopped him. "Tell you what," she said, firm but kind. "If you'll let me be something besides a preacher's daughter, I'd be willing to . . . work on things."

His hands fidgeted in his lap as he wrestled with his thoughts. "You don't have to worry about being a preacher's daughter. Afraid you'll be a convict's daughter instead, Georgia. No, I think it's best you don't associate with me."

"Why, because you're a convict?" she said. "Or because you're a sinner?"

He shook his head for a long time. "What a shame I had to become a felon to see myself truly."

"Yeah, but maybe, just maybe, if you keep being honest with yourself, we can finally know each other as we are. Two human beings made of dirt, walking the path of life."

"I'd like that," he said, nodding.

Sensing some resolution to the conversation, I stepped up to the two of them. Ronny brushed away his tears and held out his hand to me. "Fancy seeing you again," he said.

"Thank you for coming. How long you on furlough?"

"Just for today."

"The case going OK?"

"Attorney said the judge'll be favorable, since I confessed and been compliant." He looked down at his thighs. "I think my losses give him compassion for me, too. Depending on what the witnesses say, it might get lowered to second- or third-degree arson."

"You need me to give a testimony?"

"Maybe," he said, a sad twinkle in his eye. "How about that, Elijah Youngblood, witnessing."

I smiled. "I'd do it. For her, at least."

"Either way, I'm gonna be locked up next five years at least." He breathed deeply through his nose, watching all the people moving and talking under the tent, Virgil and Monty now playing instrumentals. "I reckon you count this place your church now, huh?"

"Actually," I said, winking at Georgia, "I was thinking we might go sit under that velvet-mouth Reverend Henry." Ronny squirmed a little in his wheelchair.

"He's teasing, Daddy," Georgia said. Ronny sighed in relief.

"Nah," I said, "This is a fine neighborhood, but it's no church. The Lord's here, no doubt, but we're not gathering as saints for worship, just as human beings to enjoy his good gifts of crawfish boils and folk music and bass tournaments. For what it's worth, Ronny, I don't plan to wander in the wilderness forever. I'd be glad to belong to a church again. I just have to find one that's down to earth, one that loves the world like the Lord himself does."

Ronny wrinkled his brow and, for a brief moment, a smile of contempt passed over his face. I was bracing for a snort of laughter, but instead, his forehead smoothed, and his mouth let out an inaudible sigh. "Ever think about starting one? A church, I mean. Maybe you're the man for the job."

"Nah, I'll leave that to someone else, I'm no preacher. I'm going to keep working at being a good neighbor and see what happens."

"Just fishing for bass, huh? That's too bad, but I'm not one to talk. My days of preaching are over, for sure." He let out a loud sigh. "Who knows? Maybe one day, when I'm out of prison, you'll look up and find me out on the lake, casting a line."

"Now that would be something," I said.

"Maybe you and Elijah could go together," Georgia said. "Out on his boat, father and son-in-law kind of thing."

Ronny and I paused and looked each other in the eye. "Nah," we said at the same time.

"Elijah," he said, "One last thing."

"Yessir?"

"You take better care of this girl than I did, you hear?"

"I'll do my best."

"The Lord's got his eye on you, young man," he said with a nod and half a smile and rolled his wheelchair to join Bonnie in the food line.

In between songs, Virgil said into the microphone, "All right, my friends. Few more songs and then we'll let the bride and groom dance." The band continued to play, the music echoing across the property and into the woods. I leaned over and said in

Georgia's ear, "Hey, you know where the path crosses the creek?"

"Yeah."

"Meet me there in five minutes."

Tilting her head and wrinkling her nose, she opened her mouth to ask why but then closed it. Her eyes lit up, and she nodded.

I stood next to the creek in the woods, not far from where the charred remains of the House still lay untouched, waiting in the dark. The bullfrogs croaked in the bed of the stream. Bats swooped overhead, searching for mosquitos. In the distance I could vaguely make out Virgil's lyrics. Then, rather than the footsteps I was listening for, a voice said, "Is this what I think it is?" And there she was beside me.

"You'd make a great turkey hunter, you know that?"

"You didn't answer my question."

"Yes, it's what you think it is. If you're willing."

She nodded.

We followed the creek downstream to where it met the lake. I reached out into the dark and placed my hand on a cypress tree, feeling around until I found the rope. Untying it, I pulled a jon boat out from under some low branches and heaved it a few feet onto land.

She saw the shapes of our bags already loaded in the bow of the boat and said, "I knew it. Elijah, I thought you didn't believe in eloping."

"I don't believe in stealing a man's daughter. Sneaking away with my bride? Call me a thief in the night, but that's our God-given right. As long as you're willing, of course." I glanced at the outline of her face in the dark.

"Course I am. Who else knows? Virgil, Shaw?"

"Not a soul."

"Perfect. Leaving and cleaving to one another, and no one else. Just like Monty said."

"That's the idea."

"So, where you stealing me away to? Arkansas?"

"Not quite. Just across the lake. I got us a little honeymoon getaway."

She nodded. "I'm ready." She took my hand for balance and stepped into the boat. I pushed it into the water after she sat, sinking Gerald's boots into the mud, and leapt into the stern, taking the metal seat beside Georgia. I paddled us out of the shallows, then lowered and cranked the small outboard engine, smelling the pleasant fumes of the burning gasoline. She put a hand on my leg. "I guess it's what I get for marrying the boy who kissed the preacher's daughter the day of his baptism. You've never cared a lick what people expected of you. I suppose that's why I liked you in the first place."

"Aw, is that why? I thought it was 'cause I was so handsome."

"That too."

The distant music stopped abruptly. "Shoot, we better hurry." Revving the engine as loudly as I dared, we passed out of the inlet and through the trees into the channel. The open water carried the sounds of the wedding to us more clearly than in the woods. Virgil's voice called out over the speaker. "Anyone seen the bride or groom?" Amidst the noise, I heard my father call my name. My mother gasped. Gerald roared in laughter. "Elijah!" Virgil called. "Georgia!" The commotion grew. We rode away from it all at ten miles per hour, laughing quietly to ourselves until the wedding was nothing more than a bright spot on the dark horizon of trees.

Once things were quiet, I glanced over at her moonlit dress.

"Who would've thought?" I said. "The two of us becoming one. Pretty girl like you and a rough fella like me."

"Oh, come on. We both knew it was meant to be from the moment we started passing notes at the revival."

"Just cause it was meant to be didn't mean it would be," I said. "We had a lotta things going against us. Shoot, we were dead in the grave at one point."

"Yet here we are, alive and well."

"Yes ma'am," I said, "Here we are. Imagine that."

About fifteen minutes later, arriving on the northern side of the lake, I cut off the engine and let the boat drift slowly to a pier. High up in a white sycamore on the bank, a lone flood light shone down on the property. Where the pier met the shoreline, a flight of stairs led to the screened porch of a cabin that looked out on the water. I tied the boat to the cleat. Georgia stared up at the place while I moved our things from the well of the boat to the dock. "Funny," I said, "You know what keeps going through my mind?"

"What?" she said.

"Your kingfisher."

"The painting? What about it?" she said.

"I can't get past the loss of that thing in the fire. That was worth more to me than everything else I owned. And now it's gone. You gotta paint me a copy."

"No, you don't need it no more. I'll paint something else."

"Course I need it," I said.

"No, that painting wasn't but a sign, Elijah. Why would you need the sign when you arrived where it was pointing? That kingfisher was just a promise, a hope of things to come. Now you got the real thing."

"Oh? And what's that?"

"Me," she said, stepping up from the boat onto the dock.

"Dadgum, Georgia." Shaking my head in disbelief, I picked up our bags and climbed the steps to the cabin, marveling that I no longer had to grieve what had been nor dream of what might never be.

ACKNOWLEDGEMENTS

Trying to name the influences on this book - good or bad - is almost impossible. This book grew out of the compost of a lifetime of people, experiences, and books, most of which I have forgotten. I will try to acknowledge the most recent and direct influences.

First, to my proofreaders, thank you: to Quinn Hill for making sure Elijah wasn't a heretic; to Kevin Singletary for being ever ready to listen and discuss; to Grace Eyler for her kind, sharp eye; to Joe Kendrick for reading personally; and to Jessica Elston, who somehow manages to be both my biggest fan and most honest critic. Thank you all for truly caring.

Shreveport, I am grateful to have you as a home away from Home. Despite your flaws, you are a goldmine of material for the characters, dialogue, and events that make up a novel. You don't know it, but you are as rich in culture as New York City or New Orleans or Paris, though undoubtedly of a down-to-earth sort.

It would be unfair if I didn't express my gratitude to the evangelist who brought a snake into a worship service I attended. This book was not the kind of seed you were aiming to plant, but thank you, nonetheless.

Lastly, I am thankful to God, who allows and inspires us to be like him - to create, to play, and most surprising of all, to be human.

About the Author

David began writing stories after reading Roald Dahl in first grade. Besides nonfiction, he has written *Subversive Stories*, a book of short stories based on the parables of Jesus, and *The Inlet*, a novel for children. David lives with his wife and three children in his hometown of Shreveport, LA, where he works in counseling ministry.

David enjoys hearing from readers. You can contact him and find out more about his writing at davidbelston.com

www.ingramcontent.com/pod-product-compliance
Lightning Source LLC
Chambersburg PA
CBHW020315200626

46814CB00006BA/2257

* 9 7 9 8 9 8 9 4 7 7 6 4 7 *